Vian had so rich a career that people overlooked the fact that he was one of the most powerful writers to have appeared in France since the war.
    –Roger Shattuck

Vian is one of the great iconoclasts, and more than that, one of the great comic iconoclasts.
    –J.K.L. Scott, 'From Dreams to Despair: An Integrated Reading of the Novels of Boris Vian'

'L'Automne a Pékin' could well become one of the classics of a literature which, after having exhausted with a uniformly accelerated movement all the nuances of the sinister, from Romanticism to Naturalism and from Socialism to Mysticism, notes all of a sudden that it winds up in the desert of Exopotamie; a literature where one is finally permitted to laugh!
    –Alain Robbe-Grillet

Let the entire College pay attention to this work, let it uncover its riches: they are incalculable. A great lesson that Satrap Boris Vian gives us in 'L'Automne a Pekin', using, moreover, a sacred language.
    –Noël Arnaud

BORIS VIAN AUTUMN IN PEKING

Originally published in French as L'Automne à Pékin by Scorpion in 1947

©Les Editions de Minuit 1956
©TamTam Books 2005
Translation by Paul Knobloch ©2005
Introduction by Marc Lapprand © 2005
First published by TamTam Books in the U.S.A. 2005
Printed in the United States of America

TamTam Books wants to thank Ichiro Shimizu, Les Zazous, the Boris Vian Estate, Henry Cording, Shirley Berman, Donald Morand, Lun*na Menoh, Bison Ravi, Brian Gottlieb, Prévan, Don Carlos Byas, Alistair Charles Rolls, le Major, Eva Prinz, Vernon Sullivan and Kimley Maretzo for their wisdom and assistance on this project.

TamTam Books is edited and published by Tosh Berman.

Assistance to the publisher: Carolline Kim

TamTam Books are designed by Tom Recchion

Tosh3@earthlink.net
www.tamtambooks.com

First Edition
ISBN 0-9662346-4-2

Library of Congress Control Number: 2004108149

BORIS VIAN
AUTUMN IN PEKING

Translated from the French by Paul Knobloch
Introduction by Marc Lapprand

With endnotes by
Gilbert Pestureau, Michel Rybalka and Paul Knobloch

BOOKS

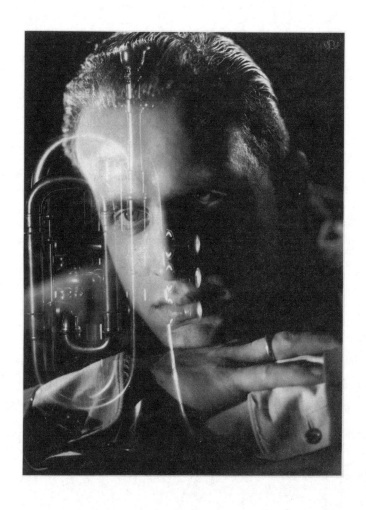

Boris Vian 1948

FOREWORD

Boris Vian was either born half a century ahead of his time or half a century too late. Indeed, on the one hand, much of his fiction is akin to that of Jules Verne, Lewis Carroll or H.G. Wells, the latter two ranking among his most favourite writers. He showed an explicit preference for two works in particular: Carroll's *Hunting of the Snark* and Wells' *Wonderful Visit*. This latter work, a novella written by one of the fathers of modern science fiction, happens to be a key to understanding *Autumn In Peking*. In Wells' story, the unfortunate Angel thinks that he has fallen into the "Land of Dreams," but he soon realizes that it is more like a land of nightmares, where humans spend most of their time inflicting pain – or avoiding it. Autumn's Angel is much of a dreamer too, in the beginning, and a succession of rather horrific events will slowly awaken him to reality. We all know that excessive sensitivity can have a negative effect on a human being in this rough world of ours, and it turns out that Vian's fiction is only one step ahead on the scale of (bureaucratic) absurdity.

Yet on the other hand, Vian was in many ways ahead of his own time, lucid and astute about such cutting edge movements as science fiction and jazz. His masters were not Racine or Mozart, but Van Vogt and Duke Ellington. This, in part at least, explains why Vian's novels remained almost entirely unknown in his lifetime, when his works are now unquestionably considered classics of 20th century French literature. One would not refute that, indeed, he belongs with us today, fully and irrevocably. Noël Arnaud, his biographer, also thought that he was writing for the next generation, as Vian's own simply could not get it, ill-equipped as it was to appreciate his innovative style and to feel at ease in his fiction. L'Automne à Pékin is his fourth novel, but when he wrote it in the fall of 1946, none of the previous three had been published. His second and third novels, Vercoquin et le plancton and L'Écume des jours, were published by Gallimard respectively in January and April of the following year, and L'Automne à Pékin later in 1947, by Éditions du Scorpion. As for his first novel, Trouble dans les andains, Vian never saw it in print, as it was published for the first time in 1966, seven years after his early death. Thus his novels met with success only in the sixties, by the end of which Vian would become an icon among the "Soixante-

II

huitards," as the participants of the May 1968 student revolution would eventually be coined.

Vian had hoped to win the 1946 Prix de la pléiade for *L'Écume des jours* and he received full support from Sartre and Beauvoir. However, the jury favoured a collection of poems of religious inspiration that year: *Terre du temps*, by (former abbot) Jean Grosjean. This setback was not only a great disappointment for Vian, but it also meant that his following novels would soon fade into oblivion, as Gallimard from then on refused to publish them. Ironically, Vian's fame was largely based on the scandal related to a certain Vernon Sullivan, whose first novel Vian claimed to have translated. It was, in fact, all a well-wrought mystification. *I Spit on Your Graves*, which TamTam Books published in 1998 for the first time in the USA, caused a sensation when it first appeared in 1947, and it was Sullivan and his hard-boiled prose that made the news, casting a large shadow on Vian's genuine novels. The next two that he would sign with his own name, *L'Herbe rouge* and *L'Arrache cœur*, would remain largely unknown until after his death.

Boris Vian (1920-1959) was born into a liberal, middle-class family. In the thirties he developed a true passion for jazz and started to play the trumpet. Because of a heart condition diagnosed at an early age, he did not have to serve when the war broke out in 1939, but would continue his studies and be trained as an engineer. In

1942 he graduated from the (still) prestigious École Centrale des Arts et Manufactures. The year before, he had married Michelle Léglise, with whom he was to have two children, Patrick and Carole. During the war, Vian devoted much time to more pleasurable activities in order to escape the dour reality of those rather depressing and gruesome years. It was the time of big jazz parties and jams. It was also the time when he started writing, first to entertain his entourage, then with more and more determination. In 1946, after Raymond Queneau secured his first publication with Gallimard (*Vercoquin et le plancton*), he would consider himself a writer and his career as an engineer, which had started in 1942, was to cease forever in August of 1947. However, his writings undoubtedly bear the mark of the engineer, as Vian remains basically a scientist. The writer and the technician are never too far apart in his fiction and this novel is no exception, as you will soon find out.

Boris Vian once wrote that "the desert is the only thing that can be destroyed by construction." This novel exemplifies such an apparently paradoxical statement. In it you will find an array of characters whose destinies converge in the building of the Exopotamian Railway. They include a technical director who is homosexual, a couple of male engineers – one of whom has a dog's name – who both happen to love the same woman, a salacious priest and a fornicating hermit, a physician obsessed with model air-

FOREWORD

planes, and an archaeologist and his team who were there long before (not to mention a sick chair which ends up being hospitalized). The astonishing onomastics would in itself justify a wholesome study, as some characters owe their names to a few actual individuals, as will be explained in footnotes.

The world in which they evolve may puzzle or irk the (Cartesian) reader, but all the characters feel at home in it. In this strange world, buses feed on catfish bones, bed covers are reluctant to be tossed back and will affectionately move up again, electricity is more like a liquid that spills when there is a failure, "Palmes académiques" are actual plants, and some objects express their feelings: the aggressive plane-motor will bite the intern's hand and the typewriter will shiver when uncovered. In the Exopotamian desert, where hepatrols blossom and children collect little animals called sandpeepers, the sun shines in an unusual way: it produces eerie black zones whose mysteries remain unexplained. Above all, Vian's peculiar way with language proves that, indeed, life in the desert is equal to none. Since unusual language is bound to produce unusual fiction, it follows that the story does not take place in the fall, nor is it set in China.

According to most critics, *Autumn in Peking* is Vian's richest, most difficult and most esoteric novel. Its complex construction hones our vigilance as the four preambles lettered A, B, C and D seem at first to have no correlation.

Nevertheless they all serve the same purpose of sending all the characters to the desert of Exopotamie where everything will unfold. It is a spiritual quest in three movements, mixed with a love story. And that's not all. To the three main groups of researchers correspond three distinct layers: underground with the archaeologist, upon the ground with the railway engineers, and in the air with the model airplane. At this point one may be inclined to believe that the novel is actually conceived with a deeper structure involving alchemy and esotericism, as was once suggested by Noël Arnaud. Be that as it may, it should not diminish our appreciation of this novel as a very witty and humorous one. Vian is a master at creating uncanny fiction, with a twist of harshness and cruelty, but at the same time with tenderness and joyful fun. Undoubtedly, the figure of Littlejohn exemplifies sheer humor and cleverness. His matter-of-fact mind may not make him a typical churchman, yet he is very convincing in his down-to-earth ways and may rank among the most farcical priests in modern French fiction, as Gilbert Pestureau once suggested.

The last "Passage" tells that with the demise of the initial project and the disappearance of several key characters, new teams will be formed and the missing people will be replaced by clones who will start anew but on the same basis. In that respect, the novel reads ad infinitum, an endless cycle like life itself. When Antenne Pernot (whose initials match those of the title) is chosen to replace Amadis Dudu as the technical director, one may

FOREWORD

feel that a similar kind of story is going to unfold. Yet the narrator warns us that "one may conceive of any solution." This final statement harbors a pleasant ambiguity: either you feel compelled to read the book again right away, if only to check that you did not overlook anything at first and assure yourself that you've completed the puzzle proposed by it, or you simply imagine a new storyline with the identical premise as laid out by the preambles A, B, C and D. Whichever way you lean, you cannot remain indifferent to the various levels of interpretations with which this novel is loaded, and you may even – at least I hope so – have fun in the process of discovering them.

In closing, I would like to pay tribute to the remarkable translation by Paul Knobloch. He has successfully managed to convey Vian's style without betraying him. All along, he remained faithful to the original text and cleverly found equivalents when a direct translation would have been either meaningless or would have simply levelled Vian's subtle play with language (see for instance the passage with imaginary birds, p. 90). In addition, the abundant footnotes will definitely help the reader understand otherwise rather obscure contextual references. Most of them are based on the Fayard edition (*Œuvres complètes, tome 3,* 1999) and constitute the most valuable and up to date information for today's reader.

Marc Lapprand

A
SHORT
NOTE
FROM
THE
TRANSLATOR

Translation is a tricky business, and translating Vian can be downright daunting. His use of neologisms, his wordplay, and his irreverent subversion of language demand that the translator remain always vigilant and at all times use the most of his or her ingenuity to solve these linguistic puzzles while at the same time remaining faithful to the text and respectful of the lyrical beauty of Vian's prose. This has been my goal with this translation and I hope, that while reading the text, you find that I have lived up to my end of the bargain, as it were. Furthermore, I feel that it is my responsibility to explain certain creative choices that I have made.

I believe it will be quite clear to the reader when I am

myself trying to find just the right English equivalents for the neologisms and puns created by Vian in the original text. Furthermore, while most of the characters' names have not been modified for this translation, I feel that I should clarify why I chose to actually translate the names of certain personages. I have done this only when the names themselves are verbal puns. For example, Professor Petereater is called "Mangemanche" in the original French. Now, Mangemanche has clear phallic and oral connotations in French and Vian is obviously engaging in some wordplay here. Thus, my use of "Petereater" should require no further elaboration. In other cases where I have translated a character's name – for example Petitjean is translated quite literally as "Littlejohn" – I have explained why I have done so in the endnotes.

I also need to comment on the names of the major female characters. Rochelle is the main female protagonist and I have chosen to keep her name the same in this translation. However, it is important to note that the root of Rochelle is "roche," which means rock. The other two female characters are called Cuivre and Lavande in the original French text. I have translated these names, quite literally again, as "Copper" and "Lavender." The reason that I have done so is that Vian is obviously associating femininity with plant and mineral life, or the earth in general, if you will. Had I not translated these names, this subtlety would have been lost on an American reader who has no working knowledge of French.

Finally, a word about the notes. Tosh Berman and I have decided not to interrupt the flow of the narrative with countless numbers and long footnotes that would only serve to break up the reading. Instead, should you come across an unclear or arcane reference, you simply need to consult the endnote section and look for the page in question on which you found the word or the phrase that you might feel calls for further clarification.

In closing, I would like to thank Tosh Berman for giving me the chance to finally get this important work published in English. I would also like to thank Marc Lapprand for his guidance and feedback and also Ursula Vian-Kübler and the Vian Foundation for their support of this project. Last, but certainly not least, I wish to express my gratitude to my wife for her assistance and for the patience she showed during the long and sometimes arduous process of bringing this translation to print. I hope this short commentary has been of help and that it will ease your transition into the world of Vian's fictional and farcical desert. As Marc Lapprand put it in his introduction, "...life in the desert is equal to none," as is the work of Boris Vian itself.

Paul Knobloch
Fall, 2004

A

*People who have not studied the
question are apt to be led astray...*

Lord Raglan, *Le Tabou de l'inceste*
Paris, Payot, 1935, p.145.

1

Amadis Dudu carelessly followed the narrow alleyway which constituted the longest of the shortcuts leading to the stop for bus 975. Every day, because he would jump off the moving bus before his destination, he had to use three and a half tickets. He checked the pocket of his vest to see if any remained. Yes. He then spotted a bird that was hunched over a pile of rubbish, and digging its beak into three empty tin cans it succeeded in playing the beginning of "Bateliers de la Volga." He stopped to listen, but the bird hit a false note and flew away in a fury, murmuring dirty little words to itself in bird-talk. Amadis Dudu then departed again, trying to finish the rest of the song. But he, too, let out a false note and started to curse.

It wasn't too sunny out, but what sun there was fell right in front of him and the end of the alleyway shone softly because the pavement was oily. Still, Amadis couldn't see it because the path turned two times, first to the left, then to the right. The women, who had come out on their doorsteps to empty garbage pails, were ripe with fleshy desire and their bathrobes hung open onto a flagrant lack of modesty. In unison, they pounded the bottoms of their rumbling trash cans, and as usual, Amadis started to march in step. That's why he liked to pass through the alleyways. It reminded him of his military service with the Yanks, when he used to eat *pineute beutteure* from a tin can, like the ones the bird was playing on, only larger.

The garbage falling all around cast clouds of dust, which pleased him because it made the sun visible. From the shadow of the red street lamp at the big number six, where undercover agents were housed (it was in reality a police station, and to avoid suspicion the neighboring whorehouse put out a blue lamp), one could tell that it was about eight twenty-nine. He had a minute to catch the bus, which meant that he had to take a step each second. But instead, he took five steps every four seconds, and this all too complicated calculation dissolved in his head and would later, as usual, be expulsed through his urine, rat-a-tat-tatting as it bounced off the porcelain. But only much later.

There were already five passengers in front of the bus stop and they were boarding the first 975 that had just arrived. But the porter refused entry to Dudu. Although he did indeed possess the little slip of paper proving he had the sixth place, there was only room for five and the bus reminded Dudu of this by letting loose four big farts as it left. It rolled off gently, dragging its tail-end while sparks shot up from the bumps on the pavement. Certain conductors would tie flint onto the rear to give this spectacle an even greater flair (especially the ones who were driving the bus right in back).

A second 975 came and stopped smack-dab in front of Amadis. The exhausted vehicle huffed and puffed and was jam-packed full of riders. A fat lady got off, followed by a cake knife that was being carried by a tiny, half-dead, old man. Amadis Dudu grabbed hold of the metal bar and presented his ticket, but the porter slapped at his fingers with his hole puncher.

"Let go of that!" he told him.

"But three people just got off!" Amadis protested.

"They were over the limit," whispered the employee confidentially, as he shot a nasty little sarcastic wink at Amadis.

"That's not true," Amadis protested.

"Yes it is," added the porter, who then jumped back up onto the bus to pull the cord, holding on to it so he could regain his position and show off his derriere to Amadis. The driver felt the tug of the pink string that was attached to his ear and he sped away.

Amadis looked at his watch and said "Boo!," hoping this little incantation would somehow make the hands run backwards. But it had no effect. Only the second hand started inching in reverse. The others kept plowing forward. He was standing in the middle of the street watching the 975 disappear while a third bus pulled up and hit him right in the ass with its bumper. He fell, and the driver continued moving the bus forward until it was directly over Dudu. The driver then opened the hot water valve, which started to spray Amadis on the neck. During this time, the two people holding the following numbers climbed aboard and when Amadis got up, the 975 sped off in front of him. His neck was all red and he was furious. He would surely be late. Meanwhile, four more people came, pressing the lever and taking tickets. A fifth person, a fat young man, even received a little spray of perfume: a bonus that the bus company offered to every one-hundredth customer. He ran away screaming because it was almost pure alcohol and a shot in the eye like that is truly quite painful. A 975 from the opposite direction passed by and crushed him complacently, putting an end to his suffering. One could see that he had just eaten strawberries.

There were still a few seats left on the fourth bus that arrived and a woman who had been waiting not quite as long as Amadis was holding on to her number. The porter called out in a loud voice.

"One million, five-hundred and six thousand, nine-hundred and three!"

"I've got nine-hundred!..."

"O.K." said the porter, "Numbers one and two?"

"I've got four," somebody shouted.

"We've got five and six," said the two others.

Amadis had already gotten on but the porter grabbed him by the collar.

"You picked that up off the ground, didn't you? Get off."

"We saw him," cried the others, "He was under the bus."

The porter puffed up his chest, hurled Dudu to the bottom of the platform, and then shot out a look of contempt that pierced straight through Amadis' left shoulder. He started to flinch in pain on the spot. The four other people boarded and the bus took off hanging its head a bit, for it was, in fact, a little ashamed of itself.

The fifth bus passed by, completely full, and all the passengers were sticking their tongues out at Amadis and the others who were waiting there. The porter even spat at him, but the bus' momentum wasn't conducive to the spit, which never hit the ground. Amadis tried to swat it down in mid-air but he missed. He was really perspiring because all this had left him in a truly furious state. When he missed the sixth and seventh buses he decided to walk. He would try to catch the next one at the following stop, where ordinarily more people got off.

He walked away with an odd sort of swagger that he affected on purpose to let everyone know just how angry he was. He had to go about four hundred meters while other 975's passed by, almost empty. When he finally reached the green boutique ten meters from the stop, seven young priests and twelve school children, carrying colored ribbons and banners with religious idols, emerged from a porte-cochère. They gathered around the bus stop and the priests deployed two of their communion slingshots to dissuade bystanders who might want to join them in waiting for the 975. Amadis Dudu made an effort to remember the password, but he couldn't; too much time had slipped away since catechism. He tried to move closer by walking backwards, but he was met with a wadded-up ball of communion bread which struck him in the back. It hit him with such force that he lost his breath and started coughing. The priests were laughing, busy using their slingshots to spit out a nonstop array of projectiles. Two 975's came and the children took up almost all the empty spaces. There was some room in the second bus, but the priests stood on the platform and stopped him from boarding. His spirits fell once again when he turned around to take a ticket and saw that

5

six people were already ahead of him. Thus he ran with all his might to get to the next stop. In the distance, he saw the burst of sparks from the back end of the 975 and he had to hit the ground because one of the priests was brandishing a slingshot in his direction. He heard the communion wafer pass over him, making a sound like burning silk as it fell into the gutter.

Amadis stood back up, filthy. He was reluctant about going back to his office in this soiled condition, but what would the time clock say? His right sartorial muscle was hurting, so he planted a needle in his cheek to ease the pain. Studying the acupuncture techniques of Dr. Deadboot was one of his pastimes. Unfortunately, his aim wasn't true and he healed himself instead of a nephritis of the calf, which set him back all the more, for he didn't happen to be suffering from this particular problem. When he arrived at the next stop there was already a hostile wall of people huddled around the number dispenser.

Amadis Dudu kept himself at a reasonable distance and took advantage of this moment of tranquility to try and calmly sort things out:

- On the one hand, if he walked to the next stop, it wouldn't be worth the trouble to take the bus at all. He would be too late.

- On the other hand, if he walked back, he risked finding more priests.

- Thirdly, he wanted to take the bus.

He laughed out loud at himself because even though he had taken care not to rush things, he had still deliberately avoided making a logical decision and continued to walk toward the next stop. He was more turned around than ever and it was obvious that his anger had only grown.

Having almost reached the next station, he could hear the 975 purring in his ear. Nobody was waiting. He started to raise his arm, but it was too late. The driver, oblivious to the presence of Amadis, just kept right on going past the metallic sign with his foot joyously pressing the accelerator pedal to the floor.

"Oh shit!" said Amadis Dudu.

"You said it," confirmed a stranger who had arrived behind him.

"You'd think he did it on purpose!" responded an outraged Amadis.

"Oh really," said the man. "On purpose?"

"I'm sure of it!" said Amadis.

"In your heart of hearts?" asked the man.

"And in the depths of my soul."

"And you would swear to it?"

"Absolutely! Damn all!" said Amadis. "A plague on that fucking asshole! Yes, I'd swear to it. And... shit!"

"I want to hear you swear," said the man.

"I swear!" said Amadis.

As the other gentleman moved his hand towards his mouth it was struck by a lob of Dudu's spit.

"You pig!" the man replied. "You're making insults about the driver of bus 975, and I'm going to give you a ticket."

"Is that so?" said Amadis.

Dudu's dander wasn't about to take this lying down.

"I'm a sworn in official," said the man as he flipped up the lid of his visor that had until now been kept down. It was an inspector for line 975.

Amadis shot a quick glance to the left and then to the right. Hearing the characteristic noise, he dashed to jump aboard the new 975 that had just rolled up beside him. He hit with such force that he burst through the bottom step of the platform and plunged several decimeters to the pavement. He had just enough time to lower his head; the rear of the bus flew up for a fraction of a second. The inspector pulled him out of the hole and forced him to pay a fine, during which time he missed two more buses. Aware of this, he darted off toward the next stop. As strange as it seems, it's nevertheless the case.

He reached the stop without any problems, but realized that his office was now only three hundred meters away. Why take the bus just for that...

So he crossed the street and followed the road in the opposite direction, on the sidewalk, towards some place where it would be worth the trouble.

2

He hurried along quickly and soon found himself at his usual stop. He decided to continue on because he was unfamiliar with this part of the route and it seemed to him that there were pertinent observations to be made about this side of the city. He hadn't lost sight of his immediate objective of taking the bus, but he wanted to turn to his advantage this series of mishaps that he had found himself the target of since daybreak. The route of the 975 covered a huge area and Amadis saw plenty of interesting things. But his anger wasn't diminishing. As a means of lowering his blood pressure, which he now felt approaching a critical level, he tried counting the trees. But he would periodically lose his place, so he instead tried tapping out the beat of popular military marches on his thigh to accent the rhythm of his stroll. Then he came upon a huge square surrounded by buildings dating from the Middle Ages which had since aged considerably. It was the terminal for route 975. He was overjoyed, and with the nimbleness of a pendulum he leaped onto the steps of the embarcadero. An employee removed a cord that was holding back a bus and Amadis could feel the machine as it departed. Turning around, he saw that same employee get struck smack in the face by the end of the cord which sliced off a chunk of his nose. It flew away like a spurt of acarus petals.

The motor was humming rhythmically, for they had just fed it a plate of catfish bones. Amadis, content to have the entire bus to himself, was sitting in the rear and to the right. On the platform stood the porter, unconsciously turning his ticket-gobbling instrument which he had just connected to a music box inside. Amadis was lulled by this threnody. He could feel the carcass of the machine vibrate and the crackling of the sparks accented the faint, mono-tone music. The boutiques flew past him in a ticklish array of colors and Amadis played at trying to capture his image in the huge mirrors of the displays as they passed by. However, he blushed when he saw himself take advantage of his convenient position in order to pilfer some of the items in the window, so he turned away.

He wasn't surprised that the driver had yet not stopped the vehicle. At this hour of the morning people are no longer on the way to their offices. The porter was asleep, sliding across the platform and looking, in his slumber, for a more comfortable position. Amadis felt overcome by a sort of intrepid drowsiness which invaded his body like a carnivorous fish. He stretched his legs out onto the seat on the other side. The trees, like the boutiques, were shining brilliantly in the sunlight, their fresh leaves brushing up against the roof of the bus and making the same sound that marine plants make when they hit the side of a little boat. The bus had yet to stop and the rolling motion was putting Amadis to sleep. At the moment he started to lose con-sciousness, he realized that they had just passed his office, but this last observation hardly troubled him now.

They were still moving when Amadis came to. It was no longer clear outside and he looked out at the road. The grey water of the two canals on either side helped him to recognize the Embarkment Highway and he contemplated the spectacle before him. He wondered if he had enough tickets to cover the cost of the trip. He turned his head and looked towards the porter. Aroused by a rather serious erot-ic dream, the man was turning his body every which way, finally twisting himself around one of the metal poles that supported the roof. Yet Amadis didn't interrupt his sleep, for he thought to himself that the life of a porter must be quite grueling. He got up to stretch out his legs. He figured that the bus must not have stopped, for he didn't see a single passenger. He had plenty of space to move around as he pleased. He went to the front and then walked back, and the noise he made while descending the steps awoke the porter. The latter knelt up and started to turn the lever of his machine, pointing his finger and screaming "Bang!, Bang! , Bang!"

He tapped the man on the shoulder and the porter proceeded to read the riot act at point blank range to a now subdued Amadis. Luckily, it was just a joke. The man rubbed his eyes and stood up.

"Where are we headed?" asked Amadis.

The porter, a man named Denis, shrugged in ignorance.

"There's no way of knowing. It's the conductor's fault. Number 21,239. He's crazy."

"So?"

"Well, we never really know how things will end with him. Usually nobody ever gets on this bus. As a matter of fact, how'd you get on?"

"Like everyone else," replied Amadis.

"I know," explained the porter. "I was falling asleep this morning."

"You didn't see me?" said Amadis.

"With this driver it's real tough," continued the porter. "Because you can't tell him anything. He just doesn't understand. What's more, you have to deal with the fact that he's an idiot."

"I pity him," said Amadis. "What a catastrophe."

"It sure is," said the porter. "There's a man who could be off fishing. And what does he do instead?"

"He drives a bus," Amadis replied.

"There you have it!" remarked the porter. "At least you're no fool."

"So what drove him mad?"

"I don't know. I'm always stuck with crackpot drivers. Think that's fun?"

"Hell no!"

"It's the Company," said the porter. "They're all insane at the Company."

"You seem to be holding up pretty well," said Amadis.

"Oh, me?" explained the driver. "I'm not like the rest of them, you understand? I'm not crazy."

He started to laugh so uncontrollably that he lost his breath. Amadis was a little disturbed as he watched the man roll around on the ground, turn all purple, then white and finally stiffen. But he calmed down when he saw that it was just an act. The porter gave him a wink, which on a contorted, rolled up eyeball is actually quite cute. In a few minutes, the man got back on his feet.

"I'm a great kidder, aren't I?" he said.

"That doesn't surprise me," responded Amadis.

"A lot of them are just miserable, but not me. Imagine staying with this driver without a sense of humor."

"What highway are we on anyway?"

The porter looked at him suspiciously.

"You mean you can't tell? It's the Embarkment Highway. He takes it once every three trips."

"Where are we going?"

"So that's the game," said the porter, "We talk a bit, I'm nice to you, I play the fool, and then you try to bribe me!"

"But, I'm not trying to bribe you. Not at all," replied Amadis.

"First of all," said the porter, "If you hadn't recognized the road, you would have asked me right away where we were. Ipso facto."

Amadis said nothing and the porter continued.

"Secondly, since you have noticed the road, you do know where we are going... and thirdly, you don't have a ticket."

He started laughing with a sort of false affectation.

11

BORI/ UIAN

Amadis felt uncomfortable. It was true: he didn't have a ticket.

"But you sell them?" he said.

"I beg your pardon," said the porter. "I sell tickets, but only for the regular route. Wait a minute."

"So what can I do?" said Amadis.

"Nothing."

"But I need a ticket."

"You can pay me afterwards," said the porter. "He could steer us right into the canal, so you might as well keep your money."

Amadis didn't argue. He tried to change the subject of conversation.

"Do you have any idea why they call this thing the Embarkment Highway?"

He hesitated repeating the name of the highway or even bringing up this subject because he was afraid the porter would lose his temper again. The little man looked down sadly at his feet and let his arms drop limply at his sides and left them there.

"You don't know?" insisted Amadis.

"You'll just be disappointed if I reply," murmured the porter.

"Of course not," said Amadis, encouragingly.

"Listen, I don't know anything about anything! Nothing, alright. No one is supposed to say that it's even possible to embark by this route."

"Where does it lead?"

"Look," said the porter.

Amadis saw a big pole holding up a galvanized metal sign. The white letters spelled out the name of Exopotamie, along with an arrow and the number of kilometers.

"That's where we're going?" he said. "Then we can get there by land?"

"Sure," said the porter. "You just have to follow the road...and not be afraid."

12

"Why's that?"

"Because we get balled out every time we return. You're not the one paying for the gas, you know!"

"In your opinion," said Amadis, "what kind of time are we making?"

"Oh, we should be there by tomorrow morning," replied the porter.

3

About five o'clock in the morning, Amadis thought it might be a nice idea to wake up, so he did just that. This allowed him to notice that he'd positioned himself quite horribly and that his back was causing him considerable pain. He felt a heavy consistency in his mouth, like the kind that comes when people don't brush their teeth. He stood up and moved about a bit in order to gather himself together and then proceeded with his intimate grooming ritual, being careful not to fall into the porter's line of sight. The latter, asleep between two rows of seats, was lost in a dream, turning his music box. It was broad daylight. The spiked wheels of the bus sung out across the pavement like so many spinning tops from Nuremberg humming over the waves of the Beebeesee. The motor roared away at a consistent rhythm, sure of getting its plate of fish when needed. To pass the time, Amadis started practicing his long jump and his last leap landed him right on the stomach of the porter. He bounded back up with such force that his head dented the ceiling of the bus and then he fell down flatly on all fours over the armrest of one of the seats. This last movement obliged him to lift up his leg rather high on the seat side so that the other could stretch out across the aisle. Just at that moment he saw a new sign outside: Exopotamie - two kilometers. He dashed for the bell, pressed one time, and the bus slowed down and pulled to the side of the road.

The porter, whose aching belly kept him from assuming a dignified posture, stood up and took his assigned position at the left side of the bus, near the cord. Amadis ran down the aisle with great agility, leaped lightly down the steps, and soon found himself nose to nose with the driver who had left his seat to find out what was happening. He started shouting at Amadis.

"Finally someone decides to ring the bell! And none too soon."

"Yes," said Amadis. "This is really a long haul."

"Finally. For God's sake!" said the driver. "Every time I take out the 975 nobody wants to ring and usually I end up coming back without having made a single stop. What kind of job do you call that?"

The porter shot a wink at Amadis from behind the driver's back, tapping his forehead as a sort of signal that any discussion was futile.

"Maybe the passengers forget," replied Amadis, seeing as the man was waiting for a response.

The driver laughed cynically.

"But that's not the case, is it, since you rang. All this nuisance..."

He leaned towards Amadis. The porter, sensing his presence superfluous, nonchalantly stepped away.

"...it's that porter," explained the conductor.

"Oh," said Amadis.

"He doesn't like passengers. He sees to it that we never leave with passengers and he never sounds the bell. I'm sure of it."

"That's true," said Amadis.

"He's mad, you see," said the driver

"That must be the case," murmured Amadis. "I found him bizarre."

"They're all insane at the Company."

"I'm not at all surprised."

"But me," replied the driver, "I have them all fooled. In

14

the land of the blind, the one-eyed man is king. You got a knife?"

"I've got a pocket-knife."

"Let me borrow it."

Amadis handed it over and the driver pulled out the large blade and thrust it energetically into his eye. He turned around. He was suffering a great deal and screaming out loud. Amadis got frightened and took off running, pumping his arms and lifting his knees as high as he could. This was no time to ignore an opportunity for exercise. He passed by a few clumps of spinifex scrub and then stopped to look back. The driver folded up the knife and slipped it into his pocket. From where Amadis was standing he could see that the bleeding had stopped. The driver had performed the procedure quite neatly and there was already a black bandana over his eye. The porter was pacing up and down the aisle of the bus and through the windows Amadis saw him consult his watch. The driver hopped back into his seat. The porter waited a few moments, looked at his watch again, and tugged on the cord several times in a row. His colleague understood the signal and the heavy vehicle took off with a clamor that grew progressively louder. Amadis watched the sparks fly as the noise diminished, grew faint, and finally disappeared. At that very moment, he lost sight of the bus. And he had reached Exopotamie without having to use a single ticket.

He picked up his step. He didn't want to waste any time because the porter might just change his mind and he wanted to keep his money.

B

A police captain slips into the room, pale as a
dead man (he was afraid of being hit by a bullet).

Maurice Laporte, *Histoire de l'Okhrana,*
Payot, 1935, p. 105.

1

On his port side, Claude Leon heard the trumpet-burst
of the alarm clock and woke up to listen more attentively.
This being accomplished, he quickly fell back asleep, only
to have his eyes pop mechanically and unintentionally open
again five minutes later. He looked at the phosphorescent
dial of the clock and knew it was time. He tossed back the
covers. Affectionately, they crawled back up his legs and
enveloped his body. It was dark and still difficult to make
out the luminous triangle of the window. Claude caressed
his covers, which had stopped their fight and decided to let
him get up. He sat up on the side of the bed, stretched out
his left arm to turn on the nightlight, realized once again
that the lamp was to the right, stretched out his right arm
and smashed it into the wooden frame of the bed as he did
every morning.

"I'll have to saw that thing off," he mumbled between
his teeth.

But his teeth unexpectedly spread open and let the
words escape abruptly into the room.

"Damn!" he thought to himself. "I'm going to wake up the house."

However, listening carefully, he was able to hear the supple and steady respiration of the house's walls and floors and he regained his composure. Around the curtains, one could see the grey lines of day creeping up amidst the pale glow of a winter morning. Claude Leon let out a sigh as his feet searched for their slippers at the foot of the bed. With considerable effort, he stood up. Sleep was stubbornly departing through his dilated pores, making a gentle sound as it left, like that of a dreaming mouse. He walked towards the door, and before flipping the light switch he turned towards his armoire. He had hastily shut off the light the day before while frowning before the mirror and he wanted to see himself again before he left for the office. He turned the lamp back on with a flip of the switch. Yesterday's face was still there. Seeing it, he laughed out loud, then it dissipated into the light and the mirror reflected back the new-morning Leon who turned his back to him and went off to shave. He hurried about his business in order to arrive at his office before his boss.

2

Luckily, he lived close to the Company. Luckily, it was winter. During the summer it's too short. There were only three hundred yards to walk on avenue Jacques-Lemarchand, named for the tax inspector from 1857 to 1870 who also happened to be the heroic, lone defender of a barricade attacked by the Prussians. They ended up catching him, finally, because they made it to the other side. The poor slob was trapped up too high and it was impossible for him to descend quickly. He fired two shots from his rifle into his mouth and what's more, the fall he took ripped off his right arm. Claude Leon was enormously interested in these little footnotes in history and in his desk drawer he kept the complete works of Dr. Cabanes, which were bound in black cloth like ledger books.

The little red pieces of ice around the sides of the pavement were cracking from the cold and the women tucked up their legs under their short fustian skirts. Claude gave a passing "hello" to the concierge and timidly approached the Roux-Conciliabuzia elevator, where three typists and one accountant stood waiting in front of the door. He greeted them with a single, collective, reserved gesture.

3

"Good day, Leon," said his boss, opening the door.

Claude jumped up and made a huge stain.

"Clumsy idiot!" howled the other man. "Always spots..."

"Excuse me Mr. Saknussem," said Claude... "but..."

"Wipe it up!"

Claude leaned over the spot and industriously lapped it up. The ink was rancid and smelled like a seal.

Saknussem seemed to be in a jovial mood.

"So," he said, "have you seen the papers? The conformists are cooking up some real trouble for us, eh?"

"Huh?... oh, yes sir," murmured Claude.

"Those bastards," said his boss. "You know, it's time we get on the ball. They're all armed, you understand."

"Ah..." said Claude.

"We saw the whole thing at the Liberationing," said Saknussem. "They hauled munitions in by the truckload. Naturally, good citizens like you and me, we don't have guns."

"Of course not..." replied Claude.

"You don't happen to have one, do you?"

"No, I don't, Mr. Saknussem," said Claude.

"Perhaps you could find me a revolver?" asked

Saknussem bluntly.

"It's just that... well, maybe the brother-in-law of my landlady...I don't know... uh..."

"Perfect," replied his boss. "I'm counting on you, alright? I want cartridges, too. And nothing really expensive. These goddamn conformists... You can't let your guard down, right?"

"Certainly not," said Claude.

"Thank you, Leon. I'm counting on you. When can you deliver it?"

"I've got to ask around," said Claude.

"Of course...Take your time...Maybe you'd like to leave a little early?"

"Not really," said Claude. "It isn't worth the trouble."

"Fine," said Saknussem. "And be careful about the spots, O.K.? Pay attention to your work, for God's sake. It's not like we pay you to sit and do nothing..."

"I'll pay attention Mr. Saknussem," promised Claude.

"And be on time. Yesterday you were six minutes late."

"No I wasn't. In fact, I was nine minutes early," said Claude.

"Yes," said Saknussem. "But usually you're fifteen minutes early, so make an effort, for God's sake!"

He left the room and closed the door. Claude, overwhelmed, picked up his pen. Because his hands were still trembling he caused another stain. It was an enormous mark that took the form of a mocking face next to a drop of kerosene.

4

He finished eating dinner. The cheese, of which only a large chunk remained, scampered about lazily on the mauve plate with its mauve holes. Claude topped off his meal with a glass of caramel-colored lithium water and felt its descent down his esophagus. The little bubbles came right back up his throat, exploding with a metallic noise inside his pharynx. Someone rang the doorbell and Claude got up to go and answer. It was his landlady's brother-in-law.

"Good evening, sir," said the man, whose honest smile and red hair betrayed his Carthaginian origins.

"Good evening," replied Claude.

"I brought something for you," said the man. His name was Jean.

"Oh, right...the,"

"That's right," said Jean.

He pulled it out of his pocket.

It was a nice little equalizer that fired ten rounds, a Walther ppk with a clip whose ebony base fit perfectly with the grooves on both sides of the grip where the hand goes.

"Well made," said Claude.

"Hell of a cannon," said the other. "Great precision."

"Yeah," said Claude. "Easy to aim."

"Fits nicely into your hand, hey?" added Jean.

"Beautifully designed," Claude replied, aiming at a flowerpot which ducked out of his line of fire.

"It's an excellent weapon," said Jean. "Thirty-five hundred."

"That's a little steep. Anyway, it's not for me. I'm sure it's worth it, but my party can't go over three thousand."

"I can't let you have it for any less," said Jean. "That's what it cost me."

"I know," said Claude. "Still, that's pretty expensive."

"Not really," said Jean.

"Well... I mean to say that guns in general are pretty expensive."

"Oh, that. I guess so," said Jean. "Anyway a handgun like this isn't easy to find."

"It certainly isn't."

"Thirty-five hundred's my last offer," said Jean.

It was certain that Saknussem wouldn't offer more than three. Claude could maybe give him the other five hundred out of his own pocket, if he resoled his old shoes instead of buying new ones.

"Maybe it won't snow any more," said Claude.

"Maybe," replied Jean.

"I can get by," said Claude. "I'll just get some new soles for my shoes."

"Really?" said Jean. "It's winter, you know? Look, I'll leave you a second clip, on the house."

"That's awfully nice of you," said Claude.

Claude would eat a bit less for the next few weeks and make back the five hundred francs. Perhaps, by chance, Saknussem would even find out about his sacrifice.

"Thank you," said Jean.

"It's me who should be thanking you," said Claude, as he led the man towards the door.

"You've got a great gun there," concluded Jean as he walked out.

"It's not for me," Claude reminded the man as he descended the staircase.

Claude closed the door and came back to the table. The cold, black equalizer had not yet said anything. It was lying, in all its heaviness, next to the piece of cheese, which, terrified, scurried away quickly to the other side of its nourishing plate. Claude's heart was beating a little harder than usual. He took the sorrowful object and held it in his hands. He was intoxicated with the power he felt at the end of his fingertips, here behind closed doors. But he knew he had to leave, to take it to Saknussem.

It was against the law to carry a handgun on the streets. He put it back down on the table and, in the silence, pressed his ear up against the wall, wondering if his neighbors might have overheard the conversation with Jean.

5

He could feel it, like a dead beast, weighing heavy and cold against his thigh. The weight tugged at his pocket and his belt and his shirt puffed out over his pants on the right side. His raincoat covered it up, but with each advancing movement of his thigh everyone would still be able to see a huge bulge under the cloth. It seemed wise to take another route, so he deliberately turned left upon exiting the building. Trusting himself to only the smaller streets, he cut a path toward the train station. It was a depressing day, cold like the night before. He didn't know this part of the neighborhood. He took the first street to the right, then realizing that this would lead him back to his regular path, continued ten paces and took the first to the left. The little side road cut the preceding one at an oblique angle of a little less than ninety degrees and was lined with sterile and unremarkable boutiques that differed from those he ordinarily passed by.

He was walking quickly and could feel the thing pressing into his thigh. He passed a man who seemed to be looking toward his pocket. Claude trembled. He turned around a few steps later and the man was staring at him. He lowered his head and quickened his pace, hurling himself to the left at the next intersection. He brutally smashed into a little girl who went sliding into a dirty mound of snow that had just been swept to the side of the pavement. He didn't dare stop to help. He simply hurried along, glancing furtively over his shoulder and keeping his hands buried in his pockets. He then came nose to nose with an old maid armed with a broom who was exiting a neighboring building. She greeted him with a blaring insult. Claude turned around. Her gaze was still fixed upon him. He picked up his step and almost knocked over a metal grill that some highway workers had just placed over a drainage ditch. To avoid doing so he had to make a rather violent maneuver and wound up tearing open the pocket of his raincoat. The workers all called him "idiot" and "imbecile," but Claude, red-faced with shame, just kept plowing right along, slipping all the way on the frozen puddles of ice. He was beginning to perspire when he smashed into a cyclist who turned into him without warning. The pedal of the bike ripped the bottom of his pants, slashing open the flesh on his ankle. The two were hurled into the muddy street and Claude let out a cry of fear, sticking his hands out in front of himself to break his fall. There was a cop not far from the scene.

Claude Leon broke himself free of the bicycle, his ankle in tremendous pain. The cyclist had a sprained wrist and blood was pissing from his nostrils. He started yelling at Claude, who became filled with rage. His heart was pounding and hot blood raced down his arms and through his body, especially at his bloody ankle and up against his thigh where the equalizer would rise with every pulsation. Suddenly, the cyclist smashed him in the face with his right hand. Claude was more livid than ever. He plunged his hands into his pocket, pulled the trigger of his equalizer, and laughed while the cyclist muttered a few incoherent words and fell back. But then he suddenly felt a blow to his hand. The cop's nightstick came down once more. He picked up the gun and grabbed Claude by the collar. Claude no longer felt the pain in his hand. He quickly turned around and let loose a kick to the belly of the cop, who doubled over and dropped the piece. With a moan of pleasure, Claude dove for the gun and carefully proceeded to fire upon the cyclist, who brought his two hands to his gut and quietly gurgled "arrgh" from the depths of his throat. The smoke made by the bullets left a nice smell and Claude blew a puff of air at the end of the barrel, just like in the movies. He put the piece back into his pocket and collapsed onto the cop. He wanted to sleep.

23

6

Just as he was getting up to leave, the lawyer turned and said, "Really, now. Why were you carrying the gun?"

"I've already told you that..." said Claude.

He repeated his testimony again.

"It was for Mr. Saknussem, my boss. Arne Saknussem."

"He claims to know nothing about it," said the lawyer. "You understand that?"

"But that's the truth," said Claude Leon.

"I know it is," said the lawyer. "Just find something else to say. You've had plenty of time!"

He walked towards the door, irritated.

"I'm leaving now," he said. "There's nothing to do but wait. I'll try to do my best for you but you really haven't been a great help."

"That's not my job," said Claude. He hated his lawyer almost as much as he hated the cyclist and the officer at the precinct who had broken his finger. Once again, he felt the heat in his arms and legs.

"Good-bye," said his lawyer as he walked out the door.

Claude just sat down on his bed and didn't bother to respond. The guard locked his door and tossed a letter onto his bed. Claude was half asleep, but when he recognized the guard's hat he sat back up.

"I'd like some...," started Claude.

"What," responded the guard.

"Some thread. And a pin cushion."

Claude scratched his head.

"Against the rules," said the guard.

"It's not like I'm going to hang myself," said Claude. "I have my suspenders. I could have already done it."

The guard stopped to consider this logic.

"Two hundred francs," he said. "I'll give you ten or

twelve meters, no more. I'm risking my neck as it is."

"Fine. Go get it," said Claude. "Just ask my lawyer for the money."

The guard looked through his pockets.

"I've got some with me," he said.

He held out a roll of some nice, solid thread.

"Thanks," said Claude.

"What are you going to do with it?" continued the guard. "No nonsense, right?"

"I'm going..." said Claude with a laugh, " ...to hang myself."

"Ah ha!" said the guard. His voice spread through the room like a flag unfurling in the wind. "That's idiotic. Like you said, you've had your suspenders all along."

"But they're new," said Claude. "They'd be ruined."

The guard looked at Claude with admiration.

"You have an iron will," said the guard. "You must be a journalist."

"No," said Claude. "Thanks, all the same."

The guard walked towards the door.

"Like I said, my lawyer will pay you," added Claude.

"Yeah," said the guard. "Just so long as you're sure."

Claude nodded his head to signal yes and the doorlock snapped shut.

7

When torn in half and woven together, it was about two yards long. Perfect. Standing on the bed, he was able to fasten it around the bar. Getting the length exactly right was a delicate matter; he didn't want his feet to touch the ground.

He tugged at it to test the strength. It held. He stood up on the bed with his back to the wall, grabbed the bar, and with difficulty, attached the cord. He slipped his head through the noose and slung himself into the void. He felt

25

a blow to the back of his head and the cord snapped. He fell to his feet, furious.

"That bastard of a guard!" he shouted out loud.

At just that moment, the guard opened the door.

"This thread is crap!" shouted Claude Leon.

"I really don't care," said the guard. "I've already been paid by your lawyer. Hey, I've got sugar today. Ten francs a packet. Want some?"

"No," said Claude. "I'll never ask you for anything else again."

"Just wait two or three months," said the guard. "You'll come around. In fact, I'm exaggerating. You'll have forgotten about this in a week."

"Probably," said Claude. "That still doesn't mean that your string wasn't a piece of crap."

He waited for the guard to leave and decided to take off his suspenders. They were brand new, made out of braided leather and elastic. They represented two weeks of savings. A meter and a half. A little more maybe. He climbed back up onto the bed and fastened one end to the stem of the bar. He then made another noose and slipped his head through. He launched himself one more time, but the suspenders stretched out too far and he landed softly over by the window. The bar broke loose and struck him in the head like a bolt of lightning. He saw three stars and said:

"Martell!..."

His back slid down the wall and he found himself sitting on the floor. His head swelled up terribly, pounding with an atrocious music. The suspenders were still in fine shape.

8

Littlejohn, the abbot, was prancing about in the prison halls, closely followed by a prison guard with whom he was playing a little game of one-upmanship. While approaching

Claude's cell, the abbot slipped on a turd left by a cat 'o nine tails and while falling made a complete revolution in the atmosphere. With his habit graciously deployed around his robust legs he looked so much like Loie Fuller that the guard, with great politeness, tipped his hat and just passed him by. Then the abbot hit the ground with a noise that traversed the room and the guard leaped, mounting him like a horse. The abbot gave in.

"I caught you," said the guard. "Your turn to pay."

The Abbot Littlejohn grudgingly acquiesced.

"No fooling around," said the guard. "Sign the paper."

"I can't sign when I'm lying on my belly," responded the abbot.

"O.K., I'll let you up," said the guard.

As soon as he got to his feet, the priest let out a thunderous laugh and took off running straight ahead. But he ran right into a solid wall and the guard had no trouble catching him.

"Charlatan!" he said. "Sign the paper."

"Compromise," said the abbot. "I'll grant you fifteen days of indulgence."

"That's peanuts," said the guard.

"Oh, all right... I'll sign."

The guard opened his notebook and tore loose the prepared form, which he handed, along with a pencil, to Littlejohn, who then signed it and moved towards Claude's door. The key inserted itself into the deadbolt and taking a liking to the little instrument, the door opened gently for her.

Claude was sitting on the bed, meditating. The loosened bar from the window created a space through which a ray of light entered. It bounced around the room, finally disappearing into the metallic latrine.

"Hello, father," said Claude Leon upon seeing the abbot enter.

"Hello, my dear little Claude."

"Is my mother alright?" asked Claude Leon.

"But of course," said Littlejohn.

"I've been touched by grace," said Claude. He passed his hand over his occiput.

"Feel it," he added.

The abbot felt it.

"Damn!..." he responded. "Our Lady sure doesn't strike with the hand of a sissy."

"Blessed be the Lord," said Claude Leon. "I'd like you to hear my confession. I want to meet my maker with a clear conscience."

"...clear as if it had been washed with parsley!..." both of them chimed in unison, according to the prescribed catholic ritual. They then made the classic sign of the cross.

"But I don't think there's any more question about you suffering the strappado," said the abbot.

"I killed a man," said Claude. "What's more, he was a cyclist."

"I've got some news," said the abbot. "I saw your attorney. The cyclist was a conformist."

"All the same, I've still killed a man."

"But Saknussem has agreed to testify on your behalf."

"I don't care," said Claude.

"My son," said the abbot, "Don't you realize that this cyclist was an enemy of the Holy Mother of the Annotated Church of Great Spires..."

"I hadn't yet been touched by grace when I killed him," said Claude.

"Bullshit," the abbot assured him. "We're going to get you out of this mess."

"I don't want you to," said Claude. "I want to be a hermit, and what better place is there for that than a prison?"

"Perfect," said the abbot. "If you want to be a hermit I'll get you out of here tomorrow. The bishop is very friendly with the director of the prison."

"But they haven't granted me a hermitage," said Claude. "And I like it here."

"Be assured," said the abbot. "We'll find you something even less attractive."

"Well," said Claude. "That's a different story. When do we leave?"

"Hold your horses, you heretic," said the abbot. "There are certain formalities. I'll pass by tomorrow and pick you up in the hearse."

"Where will we be going?" asked a quite excited Claude.

"Exopotamie has a nice little spot for a hermit," said the abbot. "We'll give you that post. You'll be miserable."

"Perfect," said Claude. "I'm praying for you."

"Amen," said the abbot. "Burr and Bamm and Ratatamm!..." they concluded in concert, following as always the prescribed rites of Catholicism, which allows them, as we all know, to dispense with the sign of the cross. The priest tapped Claude on the cheek and gave his nose a good long pinch. He left the cell and the guard locked the door.

So there stood Claude, in front of the little window. He got down on his knees and started to pray with all his astral heart.

C

*Your ideas about the inconveniences of
mixed marriages are quite exaggerated.*

Mémoires de Louis Rossel, Stock, 1908, p.115.

Angel was waiting for Anne and Rochelle. He was seated on the weathered stone of the balustrade, watching the technicians proceed with their annual clipping of the pigeons' feathers. It was a delightful spectacle. The technicians were wearing very clean white shirts and red leather aprons that were decorated with the city's coat of arms. They were provided with a special model of feather clippers as well as a product designed to lower the amount of grease in the wings of the aquatic pigeons, which made up a large portion of the bird population in the neighborhood.

Angel waited in anticipation for the moment when the down next to the skin would start to rise up to be inhaled almost immediately by cylindrical chrome recuperators mounted on top of little pneumatic carts operated by the assistants. With the down that was gathered they filled up the comforter that belonged to the Prime Minister. It made one think of the foam on the sea when the wind blows - the kind that is often seen on the sand in big clumps, undulating to the rhythm of the wind, and which if stepped on, bounds up softly through the spaces between the toes, matting up as it dries.

Anne and Rochelle were nowhere in sight.

Anne must be screwing around. He was never on time and he never had his car looked after by the mechanic. Rochelle was probably waiting for him. He was supposed to pick her up.

Angel had known Anne for five years and Rochelle not quite as long. He and Anne went to the same school, but Angel had graduated lower in his class because he didn't like to work. Anne directed a branch of the Gravel Factory which supplied the Heavy Railways, while Angel made do in a less lucrative situation working for a company that manufactured glass tubing fixtures for lamps. Angel assumed the technical direction of his company while Anne, in his position, looked after commercial affairs.

The sun, moving back and forth over the sky, seemed unable to make up its mind. The east and the west came to play in the four corners with their two other comrades, but for sheer amusement, they decided to change positions. From far away, the sun just couldn't find its bearings. People started taking advantage of this situation but the gears of the sundials started working backwards, one after another going haywire amidst a sinister array of cracking and shaking. Still, the gaiety of the playful sunlight over-shadowed the horror of these noises. Angel looked at his watch. They were a half an hour late and now it was beginning to get bothersome. He got up to move and saw in front of him one of the girls who was holding a pigeon for clipping. She was wearing a short skirt and Angel's gaze made its way over her shiny, golden knees and insinuated itself between her two long and streamlined thighs. It was hot there, and refusing to listen to Angel, who wanted to pull back, the gaze decided to do its own thing and move further on up. Angel became increasingly embarrassed and regretfully closed his eyes, leaving his look to die on the young girl's skirt. Its cadaver remained there until the girl ran her hand over her skirt and unknowingly knocked it to the ground when she stood up several minutes later.

The featherless pigeons desperately tried to fly again, but they tired quickly and fell right back to earth. At that point, they could hardly move and permitted themselves to be fixed with wings of yellow, red, green or blue silk that were furnished liberally by the municipality. After they were shown how to use their wings, the birds flew back to their nests filled with a new sense of dignity and their movement, naturally solemn, was almost hieratic.

Angel was starting to tire of this spectacle. He figured that Anne probably wouldn't show or that maybe he had taken Rochelle somewhere else, so he got back up to leave.

He crossed the garden and passed by groups of children who were amusing themselves as only children can: smashing ants with a hammer, playing hopscotch, observing the copulation of insects. The women, when not occupied with their progeny, would sew together haversacks out of waxy cloth which were fixed around the necks of the babies in order to help them swallow their mush. A few of them were knitting and others were pretending to do so just to look composed, even though it was clear that they had no wool.

Angel pushed the little wrought iron grill of the door. It slammed shut behind him as he stepped out onto the sidewalk. There were cars in the street and people walking around, but where was Anne? He waited a few minutes. He was hesitant about leaving. He thought to himself for a moment about the fact that he had no idea what color Rochelle's eyes were, and this idea made him waiver indecisively on the curb before crossing the street. The driver of the oncoming cab could see Angel advancing and he braked so hard that his vehicle started fishtailing out of control. Anne's car was right behind this one. It pulled up to the sidewalk and Angel got in.

Rochelle was seated next to Anne. Angel found himself alone in back on a cushion filled with wiry springs and layers of kapok. He leaned forward to shake their hands and Anne excused himself for having been late. The car started moving and Anne had to steer sharply to avoid the wreckage of the overturned taxi.

They followed the street to an area where trees started dotting the sidewalks and then they turned left at the statue. Anne started to accelerate because there were fewer cars on the road. The sun finally located the west and headed there on the double, like a bat out of hell trying to make up for lost time. Anne handled the car quite well and he liked to amuse himself by trying to brush up against the ears of school children who were walking on the sidewalk so that he could hit them with the car's automatic turn signals. In order to do that, he had to really hug the sides of the street and he ran the risk of putting a nasty scratch on his whitewalls. Nevertheless, he always seemed to succeed without getting so much as a single mark. Unfortunately, he passed by a little girl about nine or ten years old whose ears stuck out enormously. The turn light struck her smack in the lobe and it broke right off. Electricity fell in little pearl-like drops from the broken wire and the amperage meter gave a dangerously low reading. Rochelle gave the instrument a tap, but it was no use. The temperature dropped, the lights dimmed, and the motor slowed. After rolling several yards, Anne stopped the car.

"What's the problem?" said Angel.

He was a bit lost, realizing that he had been doing nothing but staring at Rochelle's hair for quite a while now.

"God dammit!" groaned Anne. "That stinking little brat!"

"We've got a broken turn signal," explained Rochelle as she turned towards Angel.

Anne got out of the car to repair the damage, delicately working with the fragile mechanics of the system. He tried to make a ligature out of catgut.

Rochelle turned all the way around and knelt up on the front seat.

"Did you wait for us a long time?" she said.

"It was really no bother," murmured Angel.

It was quite difficult for him to look her straight in the face. She was glowing, almost too brightly. Yet her eyes... he had to see the color of her eyes.

"Yes it was," she said. "It was so a bother. That's the biggest problem with Anne. He's always late. Myself, I was ready. And now look what he's gotten us into. He starts screwing around as soon as we take off."

"He just wants to have a good time. No harm in that."

"Yeah," said Rochelle. "He's so carefree."

During all this, Anne was busy swearing like a sailor and jumping into the air with each drop of electricity that would flow onto his hands.

"Where are we going?" asked Angel.

"He wanted to go dancing," said Rochelle. "But I'd rather see a movie."

"He really likes to be able to watch himself when he does something."

"Hey! You really shouldn't say things like that!"

"Excuse me."

Rochelle was blushing a little and Angel regretted having made this treacherous commentary.

"He's a great guy," added Angel. "My best friend."

"You know him well?" asked Rochelle.

"Five years now."

"You're not at all alike."

"No, but we really get along," Angel assured her.

"Is he..."

She stopped her phrase and started blushing again.

"Why are you afraid to say it? It's not something indiscreet?"

"Yes, it is," said Rochelle. "It's idiotic and really none of my business."

"If that's what you want to know..." said Angel, "the answer is yes, he's always been a hit with the girls."

"He's a really nice looking guy," murmured Rochelle.

She stopped talking and turned around when she noticed that Anne was coming back to take his place at the wheel. He opened the door.

"I hope it'll hold," he said. "It's not dripping much, but there's a strange sort of pressure. I just recharged the batteries."

"It's not your lucky day," said Angel.

"Why did that stupid little girl have to have such big ears anyway!..." protested Anne.

"Well no one asked you to play that dopey game with the turn signals," said Angel.

"That's true," added Rochelle.

She laughed.

"It was really quite funny!..."

Anne laughed, too. He wasn't at all mad. They departed once again but stopped almost immediately because the road refused to continue any further. They had arrived where they were headed.

The dance club was a place for music fans to assemble among the real purists and practice their routines of dislocation. Anne was a terrible dancer and Angel always felt a little embarrassed watching his rhythmless friend prance across the floor. What's more, he had never seen him dance with Rochelle.

A small, white, spiral staircase led to the basement where everything was happening. There was a large vine, neatly pruned every month, which allowed guests to hold onto something so they could descend without killing themselves. The club was also decorated here and there with red copper and there were portholes on the walls.

Rochelle entered first, followed by Anne, and Angel brought up the rear so that the next group of newcomers could use it as needed. Now and again, some careless fool would leave it down and the waiter, blinded by his serving tray, would take a nasty spill, his head getting a pounding with each successive blow.

Halfway down they could already feel the heartbeat of the pulsating rhythm section. A little further on they could hear a clarinet and a pocket trumpet trading solos with remarkable speed and dexterity. At the bottom of the staircase they perceived the entire, confused brouhaha: feet moving, torsos mingling, indiscreet laughter coupled with confidential giggling, some serious belching, and nervous conversation which played counterpoint to the continual clinking of glasses filled with carbonated liquids - all the little touches that go into the making of a not so luxurious bar. Anne scanned the room for an open table and pointed it out to Rochelle, who was the first to get there. They ordered three portos frisés.

Because of the constant sensation in the ears, the music hardly ever stopped. Anne took advantage of a languorous blues and asked Rochelle to join him on the floor. A large group of dancers sat back down, upset because of the slow tempo, while a few of the more twisted clientele made their way out to the floor. For them, the music conjured up a tango. They would keep time to the conventional beat and accent it with strange little half steps and hesitation moves. Anne figured that he was also capable of this and he decided to join in as Angel watched from a distance, ready to vomit at the sight of Anne losing all conception of the rhythm.

Rochelle was moving about quite gracefully.

When they came back to sit down, Angel asked Rochelle for a dance. She smiled, accepted, and stood up as the band started playing another slow tune.

"Where is it that you met Anne?" asked Angel.

"It was pretty recently," she responded.

"Just a month or two ago, wasn't it?"

"Yeah," said Rochelle. "At a surprise party."

"Maybe you'd like it better if I changed the subject," he asked.

"No. I enjoy talking about him."

Angel hardly knew her and he was a little uneasy.

Furthermore he would have been embarrassed to explain just why he was uneasy. Whenever he met a pretty girl he always wanted to possess her. He wanted to have the rights to her. But Anne was his friend.

"He's a remarkable guy," said Angel. "Extremely talented."

"You can tell that right off," said Rochelle. "And such scintillating eyes, not to mention a hot car."

"At school, everyone racked their brains to get ahead. Anne just seemed to succeed without even trying."

"He's got a great body," said Rochelle. "He works out all the time."

"In three years, I didn't see him fail a single test."

"And I really like the way he dances."

Angel was trying to lead because Rochelle seemed intent on working against the rhythm. Finally, he just relaxed his embrace and let her thrash it out alone.

"He's only got one fault," said Angel.

"Yeah," said Rochelle, "but that's not so important."

"The problem could be corrected," Angel assured her.

"He just needs someone to look after him, to always be there by his side."

"You're probably right. Anyway, he's already got someone looking after him."

"I wouldn't want a whole lot of people around him either," she said pensively. "Just good friends. You for example."

"I'm a good friend?"

"Exactly. You're the type of guy a girl would want to have for a brother."

Angel lowered his head. She left him no illusions about his chances. He didn't know how to smile in that certain way, the way Anne could. That must be the reason.

Rochelle continued to amuse herself while dancing off-beat, enjoying the music the whole time. It was hot and smoky in the club, but all the dancers were having a splen-

did time. The notes of music wove in and out of the spiraling smoke that rose languidly from crushed cigarette butts
anguishing in ashtrays which displayed small scale represen-
tations of bedpans and other sundry items for convalescents
as advertisement for Maison Dupont, rue d'Hautefeuille.

"What do I do? What's that supposed to mean?"

"I mean what do you do with your life?"

"I like to dance," said Rochelle. "I went to secretarial
college after high school, but I don't work any more. My
parents prefer that I get to know the world, live a little."

The music stopped and Angel wanted to stay on the
floor and wait for another tune so that he could start again
as soon as the musicians broke into another number. But
they were busy tuning their instruments. He followed
Rochelle, who was in a hurry to get back to the table and
take her place next to Anne.

"So," said Anne. "The next one's for me?"

"Sure," said Rochelle. "You know I love to dance
with you."

Angel pretended not to be listening. Other women
might have hair as beautiful, but none had a voice like that.
Impossible. And her body was nothing to scoff at either.

He certainly didn't want to be a bother to Anne. It was
Anne who knew Rochelle and it was his affair. He reached
for the bottle that was resting in a bucket full of green ice
and filled up his glass. There wasn't another woman in the
room who interested him. No one but Rochelle. But Anne
had priority.

And Anne was a friend.

2

They had to leave to go eat dinner. One can't stay out
all night long when there's work to do the next day.
Rochelle placed herself next to Anne, in front, while Angel

slid into the back seat. Anne behaved himself admirably with Rochelle. He avoided putting his arm around her waist or even leaning over towards her. He didn't even hold her hand. Angel would have done all those things, had he met Rochelle before Anne. Then again, Anne made more money than him; he deserved all the breaks. Being a crummy dancer isn't such a serious vice when there isn't any music playing. But we'll let that pass for the moment.

Every now and then Anne said something funny and Rochelle would laugh, tossing back her dazzling hair which fell onto the collar of her bright green suit...

Anne said something to Angel, but Angel was lost in his own thoughts, naturally. So Anne turned around to look at Angel and this movement threw the steering wheel off a bit. It's an unfortunate thing to recount, but a pedestrian on the pavement was struck in the side while the right front wheel of the car plowed over the curb. The man let out a loud cry and dropped to the ground, grasping at his hip as his agitated body thrashed and convulsed. Angel had already opened the door and moved outside. He was frightened to death as he leaned over the injured man. The victim was doubled over in laughter. He would stop now and then to moan and then roll around again, full of joy.

"Are you in pain?" asked Angel.

Rochelle wasn't watching. She stayed in the car, her head buried in her hands. Anne's face was all dirty. He was pale. He figured that the man must have been in real agony.

"It was you?" stuttered the man as he looked at Angel.

Once again he fell into a fit of laughter. Tears started flowing down his face.

"Get a hold of yourself," said Angel. "You must be seriously hurt."

"I'm suffering like a beast," he managed to blurt out.

The words he spoke sent him into a frenzy that somersaulted his body forward several feet. Anne stood his ground, perplexed. He turned around to glance at

Rochelle. She was crying and figured that the man was surely complaining. She was frightened for Anne. He came towards her, and through the open door placed his large hands around her face and kissed her on the eyes.

Angel caught a glimpse of this, which was the last thing he wanted, but as Rochelle's hands reached up to grasp the collar of Anne's coat, he turned back to listen once again to the wounded man who was making an effort to pull his wallet out of his pocket.

"Are you an engineer?" he asked Angel.

His laughter started to fade a bit.

"Yes..." murmured Angel.

"Well, then you can take my place. I can't, in all honesty, go to Exopotamie with a hip that's been shattered into five pieces. If you only knew how happy I am!..."

"But..." replied Angel.

"You mean you weren't the one driving?"

"No," said Angel. "It was Anne."

"That's a problem," said the other man.

His face grew sullen and his lips started to tremble.

"Don't cry," said Angel.

"But they won't send a girl in my place..."

"He's a guy..." said Angel.

The wounded man was rejuvenated.

"You must congratulate the mother..."

"I won't forget," said Angel, "but I'm sure she's gotten quite used to it by now."

"Great. Then we'll send Anne to Exopotamie. My name is Cornelius Onte."

"I'm Angel."

"You'd better inform Anne," said Cornelius. "He has to sign. Fortunately, the name's been left blank on my contract."

"How's that?" asked Angel.

"I don't think they really trusted me," said Cornelius. "Call Anne over."

Angel didn't feel so good. He looked around, took a

couple of steps, and put his hand on Anne's shoulder. He was almost in shock and there was a dazed look in his eyes. Rochelle held hers completely shut.

"Anne," said Angel. "You're going to have to sign."

"Sign what?" said Anne.

"A contract. You're going to Exopotamie."

"It's to build a railroad," clarified Cornelius.

He started moaning at the end of his phrase because the shattered pieces of his hip were grinding up against one another and making quite a disagreeable sound in his ears.

"Are you really going to go?" said Rochelle.

Anne leaned toward her again and asked her to repeat what she had just said. And he told her yes. He searched through his pockets and found a pen. Cornelius handed him the contract. Anne filled out the forms and signed at the bottom of the page.

"Shouldn't we drive you to the hospital?" proposed Angel.

"It's not worth the trouble," said Cornelius. "An ambulance will come along soon enough. Just leave me the contract. Really, I'm quite content."

He took back the contract and fainted.

3

"I don't know what to do," said Anne.

"You've got to go," said Angel. "You've signed."

"But I'll be bored stiff," said Anne. "I'll be all alone."

"Have you seen Cornelius again?"

"He telephoned. I have to leave the day after tomorrow."

"Are you really that bothered about all this?"

"No," said Anne. "I guess it'll give me the chance to see another country, after all."

"You don't want to admit it," said Angel, "but it's because of Rochelle that you're feeling uneasy."

Anne gave Angel a look of astonishment.

"I haven't even given that a second thought, really. You think she'll be mad at me if I leave?"

"I don't know," said Angel.

Angel figured that if Rochelle stayed behind, the two of them could see one another from time to time. Her eyes were so blue... And Anne would be gone.

"You know..." said Anne.

"What?"

"You should come along with me. They'll certainly need plenty of engineers."

"But I don't know anything about railroads," said Angel.

He just couldn't abandon Rochelle, not if Anne was leaving.

"You know just as much as I do."

"But you would at least understand all that stuff about the gravel, given the type of job you have."

"I just sell it," said Anne. "I don't know anything about it. People don't always know a great deal about what they sell."

"If the two of us were to go..." said Angel.

"Listen," said Anne. "She would find plenty of other men willing to look after her."

"You mean to tell me you're not in love with her?" asked Angel.

This idea stirred with a somewhat unusual force inside of him, near his heart. He tried holding his breath to stop it, but it was too strong.

"She really is a pretty girl," said Anne. "But sometimes you've got to make sacrifices."

"So what's the story?" asked Angel. "Why are you so worried about going away?"

"I'll be bored," said Anne. "If you come along, I'll at least have someone to kick around with. Why can't you? It's not Rochelle that's holding you back, is it?"

"No. Of course not," said Angel.

Very painful to say, but nothing was broken.

"Come to think of it," said Anne, "I could have her hired on by Cornelius, as my secretary."

"Not a bad idea," said Angel. "And I'll talk to Cornelius myself, see if they have some work for me."

"So it's decided then?" said Anne.

"Yeah. I guess I can't just abandon you like that."

"Great," said Anne. "You know, pal, I think we'll have ourselves a ball. Get Cornelius on the phone."

Angel sat down in Anne's chair and picked up the receiver.

"So I should ask him if Rochelle can come? And if he has a job for me?"

"Go on," said Anne. "I suppose, after all, that there are certain sacrifices that one just can't make."

D

...A similar decision was made after an
animated debate; It would be interesting to
know the positions of each of the participants
in this discussion.

Georges Cogniot. "Les subventions à l'enseignment
confessionel",
   La Pensée, n. 3, (April, May, June, 1945).

1

Professor Petereater stopped to look through the display
window, unable to take his eyes off the brilliant reflection that
the opaline light bulb absent-mindedly attached to the polished wood of a twelve-blade propeller. His heart, full of joy,
was thrashing about forcefully and shook with such might
that it touched the eighteenth set of his temporal brachial
nerves. Petereater opened the door. The shop smelled like
sawdust. Throughout the room there were little pieces of
balsa, hickory, and both hemlock and hemlock spruce, all
varying in price and size, while the window displayed ball-
bearings, mechanical objects designed for flight, and other little nameless round things that the owner had christened
"wheels" simply because they had holes in the middle.
   "Hello, professor," said the shopkeeper.
   He knew Petereater quite well.
   "Good news, Mr. Crock," said Petereater. "I have the

time to get back to work again, now that I've killed three of my clients."

"Fantastic!" replied Crock. "You must never let them slip by."

"Medicine is an amusing way to pass the time," said the professor, "but it can't compare to building these scale models."

"Don't say that," said Crock. "I started practicing just two days ago myself and I'm having a ball."

"You'll change your mind!" said Petereater. "Have you seen that new little Italian motor?"

"No," said Crock. "What's it like?"

"Terrible," he said. "We'll have to Peter-eater the thing."

"You always break me up, doctor," laughed Mr. Crock.

"Sure I do," said the professor. "But listen, there's no ignition switch."

Mr. Crock's eyes grew wider, which gave the impression that his eyelids were actually falling. He leaned toward the professor with his hands placed firmly on the counter.

"No?" he gasped.

"Afraid so..."

Petereater spoke with a clean, soft, and rosy tonality which excluded any possibility that he may have been mistaken.

"Have you seen it?"

"I've got one at my place, and it works."

"Where did you find it?"

"My Italian correspondent, Alfredo Jabes. He sent it to me."

"Can I see it?" asked Crock.

A feeling of hope highlighted his pear-shaped cheeks.

"Well," said Petereater, "...that depends."

He passed his fingers between the collar of his gold studded shirt and moved them around his cylindrico-conical neck.

"I need some supplies."

"Help yourself," said Crock. "Take whatever you like. Don't even worry about paying. But I want to come to your place later."

"Great," replied Petereater.

He took a deep breath of air and strolled around the boutique while humming a military tune. Crock just watched. He would have let him walk away with the entire store.

2

"It's incredible!..." said Crock.

The motor stopped. Petereater fiddled around with the needle and gave the propeller a spin to get it going again. On the third try it started too abruptly, leaving him no time to pull back his hand. He jumped back and let out a wail. Crock then decided to give it a spin. The engine kicked right in. In the little combustion chamber one could see air bubbles entering through the tube, each one crawling through like a slobbering snail while oil gently flowed through the two exhaust valves.

The propeller was spreading the fumes from the motor right into the face of Petereater, who had now returned to the machine. In order to regulate the compression, he tried turning the throttle of the counter-piston and ended up burning his hand quite severely. He shook his fingers and shoved his whole hand into his mouth.

"Shit, shit, shit!..." he swore.

But as the words passed through his fingers they were, thank God, difficult to understand. Crock, hypnotized, tried to follow the motion of the propeller with his eyes, spinning the two globes furiously round and round in their orbits. But soon the centrifugal force projected his crystalline lenses toward the exterior and all he could see was the inside of his own eyelids, so he gave up. The small aluminum crankcase of the machine was fastened to a heavy table which vibrated so strongly that the whole room was starting to shake.

"It's working!...." screamed Crock.

He stepped back from the table and took Petereater by the hands. They danced around as blue smoke escaped towards the back of the room.

In a perilous mid-air leap, the two men were surprised by the sound of a telephone whose sonority illustrated a preference for strident, noisy rings that resembled the hissing of a medusa. Seized in full-flight, Petereater fell flat on his back while Crock ended up head-first in the soil of a green pot that housed a huge Palme Académique.

Petereater was the first to get up and he ran to respond. Crock managed to stand up again, but still had the pot on his head and was tugging at the trunk of the palm, which he had mistaken for his neck. He became aware of his error when the soil from the pot started cascading down his back.

Petereater returned, furious. He cried out at Crock to cut the motor, which was creating an infernal blare. Crock approached the machine, turned the needle, and the engine came to a halt with the sound of a dry, lifeless, sinister kiss.

"I'm leaving," said Petereater. "Someone is ill and asking for me."

"One of your regular patients?"

"No, but I'm going to have to go."

"Sounds like a real bore," said Crock.

"You can stay and try and get it working," said Petereater.

"Whatever... you'd better get going!" said Crock.

"What a malicious bastard," replied Petereater. "You really don't give a damn about my problems."

"I couldn't care less."

Crock leaned over the brilliantly shining cylinder and gently turned the needle, then changed positions in order to restart the motor. The machine kicked in just when Petereater was walking out the door. Crock had adjusted the compression setting and with a blast of air, the raging propeller pulled the table right off the ground. The whole thing flew across the room and crashed into the wall at the opposite end. Petereater heard the noise and returned. He saw the mess in front of him, dropped to his knees, and made the sign of the cross. Crock was already at his side, deep in prayer.

3

Cornelius Onte's housekeeper brought Professor Petereater to the injured man's room. To pass the time, Cornelius had decided to start knitting. He was using one of Paul Claudel's Fair Isle patterns that he had found in an issue of *Catholic Thought and the Pilgrim Conglomerate*.

"Hello," said Petereater. "You know this is quite a bother for me."

"Really?" said Cornelius. "I'm sorry to hear that."

"So I see. You have any pain?"

"My hip's been shattered into five pieces."

"And who's been looking after you?"

"Perriljohn. I'm doing much better now."

"Then why'd you send for me?"

"I've got a proposition for you," said Cornelius.

"Go fuck yourself!" said Petereater.

"Fine then," said Cornelius. "Off I go."

He tried to get out of bed and as soon as he had a foot on the ground he re-broke the hip. He fainted almost instantaneously. Petereater grabbed the phone and called for an ambulance to transport him to his clinic.

4

"Give him a shot of Evipan every morning," said

Petereater. "I don't want him waking up as long as I'm here on duty. He's pestering me all the time with some... "

He stopped himself. His intern was listening attentively.

"Anyway, that's none of your business," said Petereater. "How's his hip?"

"We've inserted the pins," said the intern. "The large ones. That's a fantastic fracture he's got."

"Heezgot? Who's Heezgot?" asked Petereater.

"Uh..." said the intern.

"If you don't know him, don't talk about him. He happens to be a Finnish engineer who invented an exhaust system for locomotives."

"That so? ..." said the intern.

"It was later perfected by Chaplon," finished Petereater. "In any case, that's none of your business either."

He left Cornelius and his gaze drifted over to the neighboring bed. The cleaning lady came. Wanting to take advantage of the absence of a patient, she placed a chair upon the vacant bed to facilitate her routine.

"What's wrong with that chair?" said Petereater jokingly.

"It's got a fever, no less," added the intern.

"Are you kidding me?" said Petereater. "Let's stick a thermometer in it. We'll see."

He crossed his arms and waited while the intern came back with a drill and a thermometer. He turned the chair upside-down and made a small hole under the seat, blowing away the sawdust with a puff of air.

"Hurry up," said Petereater. "I have people waiting on me."

"Breakfast?" asked his intern.

"No," responded Petereater. "I'm constructing a scale model of the Ping 903. You're rather curious this morning, aren't you?"

The intern stood back up and placed the thermometer in the hole. They could see the mercury shoot up the glass, speeding past all the degrees with frightening speed. It

49

expanded into a little ball at the head of the instrument, like a bubble of soap threatening to explode.

"Take it out, fast!" said Petereater.

"Jesus!..." said the intern.

The little ball that had formed was still a bit inflated and then a rupture towards the base of the thermometer gave way and hot mercury fell onto the bed. The liquid reddened the sheets on contact. On the white material, it formed parallel lines that converged towards a small puddle of mercury.

"Put this chair back to bed," said Petereater. "And call Miss Gongourdouille."

The head nurse rushed in.

"Take this chair's blood pressure," ordered Petereater.

He watched while the intern cautiously placed the chair in the bed.

"Very interesting case..." he mumbled to himself. "And don't shake it around like that, for God's sake!"

The intern, furious, was brutally manhandling the chair, which responded with a hideous creaking noise. But aware of Petereater's stare, he began to treat it with the refined delicacy of a professional egg-eater.

5

"I think an attack wing built into the body would be your best move," said Crock.

"No," replied Petereater. "A classic outer casing of 15 tenths of balsa will be a lot lighter."

"With that motor," said Crock, "if it hits something, it's finished."

"We'll find the right place," said Petereater.

They were working on a large scale model of the Ping 903 which Petereater was modifying to accommodate the motor.

"It's going to be dangerous," observed Crock. "I wouldn't want to find myself in its path."

"You're a pain in the ass, Crock. Don't worry about it. I'm a doctor, after all."

"O.K. I'm going to go find the pieces that are still missing."

"And get good parts, too. I'll pay whatever it costs."

"I'll choose the goods as if I were buying them for myself," said Crock.

"No!... I'd prefer that you don't forget that they're for me. You have bad taste. Anyway, I'll leave with you. I have to see my patient."

"Let's go," said Crock.

They stood up and left the room.

6

"Listen," said Cornelius Onte.

He spoke in a vague and muddled voice and had trouble keeping his eyes open. Petereater took a harsh tone with him.

"Your Evipan isn't enough, hey? You're not going to start in again with your grand propositions are you?"

"Of course not..." said Cornelius. "It's just that this chair..."

"So what's the problem?" said Petereater. "It's sick and we're healing it. What do you think we do at hospitals?"

"Come on," groaned Cornelius. "Just take it away. It's been making these grinding noises all night long."

The intern was standing next to Petereater. He too seemed to be at his wits' ends.

"Is it true?" Petereater asked his assistant.

The intern indicated that this was indeed the case.

"We could just toss it out the window," he said. "It's just an old chair."

"That chair is a Louis XV," replied Petereater. "And

51

furthermore, was it you or me who brought up this business of the chair having a fever?"

"It was me," said the intern.

He became furious whenever Petereater got involved with the chair.

"So take care of it."

"But I'm going nuts!..." moaned Cornelius.

"All the better," said Petereater. "You won't be hounding me anymore with your propositions. Give him another shot," he added, turning towards the intern as he singled out Cornelius.

"Ouch!... Jesus..." cried Cornelius. "I can't even feel my ass any more!"

At that moment, the chair let out a series of bony, crackling squeaks. A foul odor engulfed its bed.

"All night it's like this," murmured Cornelius. "I want to change rooms."

"You're all alone in a two-bed room and you're still not happy?" the intern protested.

"Two beds and a chair that reeks," added Cornelius.

"It's not that bad," said the intern. "You think that you smell so great?"

"Be polite to my patient," Petereater intervened. "What exactly is wrong with the chair? Does it have a perforated occlusion?"

"I think so," said the intern. "What's more, its blood pressure is forty-nine."

"O.K." said Petereater. "You know what you have to do. I'll see you later."

Trying to get a laugh out of Cornelius, Petereater gave him a little tap on the nose. He then left the room. Crock was waiting at home with the Ping 903.

7

Crock was chewing nervously on his lip. In front of him there was a piece of paper covered with unfinished calculations and hesitant equations of the twenty-seventh degree. Petereater was pacing up and down the length of the room, and to avoid having to turn around he would start walking backwards every time he'd come to the wall painted in bedbug blue.

"It's impossible here," spouted Crock after a long silence.

"You're a lousy pessimist, Crock," responded Petereater.

"But there's not enough space. You'll need four kilometers for every minute of flight time. You understand that, don't you?"

"So what do we do?" said Petereater.

"We'll need a desert."

"I've got to stay here to take care of my patients."

"You could get a medical appointment in the colonies."

"That's a ridiculous idea. I'd wander around from one village to the next and never have any time to work on the Ping."

"Then take a vacation."

"That just isn't done."

"Well then, our hands are tied."

"What to do..." said Petereater.

"What to do, indeed," replied Crock.

"Damn! I've got to get to the hospital. Keep working on your calculations."

He came down the stairs, walked through the cylindrical hallway, and left the building. His car was waiting for him next to the curb. Since the death of one of his most valued clients, Petereater worked almost exclusively at the hospital and rarely received patients at his office.

When he entered Cornelius' room he saw a young man, blond and well-built, sitting on the bed where the chair was resting. He rose to his feet when he saw the doctor.

"My name is Anne," he said. "How do you do?"

53

"Visiting hours are over," said the intern, who had followed the professor into the room.

"He's been sleeping continuously," said Anne. "I have to stay until he wakes up."

Petereater turned around and looked at his intern.

"What's wrong with you?"

"Oh, it's nothing."

His hands were trembling like a bell mallet and his black eyes sank deep into his skull.

"Didn't you get any sleep?"

"None... It's that chair..."

"Really? Not doing so well?"

"The bitch!..." replied the intern.

The chair started to crack and shake, emitting the same foul odor as before. The intern, furious, started after it but Petereater held him back.

"Calm down," he told him.

"I can't take any more!... She's toying with me!"

"Did you give her a bedpan?"

"Yes, but it's no use," said the intern. "She just wants to crack, squeak, run a temperature, and drive me out of my goddamn mind."

"Be polite," Petereater reminded him. "We'll take care of her later. Now, what do you want?" he said, addressing his question to Anne.

"I'd like to speak to Mr. Onte. It's about my contract."

"Don't waste your time talking to me about that. I don't know anything."

"Mr. Onte hasn't made you any propositions, has he?"

"Mr. Onte is so talkative that I have to knock him out for days on end."

"I beg your pardon," said the intern. "But it's me."

"Fine," said Petereater. "It's you, O.K., if that makes you feel better."

"I know about these propositions," said Anne. "I can explain them."

Petereater gave a signal to his intern who started searching through his pockets. He took up position right behind Anne.

"Is that so?" said Petereater. "Very interesting. Go on."

The intern pulled out a big needle and planted it in the fatty tissue of Anne's right bicep. Anne tried to fight the effect, but he soon fell unconscious.

"Where do I put him?" asked the intern, because Anne was quite heavy.

"Just handle it," said Petereater. "I've got to do my rounds. Anyway, Onte should be just about ready to wake up."

The intern opened his arms and let Anne slide to the ground.

"I could put him where the chair is..." he suggested.

The chair responded with a series of sniggering explosions.

"Leave her alone," said Petereater. "And if I catch you giving her a hard time..."

"Fine," said the intern. "I'll just leave him here."

"Do whatever you want."

The professor straightened out his white shirt and walked out of the room with a velvety suppleness. He disappeared into the glossy corridor.

The intern was all alone. He approached the chair and covered it with a look that screamed pure wickedness. He was so tired that he couldn't keep his eyes open. A nurse interrupted him.

"Did you leave her a bedpan?" asked the intern.

"Yes," said the nurse.

"Well then?"

"She's got an intestinal woodworm. Furthermore, she left her bed all by herself the other day. She just goes ambling about. It's not a pleasant spectacle to behold, either. I was terrified."

"I'll take her pulse," said the intern. "Pass me some

clean linen."

"Here."

The nurse had opened her blouse for him as she usually did, but he didn't even have the energy to slip his hand between her thighs. Feeling spited, she passed him the towel and left, rattling the galvanized metal of the bedpan. The intern sat down on the bed and pulled the covers off the chair. He struggled not to inhale because it was creaking more than ever.

8

When Petereater came back from his rounds he found the intern stretched out across Anne's body, fast asleep at the foot of Cornelius' bed. The professor noticed something a bit unusual in the neighboring bed and quickly went over to examine the Louis XV chair. Its legs had stiffened up and it had aged about twenty years. It was suddenly a cold, inert Louis XVI. The curves of its back, rigid and erect, testified to the great agony it must have experienced. The professor noticed that the wood had taken on a bluish-white sort of hue. He turned around and gave his intern a swift kick in the head but the man refused to move. He was snoring. The professor kneeled down next to him and gave him a good shake.

"What's going on?...Are you sleeping?...What have you done?"

The intern stirred about and opened a groggy eye.

"I took a shot myself," he murmured. "Evipan. Slept too long."

He let out a cavernous snore and closed his eyes again. Petereater shook harder.

"And the chair?"

The intern snickered slowly.

"Strychnine."

"Bastard!...." replied Petereater. "All we can do now is put her back on her feet and have her stuffed."

Petereater stood up, feeling a bit vexed. The intern, as well as Anne and Cornelius, were all sleeping quite contentedly. Petereater yawned. Delicately, he picked up the chair and put it down at the foot of the bed. She let out one last squeak, soft and dead, and then he sat down on her. His head swung from right to left, and just when he found himself in a comfortable position someone knocked on the door. The professor heard nothing. Angel knocked once more and entered the room.

Petereater's two vitreous eyeballs, stripped of all expression, turned towards him.

"It will never be able to fly," mumbled the doctor.

"What's that you said?" Angel asked politely.

It was hard for the professor to pull himself out of his drowsiness. With a massive effort, he managed to say a few words.

"I'll never have enough open space in this country to fly my Ping 903. I give you my word as a Petereater!... There are just too many trees."

"What if you came with us?" asked Angel.

"With who? You?"

"With Anne and me. And Rochelle."

"Where?"

"Exopotamie."

The veil cast by Morpheus had now been lifted and Morpheus himself hurled a stone against the doctor's forehead. He was completely revived.

"Christ almighty! That's a desert, isn't it?"

"Yes," said Angel.

"It's exactly what I need."

"Then we're in agreement?"

"Agreement on what?" asked the professor, no longer sure of what Angel meant.

"After all, Mr. Onte made you a proposition, didn't he?"

BOR1/ UIAN

"Mr. Onte is a pain in the neck," said Petereater. "For eight days now I've had to inject him with Evipan just to keep him calm."

"But he just wanted to offer you a position in Exopotamie. We need a doctor for the camp."

"What camp? When?"

"The camp for the railroad we're building out there. In a month. We're leaving tomorrow, that is Anne, myself, and Rochelle."

"Who's Rochelle?"

"A friend."

"Pretty?"

Petereater stood up. He was rejuvenated.

"Yes," said Angel. "At least I think so."

"You're in love with her," affirmed the professor.

"Not at all!" said Angel. "It's Anne that she loves."

"Still, you love her?"

"Yes," said Angel. "And that's why Anne must love her as well, since she loves him. That way, she'll be happy."

Petereater scratched his nose.

"I suppose it's your business," he said. "But I'd be skeptical about that sort of reasoning. So, do you think there's enough space for me to fly a Ping 903?"

"All the room you need."

"How do you know?"

"I'm an engineer."

"Marvelous!"

The professor pressed the buzzer that was on Cornelius' night stand.

"Wait," he said to Angel. "I'm going to wake them."

"How's that possible?"

"A shot," Petereater assured him. "It's quite simple."

He stopped for a moment to consider something.

"What are you thinking about?" asked Angel.

"I'm going to bring my intern along with me," said Petereater. "He's a good lad."

58

He felt a bit uncomfortable on the chair but continued nevertheless.

"I hope they've got a job for Crock as well. He's a great mechanic."

"I'm sure they will," said Angel.

The nurse finally entered with all the items necessary for the injections.

PASSAGE

It's time to stop for a minute, because now things are going to become linked together in ordinary chapters. And there is a reason why: already there's a girl, a pretty girl. Others will follow and nothing can endure in these conditions.

If that were not the case, things would be much more lighthearted, but where women are involved, sadness necessarily follows. It's not that women love sadness - at least they say they don' t - it's just that they bring it with them. Especially the pretty ones. As for the ugly, I wouldn't know; it's enough that they exist. Anyway, all women are pretty.

One will be called Copper and another Lavender. Names of certain others will follow later but neither in this book nor in the same story.

Because it is a desert, there will be plenty of people in Exopotamie. People like to get together in the desert because there's plenty of space. Once there, they try to recreate the same projects that they were occupied with elsewhere, for in the desert these undertakings somehow seem new. The reason for this is that the desert constitutes a background which brings out the best in everything, especially if the sun is gifted with those most special of hypothetical properties.

The desert is often a very useful site. Arthur Eddington developed a method for gathering together the entire number of lions it contains. All you have to do is pass the sand through a strainer and the lions remain on the screen at the bottom. This involves an important phase, which is the most interesting: the phase of agitation. At the end, you surely do have all the lions on the screen. But Eddington forgot about the pebbles that also remain. I think, from time to time, I'll talk about the pebbles.

FIRST MOVEMENT

*Now there is a truly advantageous process. Given
the quality of the fiber and the reasonable cost, we have
here a particularly interesting method.*

René Escourrou, *Le Papier,*
Armand Colin, 1941, p.84.

I

Seeing as he was hungry, Athanagore Porphyrogenete put
down his archaeological hammer and, faithful to his motto
(sit tibi terra levis), entered the tent to have lunch, setting
aside the Turkish pot whose cleaning was nearly completed.

Then, for the convenience of the reader, he filled out
the following information card, which is reproduced here
in extenso (that is the typographical information, not the
card itself).

Height: 1.65 meters
Weight: 69 kilograms
Hair: greying
Residual body hair: poorly developed
Age: uncertain
Face: long
Nose: fundamentally straight
Ears: university type that stick out like the two handles
on an amphora vase
Wardrobe: generally neglected, with strangely shaped

and unscrupulously crammed pockets

Other noteworthy characteristics: none of any significance.

Habits: sedentary, except during periods of transition

Having filled out the card, he then ripped it up because he had no use for it. This was especially so seeing that since the days of his youth he had always practiced that little Socratic exercise commonly known as:

γνωθι σε∝υτον

Atha's tent was constructed from a specially cut and measured piece of cloth, furnished with eyelet-holes at certain judiciously chosen spots. It lay over the ground, supported by an intermediary of wooden bazooka cylinders that made for a firm and sufficient foundation.

Above this piece of cloth, another was extended out at a convenient distance, subjugated by means of cords attached to metal stakes, which held everything to the ground and helped fend off the disagreeable gusts of wind.

The mounting of this tent, superbly realized thanks to the care of Martin Lardier, Athanagore's factotum, provided the ever-possible future visitor with an ensemble of sensations in keeping with the quality and acuteness of its intrinsic faculties. In reality, the tent only covered a surface of six square meters (and a fraction more, because it came from America and Anglo-Saxons express in feet and inches what others are used to expressing in meters. This left Athanagore thinking: in this country where the foot is master, it would be a good idea for the meter to set foot) and there was still plenty of space to the sides.

Martin Lardier, who was busy nearby tightening up the frame of his magnifying glass which had been bent out of shape by too massive an enlargement, rejoined his master under the tent. It was his turn, so he filled out a card. Unfortunately, he tore it up before we could copy it. But we'll corner him later. Just from a quick glance one could see that he had brown hair.

63

"Serve the meal, Martin," requested the archaeologist, who ruled with an iron fist on his excavation site.[1]

"Yes sir," responded Martin, without any vain concern for originality.

He put the plate on the table and sat down facing Athanagore. The two men noisily clinked together their five-pronged forks, digging into, with common accord, the big can of condensed stew that Dupont, their black servant, had just opened.

Dupont, the black servant, was in the kitchen preparing another batch of canned food for the evening meal. First of all, he had to cook the fibrous meat of the mummy in a big pot of water with ceremonial seasoning over a fire rigorously kept at medium heat by means of igniting sacred vine shoots. Then he had to distill the solder, fill the corrugated tin box with the mixed grain and the food cooked in the large pot of water and finally, only after having emptied all the cooking water into the little sink, weld the cover shut with the solder so that it was ironclad. This yielded one can of food for the evening meal.

Dupont, the son of hard-working craftsmen, had killed his parents in order that they might finally stop laboring and rest in peace. Brushing aside the conspicuous congratulations, he lived in solitude, a devoted and religious man. He hoped to be canonized by the Pope before he died, just like father Foucault with his fire and flintstone sermons. Generally speaking, he tended to swagger around and stick out his chest. At the moment, he was busy piling up twigs over an unstable fire, using a bill hook to baste the moist pieces of cuttlefish whose ink he tossed to the pigs before dropping the fish in mineralogical water that was boiling in a pot constructed out of tightly bound strips from a red-hearted tulip tree. The cuttlefish took on a beautiful indigo tint when it touched the boiling water. The light from the fire bounced off the trembling liquid surface, painting the ceiling of the kitchen with

---

[1] Thus producing induced currents which passed through the solenoids and lit up the space. (author's note)

reflections whose shapes resembled those of cannabis indica but whose scent mimicked more closely the aromatic lotions of Patrelle that one finds in all the better hair salons, especially those of André and Gustave.

Dupont's shadow danced across the room in disjointed, angular gestures. He was waiting for Athanagore and Martin to finish their meals so that he could clear the table, but Martin struck up a dialogue in order to offer his mentor a narrative account of the morning's events.

"So what's new?" said Athanagore.

"Nothing, as far as the sarcophagus is concerned," replied Martin. "There isn't any."

"Still digging?"

"Still digging. Every which way."

"We'll narrow it down to one direction as soon as we're able to."

"We saw a man in the area," remarked Martin.

"What was he doing?"

"He came on bus 975. His name's Amadis Dudu."

"So," sighed Athanagore. "We've finally encountered a traveler."

"He's already settled in," said Martin. "He's borrowed a desk and he's writing letters."

"Who did he borrow a desk from?"

"I don't know, but he seems to be working quite hard."

"That's interesting."

"And as for the sarcophagus?" said Martin.

"Listen, Martin, don't lead yourself to believe that we're going to find a sarcophagus every day."

"But we haven't found even one!"

"Which just goes to show how rare they are," concluded Athanagore.

Martin shook his head. He'd had enough.

"This site is worthless," he said.

"We've hardly even begun," declared Athanagore. "You're in too big a hurry."

"Excuse me, master," said Martin.

"It doesn't matter. You're going to do two hundred lines for me this evening."

"What sort, master?"

"I want a Greek translation of Isidore Isou's lettrist poetry. Take one of the longer ones."

Martin pushed back his chair and left the room. It was quite hot and he had enough work to keep himself busy until at least seven o'clock.

Athanagore finished his meal. He wanted to complete the cleaning of the Turkish pot, so he took his archaeological hammer with him and left the tent. Still, he had every intention on making it a quick job. This Amadis Dudu fellow was beginning to interest him.

The pot was large and made of a crude porcelain. There was an eye painted at the bottom that was half covered with calcium and silicon residue. With small, precise blows, Athanagore knocked away the petrified fragments, making visible the iris and the pupil. In its entirety, it was a rather attractive blue eye, a bit severe looking with pleasant, curled eyelashes. Athanagore directed his gaze toward the sides, shying away from the insistent interrogation facing him in the expression on the ceramic pot. The cleaning accomplished, he filled the pot with sand in order to avoid seeing the eye. Then he turned it upside down, smashed it with several blows from his hammer, and picked up the fragments that lay strewn about. This way, the pot took up very little space and could fit into a standard size box without disturbing the regularity of the collection of the professor, who pulled said container out of his pocket.

Having accomplished this task, Athanagore picked himself up and headed off in the presumed direction of Amadis Dudu. If the latter turned out to be of an inviting disposition there was all the more reason for the archaeologist to be interested in him.

An infallible intuition that guided the archaeologist in

his wanderings eventually led him to the right spot. Seated at a desk was none other than Amadis Dudu, making a phone call. Atha saw a desk blotter under Dudu's left arm and the paper already bore the marks of an intense undertaking. There was a pile of letters waiting to be sent out as well as a basket containing mail already received.

"Do you know where we can eat lunch around here?" asked Amadis, who covered the receiver with his hand as soon as he saw the archaeologist.

"You're working too hard," responded Athanagore. "This sun is going to kill you."

"It's a charming country," replied Amadis. "And there's plenty to be done."

"Where did you find the desk?"

"One can always find a desk. I can't work without a desk."

"You came on the 975?"

The party on the other end of the line must have been getting impatient because the receiver was twisting about violently in Amadis' hand. With a nasty grin, he took a needle out of the pencil holder and jammed it into one of the small round holes of the mouthpiece. The receiver straightened back out and permitted Amadis to hang it back up.

"You were saying?" enquired Amadis.

"I asked if you came on the 975."

"Yes. It was convenient enough. I take it everyday."

"I've never seen you around here."

"I don't take *that* 975 everyday. As I was saying, I've got a lot to do here. Incidentally, could you tell me where we might eat lunch?"

"We should be able to find a restaurant," said Athanagore. "I admit that since my arrival here I haven't really taken the time to locate one. I brought supplies and you can always fish in the Giglyon."

"How long have you been here?"

"For five years," indicated Athanagore.

"Then you must know this country."

"Pretty well. But I've been working underground. There are some siluro-devonian folds. Real marvels. I'm also interested in certain Pleistocene sites where I discovered traces of the city of Glure."

"Never heard of it," said Amadis. "And on the surface?"

"As far as that's concerned, you had better ask Martin to help you," replied Atha. "He's my factotum."

"A homosexual?"

"Yes," said Athanagore. "He's in love with Dupont."

"That doesn't matter to me," said Amadis. "And it's really too bad for Dupont."

"You're going to hurt him," said Atha. "And then he won't cook for me."

"But since there's a restaurant..."

"Are you sure about that?"

"Come along with me," said Amadis. "I'll lead you there."

He stood up and pushed back his chair. In the yellow sand it was easy to make it sit upright.

"This sand is clean," said Amadis. "And I like the area. Is there ever any wind?"

"Never," Athanagore assured him.

"If we walk down the length of that dune over there, we'll find the restaurant."

Long green weeds, stiff and waxy, painted the earth with threadlike spots of shade. Not a sound was made by the feet of the two walkers, who left behind conical footprints with softly rounded edges.

"I feel like a new man here," said Amadis. "The air is really clean."

"There is no air," said Athanagore.

"Well that clarifies everything. Before coming here I was often quite shy."

"That no longer seems to be a problem," said Athanagore. "How old are you?"

"I really can't give you a number," said Amadis. "I don't remember when it began, so the best I could do would be to repeat something that someone else has told me, in which case I'd be uncertain. I'd rather not do that. In any case, I'm still young."

"I'd say you're about twenty-eight," replied Athanagore.

"Thank you," said Amadis. "I would never have guessed. I'm sure that you'll find someone around here who will be pleased to know that."

"Oh, fine!..." said Atha.

He was a bit irritated.

The dune now slanted downward at a sharp angle and another one, just as high, was now masking the ochre horizon. The adventitious dunes turned into smaller and smaller folds, creating a series of passageways through which Amadis steered himself without the slightest hesitation.

"I'm pretty far away from my tent," said Atha.

"That's no problem," said Amadis. "Just follow your footprints when you return."

"But what if I take the wrong path when I leave?"

"Well then, you'll get lost on the way back. Simple."

"That's a troubling thought," said Atha.

"Don't worry. I'm sure to find it. There, look."

Behind the huge dune, Athanagore glimpsed the Italian restaurant: "Joseph Barrizone, proprietor." They called him Pippo. There were red cloth drapes that livened up the lacquered, wooden walls. White laquer, to be precise. In front of the red brick foundation, wild hepatrols flourished without respite in varnished earthenware pots. They were also growing in the windows.

"This will do just fine," said Amadis. "And they should have some rooms. I'll have my desk brought over."

"You're going to stay here?" said Atha.

"We're going build a railroad," said Amadis. "I've written to my company about it. The idea came to me this morning."

"But there won't be any passengers," said Atha.

"You think that you need passengers in order to have a railroad?"

"No," said Athanagore. "I suppose you really don't."

"And therefore, no one will use it," said Amadis. "That way we won't have to figure for the cost of future wear and tear. Understand?"

"But that's nothing but an item on a balance sheet," Athanagore observed.

"What do you know about business, huh?"

"Nothing," said Athanagore. "I'm just an archaeologist."

"So let's eat."

"I've already had lunch."

"At your age, you should be able to eat lunch twice," said Amadis.

They arrived at the glass door. The entire facade of the first floor was in fact made of glass and one could see the rows of small, clean tables and white leather chairs.

Amadis pushed open the swinging doors and set off the furious ringing of a bell. Joseph Barrizone, known to most as Pippo, was over to the right behind the large counter, perusing the oversized headlines of the newspaper. He was wearing an attractive white jacket and black slacks. The collar of his shirt was unbuttoned because it was, after all, relatively hot.

"Facce la barba à sept houres c'to matteigno?" he asked Amadis.

"Si," responded Amadis.

It was possible for him to recognize the jargon of Nice, if he ignored the spelling.

"Great!" answered Pippo. "Are you here for lunch?"

"Yeah. What do you have?"

"All that one could ask for from a terrestrial and diplomatic restaurant," replied Pippo with a first-rate Italian accent.

"Minestrone?"

"Minestrone and also spaghetti à la Bolognese."

"Avanti!" added Athanagore, wanting to fit in.

Pippo disappeared in the direction of the kitchen. Amadis picked out a table near the window and sat down.

"I'd like to meet your factotum," he said. "Or your cook. Whomever you please."

"Well you sure have the time."

"Not necessarily," said Amadis. "I've got a load of work to do. Pretty soon, you know, there's going to be a horde of people around here."

"Charming!" said Athanagore. "The good life. Maybe we could have some get-togethers?"

"What do you mean by a get-together?"

"It's a social gathering," explained the archaeologist.

"Listen to you," said Amadis. "As if we're going to have the time for get-togethers."

"Oh, damn it all! " said Athanagore.

All of a sudden he felt disappointed. He took off his glasses and spat into the lenses to clean them.

II

MEETING

To this list, we can easily add ammonium sulfate, dried blood, and mud.

Yves Henry, *Plantes à fibres*, Armand Colin, 1924.

1.

As usual, the usher arrived first. The meeting of the administrative board was scheduled for ten-thirty. He had to open the room, set ashtrays next to all the desk blotters, and place pornographic pictures well within the reach of the board members. He also had to straighten out the backs of the chairs to make them perfectly parallel with the sides of the oval table, as well as spray the room with disinfectant because several of the gentlemen suffered from a contagious skin shedding sickness. The usher limped around, careful about taking his time, for dawn had yet to chase away all the darkness. He was sporting an old but nevertheless very chic serge suit that was of a somber green color and a bit musty. Around his neck hung a gold chain upon which his name was engraved, in case anyone cared to read it. He walked around with jerky movements, his crippled limb cutting through the air in a spiral motion with each fragmentary progression.

He held in his hand the elaborate key to the cabinet which housed the accessories and he moved towards the corner of the room, adjacent to the meeting place, where certain indispensable items were stored. He hurried about with great effort. The shelves hidden behind the panels were smartly garnished with a festooned, pinkish paper that had been painted by Leonardo da Vinci in a bygone era. The ashtrays were shelved away in discrete order, suggesting rather than imposing themselves, but in disciplined fashion. Diverse models of pornographic cards, some multicolored, were tucked away in assorted envelopes. The usher was more or less aware of the preferences of each board member. He smiled when he saw out of the corner of his eye an innocent little packet in which he had gathered together his own personal favorites. He started to unbutton his fly, but upon contact with his pathetic member his wrinkled face grew somber. He remembered the date and realized that it would be a couple more days before anything would be happening down there. It wasn't so bad for someone his age, but he recalled a time when he could do it as often as twice a week. This thought gave him bit of happiness. Around the dirty corners of his mouth, shaped like an old rooster's sphincter, was the hint of a smile and a treacherous little glimmer sparkled in his otherwise dim eyes.

He took the six ashtrays that he needed and placed them on a Japanese tray with a glass base that he often used for this kind of transport. Then he consulted the index card that was pinned on back of the door and one by one chose four cards for each board member. He knew without having to verify it that the president liked cyclical groups with double bonds - a result of his background in chemistry - and he examined the first card with great admiration, for it displayed a truly acrobatic performance. Without further hesitation, he shook his head with complicity and quickly finished choosing.

2.

The Baron Ursus de Janpolent was arriving by automobile to the meeting place.

3.

Three of them arrived at the same time, at roughly a quarter to ten, and the usher offered his respectful salutations. They carried lightweight pigskin briefcases that had a sort of dull veneer and sported double-breasted suits with vests that were rather extravagant but whose assorted hues nevertheless fit nicely with the rest of the material of their ensemble. They wore boleros and spoke very seriously in a language peppered with clean and decisive inflections, all the time holding their chins high and making gestures with their right hands while grasping their briefcases in the other. One might also note, without undue prejudice to the chain of events, that two of the three briefcases opened by means of a zipper which ran along three sides, the fourth functioning as a sort of hinge. The third briefcase was still in the hand of its embarrassed owner, who pointed out to the others every few minutes that he would acquire this afternoon a model identical to theirs, and in light of this fact, the two others continued to exchange their decisive inflections with him.

4.

They were still waiting on two other members, not counting the Baron Ursus de Janpolent who was arriving by automobile to the meeting place.

One of them, Agathe Marion, entered the building at ten twenty-seven. He stopped and turned around in the light of the doorway in order to examine the tip of his shoe which had just been scuffed by some careless passerby. The shiny leather had a gash in it and the small triangular piece of material that was popping up, which now cast a strange shadow in response to the change in its contour, was a horrible sight. Agathe Marion shivered and shrugged his shoulders to try to chase away the goose bumps that had popped up along his spine. He turned back around and continued walking, saying hello to the usher as he passed, and his first foot crossed the lightly material plane made by the doorframe of the meeting place just one minute before the prescribed time.

5.

The Baron Ursus de Janpolent was three meters behind him.

6.

The last member was late and the conference started without him. That makes five people plus the usher, with another arriving later who also counts, which makes seven in all. A round number? Unfortunately not, because there only exists one number that is less than ten that also happens to be round: zero. And seven is different from zero.

"Gentlemen, the meeting is called to order. I give the floor over to our spokesperson who is going to explain to you, much better than I would be able to, the progress we've made since our last meeting."

"Gentlemen, you will remember that our firm, brought together at the behest of our technical director Amadis Dudu, has devised a plan for the construction and exploitation of a railroad in Exopotamie."

"I am not of that opinion."

"Of course you are. I'm sure you remember it."

"Oh, right. I was just a bit lost."

"Gentlemen, since our last meeting, we have received from director Dudu a series of important studies that the technical services branch of our firm has examined in detail. We have concluded that Amadis Dudu is in urgent need of a supervisory staff as well as workers for the actual execution."

"After our last discussion, the secretary was given the task of recruitment and will now communicate to you the results of his undertaking."

"Gentlemen, I have secured for this enterprise the help of one of our generation's most remarkable railroad technicians."

"I am not of that opinion."

"Listen, you know very well we're not talking about that!"

"Oh... right!"

"I've hired Cornelius Onte."

"That's all?"

"Unfortunately, Cornelius Onte has become the victim of an automobile accident. Yet thanks to the incessant work pace we've adopted since then, I've succeeded in finding an engineer of great merit to replace the remarkable technician we had found in Mr. Onte. What's more, I've killed two birds with one stone by signing on another gifted engineer as well as a ravishing secretary. Notice the fourth card of Mr. Agathe Marion; although a bit disfigured by the rigorous activity, the profile of the face in the upper left-hand corner is almost identical to that of the secretary I've just mentioned."

"Gentlemen, pass the card around."

"I'm not of that opinion."

"You're causing us to waste time with your perpetual interruptions."

"Excuse me. I was thinking about something else."

"And the construction workers?"

"Things are looking good."

"Gentlemen, I've also hired a doctor and an intern whose presence will surely prove precious as soon as all of the work injuries start to take their toll."

"I am not of that opinion."

"And the construction workers?"

"In accordance with a contract signed on the site by director Dudu, room and board for the technical personnel involved will be furnished by the Restaurant Barrizone."

"Gentlemen, the work accomplished by the secretary has already put us on a promising path. I would like to suggest, furthermore, that my nephew, Robert Gougnan du Peslot, seems to be the perfect person to handle the post of director of marketing for this project. I propose to you that he be given the authority to appoint his own personnel and to hire a secretary."

"Absolutely."

"As far as the technical crew is concerned, we could initiate their contracts right away and furnish them with a stipend for the relocation."

"I am not of that opinion."

"This time he's right."

"What's a technician anyway? It doesn't take any special talent. It's just a matter of mechanically going about doing what one's been taught to do."

"No stipend for relocation."

"A small stipend for relocation."

"We'll have to think it over."

"Gentlemen, the meeting is adjourned."

"Pass me my card."

"We haven't talked about the construction workers."

"We'll have to do it next time."

"I am not of that opinion."

They all stood up together, inharmoniously bustling about, and left the room. The usher waved goodbye in the hallway, dragging his gimpy foot, and started moving back in the direction of the now defunct meeting place, which was steeped in revolting vapors.

III

It seems well established that small children and young animals will suckle anything that comes into contact with their mouths, and that they must be taught to suckle in the proper place.

Lord Raglan, *Le tabou de l'inceste,* Payot, 1935, p. 2.

Anne found his suitcase quite heavy. He asked himself if he hadn't made a mistake and taken along too many cumbersome items that were not really necessary. But out of pure spite, he refused to respond to the question he had just posed himself and as a result, missed the last step of the varnished staircase. His foot shot out in front of him and his right arm simultaneously hurled his suitcase through the glass in the transom. He quickly stood back up, ran through the door, and grabbed his valise as it came back down on the other side. The weight of it made him hunch over, and the physical exertion caused his neck to bulge and break the button of the radiant metal shirt collar he had purchased some five years ago during a Thanksgiving's day bazaar. His tie had grown several inches too loose as well; he was going to have to remake himself. He picked up his suitcase and with a cruel effort tossed it back through the transom, ran back to the foot of the stairs where he caught it again and proceeded to walk backwards up the last ten steps of the staircase. He let out a sigh when he saw that his tie had straightened itself back out, and he could feel once again the button of his collar tickling his Adam's apple.

This time he was able to leave his house without hindrance. He turned and walked down the sidewalk.

Rochelle was also leaving her apartment. She was in a hurry to arrive at the train station before the conductor fired the pistol shot which signaled the departure. In order to save money, the National Train Line used soggy, old gunpowder in their firearms and therefore the conductor would pull the trigger a half an hour in advance so that the pistol would ignite at the right time. But now and then the shot would go off right away, and Rochelle had wasted a lot of time dressing up for the voyage. The result was nevertheless exceptional.

The opening of her light, crimped-wool coat gave way to the very simple cut of a lime green dress. Her legs fit snugly into a pair of sheer nylons and her delicate feet were slid into shoes covered with fauve leather. Her suitcase followed closely behind, carried by her brother. He had been nice enough to offer his assistance and as compensation she conferred upon him this job which demanded the utmost precision.

The mouth of the metro entrance hung wide open, luring imprudent groups of passengers toward its obscure orifice. At regular intervals the flow would reverse itself, and its throat would painstakingly vomit up a pile of pale and lifeless individuals who carried on their clothes the putrid scent of the monster's entrails.

Horrified by the idea of taking the metro, Rochelle turned her head from right to left in search of a taxi. With a sucking sound, the eyes of Rochelle drank in the spectacle of the five people around her, three of whom were obviously from the country, for they were carrying basketfuls of geese. She had to shut her eyes in order to get a hold of herself. There wasn't a single taxi in sight. The waves of cars and buses that came tearing down the steep incline of the street gave Rochelle a sensation of spiraling vertigo. She was exhausted and almost ready to let herself be gobbled up by

79

the insidious staircase of the metro when her little brother caught up to her and held her back by grabbing the bottom of her dress. Men started to faint as they saw Rochelle's ravishing thighs, which were now unveiled thanks to her brother's gesture. As she stepped back off that fatal step, she thanked him. Fortunately for her, the body of one of the ravished men fell right in front of an available taxi whose wheels went pale as it screeched to a halt.

She ran and gave the address to the driver, who took the suitcase from the hands of her brother. He watched her disappear as she blew him kisses with her right hand through the back window, where a macabre toy dog was hanging from a cord.

The ticket that Angel had picked up for her the night before had all the usual markings and the indications given her by five successive employees matched with the information she found posted on the signs. She located her compartment without any trouble. Anne had just arrived and was putting his luggage on the rack. His face was drenched with sweat. He had already placed his jacket above his seat and Rochelle was admiring his bicep through the taffeta weave in his wool shirt. Her scintillating eyes were shining with happiness as he said hello and kissed her hand.

"Marvelous! You're on time!"

"I'm always on time," said Rochelle.

"Still, you're not used to having a regular job."

"It's not something I'm in a hurry to get used to," said Rochelle.

She was still holding her suitcase, so he helped place her things.

"Excuse me. I was staring at you."

Rochelle smiled. She was amused by his need to explain.

"Anne..."

"What?"

"Is it a long trip?"

"Real long. We'll have to take the boat later and then another train. And a car across the desert."

"It's marvelous."

"It's super-marvelous."

They sat down together in the seat.

"Angel is here..." said Anne.

"Ah!..."

"He took off looking for some food and some things to read."

"How can he think about eating when the two of us are sitting here..." murmured Rochelle.

"It doesn't have the same effect on him."

"I really like Angel," said Rochelle, "but there's nothing poetic about him. Nothing at all."

"He's got a bit of a crush on you."

"Well then he shouldn't be thinking about eating."

"I really don't believe he's thinking just of himself," said Anne. "Maybe so, but I doubt it."

"Well I can't think about anything else but this trip...with you..."

"Rochelle..." said Anne.

He spoke softly.

"Anne.."

"I'd like to kiss you."

Rochelle pushed herself away and said nothing.

"You're ruining everything," she let out. "You're just like all other men."

"Would you rather I say that you have no effect on me whatsoever."

"You're not very poetic."

Her tone revealed disenchantment.

"It's impossible to be poetic with a pretty girl like you," said Anne.

"You know what I think? I think you'd want to kiss any idiotic girl that comes your way. That's what I think."

"Don't be that way, Rochelle."

"What way?"

"That way... nasty."

She moved closer to him, but was still pouting.

"I'm not nasty."

"You're adorable."

Rochelle really wanted Anne to kiss her, but she had to keep him in line. One can't just always let men have their way.

Anne didn't lay a hand on her. He didn't want to rush things, not all at once. Furthermore, this was a very sensitive woman. Quite sweet. Young, tender. Don't kiss her on the mouth. Too vulgar. Caress her, around the temples, maybe the eyes. Around the ear. Then put your hand around the waist.

"I am not adorable."

She acted as if she were ready to push away the arm that Anne had just slipped around her waist. He didn't resist much. Had she wanted him to, he would have removed it.

"Am I annoying you?..."

She really wasn't in the mood.

"You're not annoying me. You're just like all the others."

"That's not true."

"We both know exactly what you're going to do."

"Not at all," said Anne, "if you don't want to be kissed, I'm not going to kiss you."

Rochelle lowered her eyes and offered no response. Anne's lips were resting close to her hair. He was talking into her ear and she could feel his breath, light and restrained. She pushed herself away once more.

Anne didn't appreciate this. That last time, in the car... just what was it that got her so turned on?... She just let herself go. Now, all of the sudden, she's stuck-up. You can't just run down some poor slob every time you want to kiss a girl. Just to put her into that receptive state of mind. He deliberately moved close once again, took her face, and planted his lips on Rochelle's rosy cheeks. She resisted a bit, but not for long.

"No..." she murmured.

"I don't want to be a bother," Anne sighed.

She turned her head a bit and made an offering of her lips. Then she gave him a little bite, just to be playful. Such a big boy. But they too have to be taught. She heard a noise on the other side of the door and without changing position was able to look and see who it was. It was Angel that she saw passing through the car's corridor.

Rochelle sat caressing Anne's hair.

IV

Those little contraptions like that are starting to become a nuisance, and from now on, I'll only put them here and there.

Boris Vian, *Pensées inédites.*

Flying down the road was none other than Professor Petereater, who was making his way to Exopotamie by his own means. The product of these means bordered on the extreme, defying all description. Still, description threw down the gauntlet and accepted the challenge and the result is as follows:

> To the right and in the front, one wheel;
> to the left and in the front, one wheel;
> in the back and to the left, one wheel;
> in the back and to the right, one wheel;
> in the middle and at an incline plane of 45°

whose position was determined by three of the centers of said wheels (in which case one may as well add a fourth), a fifth wheel, which Petereater named the "steering wheel." Under the influence of this last wheel, the ensemble would, now and again, move as an ensemble, which is, of course, normal.

Inside the machine, between the sheet metal and cast iron walls, one could have also observed a great number of other wheels of diverse sizes and shapes, but only at the expense of getting one's fingers all greasy.

We should furthermore mention the presence of iron, cloth fabric, quartz halogen, oil, combustion fuels, a radiator, a rear axle, voluble pistons, track rods, a crankshaft, magma, and the intern, who was sitting next to Petereater in the throes of a good book: *La vie de Jules Gouffé*, by Jacques Loustalot and Nicolas. A strange and ingenious system built around a needle from a haystack immediately displayed the velocity for Petereater, who looked on as the speedometer wagged its finger at him.

"We're really moving," said the intern, raising his eyes. He put down his book and took another one from his pocket.

"Yeah," said Petereater.

His yellow shirt was a joyous explosion in the face of the oncoming sun.

"We'll be there tonight," said the intern, rapidly thumbing through his new manuscript.

"Indeed," responded Petereater. "But we're not there yet and the pitfalls could multiply."

"Multiply by what?" said the intern.

"By nothing," said Petereater.

"Then there won't be any pitfalls," said the intern, "because anything multiplied by nothing is always nothing."

"You really get on my nerves," said Petereater. "Where did you learn that?"

"In this book," said the intern.

It was *A Mathematics Course*, by Brachet and

Dumarqué. Petereater ripped the book out of his hands and hurled it overboard. It was swallowed up by a ditch in a great gush of luminous rays.

"That's that," said the intern. "Brachet and Dumarqué are dead for sure."

He began to cry bitterly.

"This isn't the first ditch those two have seen," said Petereater.

"Is that what you think?" said the intern. "Everyone likes Brachet and Dumarqué. What you've done is paramount to witchcraft turned inside-out. It's punishable by law."

"And what about taking chairs that never did you a bit of harm and then injecting them with strychnine?" said the professor, quite severely. "I suppose that's not punishable by law?"

"It wasn't strychnine," the intern sobbed. "It was methylene blue."

"Same thing, more or less," said Petereater. "Just stop pestering me, or it'll come back to haunt you. I can be real mean."

He laughed.

"That's true," said the intern.

He sniffled and passed his shirtsleeve under his nose.

"You're a rotten old bastard," he said.

"It's deliberate," said Petereater. "I do it in order to exact my vengeance. It's been like that ever since Chloë died."

"Why don't you stop thinking about it!" said the intern.

"I'm forced to think about it."

"And why do you still wear those yellow shirts?"

"That's none of your business," said Petereater. "I tell you that fifteen times a day, but you never learn."

"I hate your yellow shirts," said the intern. "Looking at that all day long, it's enough to drive a guy mad."

"I don't see them," said Petereater.

"Yeah, I know," said the intern. "But what about me?"

"I don't give a damn about you," said Petereater. "You signed a contract, right?"

"So this is blackmail?"

"No. The truth of the matter is that I needed you to come."

"But I'm useless when it comes to medicine!"

"You're right," observed the professor. "That's a fact. As far as medicine is concerned, you're useless. Rather dangerous, I might add. But I'm going to need an able-bodied lad to turn the propeller on my model airplanes."

"That's not tough," said the intern. "You could have taken anybody. Those things start with a quarter turn."

"You think so? Maybe with a combustion motor. But I'm also building motors out of rubber-bands. Do you know what that takes, getting a rubber-band motor up to three thousand revolutions?"

The intern squirmed in his seat.

"There are ways," he said. "With a drill, for example. It's very simple."

"No drills," said the professor. "It screws up the propeller."

The intern sulked in his corner. He was no longer crying. He was grumbling about something.

"What?" said Petereater.

"Nothing."

"Nothing," said Petereater. "Nothing always equals nothing."

He laughed once more and saw the intern rest his head against the door, pretending to sleep. He sang out joyously as he pressed the accelerator to the floor.

The sun had shifted and its rays now bounced obliquely off the car. To the adequately placed observer, the vehicle appeared brilliant against the dark background, thanks especially to the ultramicroscopic principles applied by Petereater.

V

The boat made its way alongside the breakwater in order to build up the needed momentum and clear the sandbar. It was crammed full of people and materials bound for Exopotamie and almost hit bottom when it had the misfortune of dipping in between two waves. On board, Anne, Rochelle, and Angel were occupying three uncomfortable cabins. The director of marketing, Robert Gougnan du Peslot, was not along for the trip: he was to arrive as soon as the construction of the railroad was completed. For the time being, he would receive his salary without leaving his former position.

The captain was in the steerage, pacing back and forth, looking for his bullhorn so that he could signal his orders. He just couldn't seem to find it and if the boat kept this bearing without receiving new commands it would be smashed to bits against La Toupie, a reef named for its savage fierceness. He finally located the instrument lurking behind a ball of cord, on the lookout for a seagull it could pounce upon. The captain seized it and strode forcefully down the gangway and up the stairs to the deck, finally reaching the bridge. He was just in time. They had sighted La Toupie.

Huge waves, white with foam, were racing by one after the other. This caused the vessel to toss and turn ever so lightly in the wrong direction, throwing it off course and slowing down the progress. A fresh breeze, smelling of ichneumon and iodine, swept into the folds of the helmsman's ears, producing a sweet music that was like the song of a curlew resonating in D sharp.

The crew was busy cooking up a soup of deep sea biscuits that the captain had procured from the government by special favor. Imprudent fish were hurling themselves head-first against the hull of the vessel and the deafening blows gained the attention of certain debutante voyagers, especially Didiche and Olive. Olive was the daughter of Marin and Didiche the son of Carlo. Marin and Carlo were two construction workers hired on by the company. They had other children as well, but they were hidden away in other parts of the ship, busy examining the boat and each other. The foreman, Arland, was also on board. A real bastard.

The stem of the boat was slowly crushing the waves that passed under her. Because it was a commercial vessel, it was not built for speed, and the movement was like the grinding of a mortar and pestle. Nevertheless, this motion produced an exquisite effect in the hearts of the onlookers, no doubt a result of the salt water which purifies all things. As usual, the seagulls screeched constantly, soaring aggressively around the largest mast and finally coming to rest on the fourth topsail high up to the left, where they all lined up in a row to watch a cormorant who was attempting a mid-air spin.

At that very moment, Didiche was showing Olive how he could walk on his hands and the cormorant, who caught a glimpse of this, was distracted. He wanted to fly upwards but started off in the wrong direction. He smashed head-first into the floor of the bridge. The impact made a sharp sound. He was bleeding from the beak and had to close his eyes because the pain was causing him to blink incessantly. The captain turned around and shrugging his shoulders, passed him a grimy handkerchief.

Olive had seen the cormorant fall. She ran to ask if she could hold him in her hands. Didiche was still turned upside down, calling out for Olive to watch him, but she was no longer there. He stood up and cursed without any ostentation - a rather filthy word, but well suited to the occasion - then took off after Olive, without hurrying too much, because after all, women always tend to exaggerate. About every two steps, he tapped the guardrail with the palm of his dirty hand, causing it to resonate throughout with a beautiful vibration. It made him feel like singing.

The captain truly welcomed these uninvited visits to the bridge because he really detested the gendarme and furthermore the two were strictly forbidden to speak. He smiled at Olive. He admired her shapely legs, her straight blond hair, and her sweater, which, a bit too tight, accented the two little bulges that the good lord had bestowed upon her just three months ago. At this very moment, the ship was passing alongside La Toupie and the captain brought the bullhorn to his mouth so that he might give his orders and impress Olive and also Didiche, whose head could be seen making its way up the metal ladder. He cried out forcefully. Olive didn't understand a word of what he was saying and the cormorant had a terrible headache.

The captain dropped his bullhorn and turned towards the children with a satisfied grin.

"Who are you shouting at, sir?" said Olive.

"Call me captain," said the captain.

"But who are you shouting at?" repeated Olive.

"The castaway," explained the captain. "There's a castaway on La Toupie."

"What's La Toupie, captain?" asked Didiche.

"A huge reef," said the captain.

"Is he always there?" asked Olive.

"Who?" said the captain.

"The castaway," explained Didiche.

"Of course," said the captain.

"Why?" inquired Olive.

"Because he's an idiot," said the captain, "and also because it would be very dangerous to go rescue him."

"Does he bite?" asked Didiche.

"No," said the captain, "but he's quite contagious."

"What does he have?"

"We don't know," said the captain.

He hoisted the bullhorn to his lips once more and

shouted into it, causing all the sea-flies within a cable's length to fall dead.

Olive and Didiche were leaning against the guardrail of the bridge. They were watching as enormous jellyfish turned furiously around themselves, producing vortexes into which imprudent fish would wander and be caught: a method initially invented by Australian jellyfish and now all the rage along the coast.

The captain set his bullhorn down at his side, delighted in his observation of how the wind was separating Olive's hair and tracing a white part across her round head. Now and again her skirt would rise up over her thighs and flap in the wind as it encircled her legs.

The cormorant, saddened by the fact that no one was paying attention to him, let out a painful groan. Suddenly, Olive remembered why she had come to the bridge and turned towards the injured party.

"Captain," she said, "can I take him?"

"Sure," said the captain, "if you're not afraid that he'll bite you."

"But birds don't bite," said Olive.

"Ah! Ah!," said the captain. "That's no ordinary bird!"

"What is it?" asked Didiche.

"I don't know," said the captain. "And that alone proves that it's no ordinary bird, because I'm familiar with the common varieties. There's the magpie, the kittyhawk and the hawse-hole, the duckboard, and also the horsefeather, the sparrowgull, the woodpeeper, the silly goose and the cantroupe, the verdant beechcomber, the chicken à la king and the chicken-in-a-basket. Along with that you can add the seagull and your garden-variety hen, which in Latin is called cocota deconans."

"Wow!" murmured Didiche. "You sure do know an awful lot."

"The result of hard study," said the captain.

All the same, Olive had taken the cormorant in her

arms, rocking it gently and whispering sweet little nothings in an attempt to calm him down. He happily sunk back into his feathers, purring like a tapir.

"You see, captain," she said. "He's very gentle."

"Well, then he must be a kittyhawk," said the captain. "Charming birds. They're in the book."

The cormorant was flattered and assumed a gracious and distinctive posture while Olive caressed him.

"When do we arrive, captain?" asked Didiche, who also liked birds, if a bit less passionately.

"It's still far off," said the captain. "We've got quite a ways to go, you understand. Where are you two headed?"

"We're going to Exopotamie," said Didiche.

"You don't say!" remarked the captain, obviously impressed. "Just for that, I'll give the wheel one more spin."

He completed the maneuver and Didiche thanked him.

"Are your parents on board?" asked the captain.

"Yes," replied Olive. "My dad is Marin and his is Carlo. Me, I'm thirteen. Didiche is thirteen and a half."

"Ah ha!" said the captain.

"They're going to build a railroad just for themselves."

"And us, too. We can ride it."

"Aren't you a couple of lucky ducks," said the captain. "If I could, I'd come along with you. I've had my fill of this boat."

"But isn't it fun being the captain?"

"Certainly not!" said the captain. "I'm really nothing more than a foreman."

"That Arland, he's a real bastard," Didiche affirmed.

"You're going to get in trouble," said Olive. "You're not supposed to talk like that."

"That's O.K.," said the captain. "I won't repeat it. It's just between us men, right?"

He caressed the cheeks of Olive's buttocks. She was flattered to be considered one of the boys and interpreted the gesture as a sign of some sort of male bonding. The captain was blushing.

"Why don't you join us, captain." said Didiche. "Our parents would be happy to have you."

"Sure," said Olive. "It would be fun. You could tell us about adventures on the high seas and we could play pirates!"

"Great idea!" said the captain. "You think you're strong enough for that?"

"I get it," said Olive. "You want to feel my muscles?"

The captain pulled her close and took hold of her shoulders.

"You'll do," he said.

He was having trouble speaking.

"But she's a girl," said Didiche. "She won't be able to fight."

"And what makes you say she's a girl?" said the captain. "Those two little things there?"

"What things?" asked Didiche.

He touched them to show Didiche.

"They aren't that small," said Olive.

In order to let them see, she set the cormorant down at her side and stuck out her chest.

"Maybe not," said the captain. "Not so little after all."

He motioned to her to approach.

"If you tug on them every morning," he said, keeping his voice low, "they'll grow even bigger."

"How?" said Olive.

Didiche was a bit uncomfortable seeing the captain all red, veins bulging in his forehead. He turned away, embarrassed.

"Like this..." said the captain.

Didiche could hear Olive cry out as he started to pinch her. She was fighting back, but he could see that he captain had hold of her and that it was painful. He took the captain's bullhorn and with all his force, smashed it up against his head. The captain cried out an obscenity and released Olive.

"Get the hell out of here, you lousy brats!" the captain

blared.

One could see the mark on his face where Didiche had struck him. Huge tears were flowing down Olive's cheeks and she was holding onto her chest in the place where the captain had just pinched her. She climbed back down the metal ladder. Didiche followed. He felt angry, even furious. He didn't understand exactly why he was so livid, but he had the impression that he had been double-crossed. The cormorant, hurled forward by a kick from the captain, came crashing down at their feet. Olive bent over and picked it up. She was still sobbing. Didiche put his arm around her and with his other hand brushed aside the strands of yellow hair that were stuck to her tear-soaked face. He kissed her on the cheek, as gently as possible. She stopped crying. She looked at Didiche and then lowered her eyes, holding the cormorant snugly against her as Didiche took her in his arms.

VI

Angel made his way to the deck. The boat had now reached deep sea and the winds from the back were challenging those from the front. This resulted in cross-like pattern, a fairly normal phenomenon given the proximity of the Pope and his Popedom.

Anne and Rochelle had just tucked themselves into their cabin and Angel wanted to get away. It was hard, nevertheless, for him to think about anything else. Anne was as congenial as ever toward him and what's worse, so was Rochelle. But those two, alone in the cabin, they weren't going to be talking about Angel. They weren't going to be talking period. They weren't going to be... Or maybe... Maybe they were...

Angel's heart was pounding. He couldn't stop thinking about Rochelle, down there with Anne in the cabin, naked, behind closed doors. That must be what's happening or the door wouldn't have been shut.

The way she was looking at Anne had, for several days now, made Angel feel very uncomfortable. Her eyes were like Anne's eyes had been when he kissed her in the car: possessed, with that faraway, vague look. They were horrible orbs that drooled, with eyelids like murdered flowers, the petals all crushed, spongy, and translucent.

The wind was singing in the wings of the seagulls, attaching itself to things that were beyond the boundaries of the ship and shooting up a vaporous tail when it brushed against harsh surfaces, like a feather of snow gusting atop Everest. The sun was shining into the eyes of the voyagers, sparkling and white in the places where it bounced off the surface of the sea. The seafood and the veal in white wine sauce matured in the warm atmosphere and gave off a wonderful odor. The pistons of the machine churned away consistently and the hull vibrated with steady regularity. A blue smoke rose above the slits in the roof of the ventilation conduit that serviced the mechanic's quarters. Angel would watch as the wind quickly carried it away. An ocean voyage, it's something that can comfort you; the gentle hiss of the water, the froth clinging to the side of the hull, and the cries and screeches of the seagulls all came pouring into his head and his spirits were soothed. In spite of Anne, who was down below with Rochelle, he could still feel his blood dancing through his veins like a fine champagne.

The air was light yellow and watery turquoise blue. The fish continued to bump into the hull every now and then. Angel would have liked to have gone down to see if they were causing any serious dents in the already old and worn sheet metal. But this idea quickly vanished, as did his images of Anne and Rochelle, for the flavor of the wind was exquisite and the shiny cracks in the dull tar that covered the bridge broke through brilliantly, like the veins in a wayward leaf. He made his way toward the front of the boat, for he wanted to lean against the guardrail. Olive and Didiche were there, propped over the side and watching as spots of foam applied their white moustaches to the chin of the stem - a rather curious place for moustaches. Didiche was still holding on to Olive, and the wind tousled the hair of the two children as it whispered its music into their ears. Angel stopped and rested his elbows next to theirs. They were aware of his presence. At first, Didiche was quite suspicious, but after a while he calmed down. Angel could see the traces of tears on the cheeks of Olive and she was still sniffling into her coat sleeve.

"So," said Angel. "Are you having a good time?"

"No," said Didiche. "That captain's a dirty old man."

"What did he do to you?" asked Angel. "Did he chase you off the bridge?"

"He tried to hurt Olive," said the child. "He pinched her. There."

Olive pointed to the area in question and let out a loud whimper.

"It still hurts," she said.

"What a filthy old pig," said Angel.

He was quite furious with the captain.

"I smashed him in the head with that funnel of his," remarked the boy.

"Yeah," said Olive, "it was funny."

She started to laugh a little and so did Didiche and Angel when they imagined the face of the captain.

"If he tries anything else," said Angel, "you come and get me. I'll break his face."

"You're O.K., mister," remarked Didiche.

"He wanted to kiss me," said Olive. "His smelled like

95

red wine."

"You're not going to pinch her are you?"

Didiche was concerned all of the sudden. One should-n't be too quick to trust an adult.

"Don't be scared," said Angel. "I won't pinch her and I won't try to kiss her."

"But I'd like that. I mean if you want to kiss me. It's the pinching that hurts."

"I couldn't care less if you kiss Olive," said Didiche. "I could do quite a nice job of that myself, if I wanted to..."

"So, you're jealous, eh?" said Angel.

"Not at all."

Didiche's cheeks took on a lovely purplish hue and he deliberately avoided looking at Angel. To do so, he had to hold his neck at an extremely uncomfortable angle. Angel laughed. He grabbed Olive under the arms, hoisted her up, and gave her a kiss on the cheeks.

"There," he said, placing her back on the ground, "now we're pals. Let's shake on it," he said to Didiche.

The boy half-heartedly offered him his dirty paw but he lightened up when he saw Angel's face.

"You're just taking advantage of the fact that you're older. But I really don't care. I kissed her before you anyway."

"Well, congratulations, then," said Angel. "You're a man of fine taste. She's a charming girl to kiss."

"Are you coming to Exopotamie, too?" inquired Olive. She wanted to change the subject.

"Yeah," said Angel. "I'm one of the engineers."

"Our parents are the construction workers," she said proudly.

"They're the ones who do all the work," finished Didiche. "They say that without them, engineers would be useless."

"And they're right," Angel assured them.

"Then there's the foreman, Arland," added Olive.

"He's a real bastard," clarified Didiche.

"I guess we'll see," said Angel.

"Are you the only engineer?" asked Olive.

Then Angel remembered that Anne and Rochelle were alone together, down below in their cabin. A wind kicked up and the sun hid itself as the ship started dancing a bit more forcefully. The cries of the seagulls grew aggressive.

"No..." he managed to blurt out. "One of my friends is coming as well. He's down below."

"What's his name?" asked Didiche.

"Anne," replied Angel.

"That's funny," observed Didiche. "That's a dog's name."

"It's a pretty name," said Olive.

"It's a name for a dog," repeated Didiche. "It's stupid, a guy with a name you'd give a dog."

"It is stupid," said Angel.

"You want to come see our cormorant?" proposed Olive.

"No," said Angel, "it's best not to wake him."

"Did we say something to bother you?" asked Olive, in a soft voice.

"Of course not," said Angel.

He touched Olive's hair and caressed her round head, then sighed.

Up above, the sun was hesitating to come back.

VII

...and sometimes it's not a bad idea to put
a little water in one's wine...

Marcel Veron, *Traité de chauffage,*
Dunod, volume 1, p. 145.

Someone had been knocking at Amadis Dudu's door for a good five minutes now. Amadis looked at his watch and calculated just how long it would take before his patience would start to wear thin. Finally, at six minutes ten seconds, he stood up and slammed his fist against the table.

"Come in," he howled, his voice filled with rage.

"It's me," said Athanagore, as he pushed open the door. "Am I disturbing you?"

"Naturally," said Amadis.

With superhuman effort he attempted to calm himself.

"That's perfect," said Athanagore, "that way, you're sure to remember my visit. You haven't seen Dupont, have you?"

"No, I haven't seen Dupont."

"Now you're pushing things," said Athanagore. "Come on, where is he?"

"Christ! For the last time," said Amadis, "is it me or is it Martin who's screwing Dupont? Go ask Martin!"

"Fine! That's all I wanted to know," replied Atha. "So you still haven't been able to seduce Dupont?"

"Listen, I don't have any time to waste. The engineers and the material are arriving today and everything's all topsy-turvy."

"You're talking like Barrizone," said Athanagore. "You must be very impressionable."

"Oh, fuck off," said Amadis. "Just because I happen to

blurt out by chance some diplomatic expression of Barrizone's is no reason to accuse me of being impressionable. Impressionable? You make me laugh,...really!"

Amadis started to chuckle, but Athanagore was staring at him and once again he became furious.

"Instead of standing around," he said, "why don't you help me prepare for their reception?"

"What's to prepare?" asked the archaeologist.

"Their offices. They're coming here to work. How are they supposed to work without offices?"

"I work just fine without an office," said Athanagore.

"Work?... You?... Well, I'm talking about serious work and that's hard without an office. Right?"

"As far as I'm concerned, I work just as hard as anyone else," said Athanagore. "You think it's easy to swing an archaeological hammer? Or break pots all day long in order to stuff them into standard size boxes? You think that's some sort of fun and games? Watching over Lardier, yelling at Dupont, taking down information in my notebooks, and then not knowing what direction to dig in. All that means nothing?"

"It's just not serious," said Amadis Dudu. "Try writing memos and sending service reports, on time! It's not like digging holes in the sand."

"What is it you hope to accomplish anyhow?" said Athanagore. "With all your memos and reports? You're going to construct some contemptible little railroad, all stinking and rusty, that'll end up spreading smoke all over the place. I'm not saying that it'll be completely useless but you're not talking about any desk job either."

"You'd best know that this plan has been approved by the administrative council as well as Ursus de Janpolent," Amadis said smugly. "You are in no position to judge its usefulness."

"You're a pain in the ass," said Athanagore. "And what's more, you're a homosexual. I shouldn't be keeping company with you."

"You needn't worry," said Amadis. "You're a bit too old

for me. I'll have Dupont, when the time is right."

"Enough already with Dupont. What are you waiting for today, anyway?"

"Angel, Anne, Rochelle, a foreman, two construction workers and their families, and the material. Doctor Petereater is arriving on his own, with an intern, and a mechanic called Crock will also be joining us shortly. We'll recruit the four other indispensable construction workers from the immediate area, if there is any need. But I doubt there will be."

"That's a considerable number of workers," said Athanagore.

"If need be," remarked Amadis, "we'll hire away your crew by offering them a superior salary."

Athanagore looked at Amadis and started to laugh.

"You're amusing, you and your little railroad."

"What's so funny about it?" asked Amadis, vexed.

"You think you'll entice my crew away just like that?"

"Certainly," said Amadis. "I'll offer them a special bonus for productivity, social advantages, a worker's council, a cooperative, and an infirmary."

A saddened Athanagore shook his head and the greying hair upon it. This utter meanness was melting him into the walls and Amadis actually thought he saw him disappearing, if one may in fact be permitted to express it thusly. He made an accommodating effort and an inert Atha emerged once again in his field of vision.

"You won't succeed," assured Athanagore. "They're not crazy."

"You'll see," said Amadis.

"They work for nothing with me."

"All the more reason."

"They like archaeology."

"They'll like building a railroad."

"Whatever the outcome might be," said Athanagore, "I'd like to know, have you studied political science?"

"Yes," said Amadis.

Athanagore remained silent for a moment.

"Even so," he finally said. "You had predispositions. Political science isn't a sufficient explanation."

"I have no idea what you're trying to say, but in any case, I'm not interested. Do you want to come along? They're arriving in twenty minutes."

"I'll follow you," said Athanagore.

"Do you know if Dupont will be there tonight?"

"Would you just leave me out of this Dupont nonsense," replied a rather exasperated Athanagore.

Amadis mumbled something and stood up. His office was now housed in a room on the second floor of Barrizone's restaurant and through the window one could see the dunes and the stiff, green weeds upon which clung little yellow snails and sandpeepers, aglow in all their changing iridescence.

"Let's go," he said to Athanagore as he insolently passed him by.

"I'll follow you," said the archaeologist. "All the same, you sure didn't look like any important administrator while you were waiting for the 975..."

Amadis Dudu blushed. As he descended the cool, dimly lit staircase, shiny brass objects emerged from the shadows.

"How did you know?"

"I'm an archaeologist," said Athanagore. "Old secrets are nothing new to me."

"O.K., you're an archaeologist. But that doesn't make you a psychic."

"Let's not argue," said Atha. "You're a young man with a poor upbringing... I'd like to help you welcome your staff but you're ill-mannered, and no one can change that. You've been poorly raised and also raised to a position of importance... It's unfortunate."

They arrived at the bottom of the staircase and crossed the hallway. In the dining room of the restaurant, Pippo was still sitting behind the counter reading his newspaper, shaking his head and murmuring in his provincial dialect.

"Salut, la Pipe," said Amadis.

"Hello," said Athanagore.

"Bon giorno," said Pippo.

Once outside the hotel, Amadis and Athanagore departed. It was hot and dry and the air was undulating above the yellow dunes. They moved in the direction of the highest hill, a massive lump of sand crowned with a few green weeds that offered a good panoramic view.

"Where are they coming from?" asked Amadis.

"Oh, they could arrive from any direction," said the archaeologist. "Especially if they took the wrong road."

He watched attentively, pivoting his body around and coming to a dead stop when his plane of symmetry intersected that of the two poles.

"Over there," he said, pointing to the north.

"Where?" asked Dudu.

"Flush out your pipes!" said Atha, resorting to typical archaeologist slang.

"I see," said Amadis. "It's just one car. It must be Professor Petereater."

All they could see was a small and shiny green spot, followed by a cloud of dust.

"They're on time," said Amadis.

"What does that matter?" said Athanagore.

"The time-clock, what should we do about that?"

"Isn't it arriving with the material?"

"Yes, but seeing that it isn't here, I'll clock them in myself."

Athanagore stood contemplating him, dumbfounded.

"I wonder what on earth makes you tick? What's inside?" he asked.

"The same load of vile rubbish that's inside everybody else," said Amadis...

He turned in the opposite direction.

"...guts... shit... Here come the others," he announced.

"Should we go and meet them?" proposed Athanagore.

"We can't," said Amadis. "They're coming from opposite sides."

"How about we each go in one direction, separately?"

"And leave you alone to fill them with a bunch of lies? Forget it! Anyway, I have my orders. I have to welcome them myself."

"Fine," said Athanagore. "Then just leave me the hell alone. I'm going."

He left the befuddled Amadis planted in the soil, where his feet took root under that first accommodating, superficial layer of sand. Athanagore descended the dune. He was off to meet the large convoy.

Petereater, meanwhile, was making swift progress through the hills and hollows with incredible speed. The intern, nauseous, was hunched over in a fetal position, his head resting in a damp sponge while he hiccuped unpleasantly. Refusing to let such a small inconvenience put a damper on things, Petereater continued humming a little American ditty entitled, "Show Me the Way to Go Home," whose words and melody were well suited to the occasion. When he reached the top of one of the more elevated areas of terrain, he deftly worked in the melody of Vernon Duke's "Taking a Chance for Love," while the intern let out groans that would have melted the heart of even the most hardened of black-market gun runners. Petereater then accelerated on the downslope, which forced the intern to shut his mouth because he was unable to vomit and moan at the same time: a skill he unfortunately lacked thanks to an overly bourgeois education.

With one last roar of the motor and a grunt from the intern, Petereater finally stopped in front of Amadis, who was watching with a wrathful eye as the archaeologist made his way toward the convoy.

"Hello," said Petereater.

"Hello," said Amadis.

"Uurrgh!..." said the intern.

"You're on time," Amadis observed.

"No," said Petereater. "I'm early. And tell me, why aren't you wearing yellow shirts!"

"They're hideous," said Amadis.

"Yes," said Petereater. "With your earth-like skin tones that would be a disaster. Only handsome men can be permitted this luxury."

"You find yourself good-looking?"

"First of all, if you wish to address me, I have a title," said Petereater. "I'm not just anybody, I am Professor Petereater."

"That's of little importance," said Amadis. "In any case, I find Dupont much prettier than you."

"Professor," Petereater reminded him.

"Professor," Amadis repeated.

"Or doctor," said Petereater. "Whatever you prefer. I suppose you're a homosexual?"

"Can you love men without being a homosexual?" said Amadis. "In the long run, you all turn out to be a pain in the ass!..."

"Aren't you a nasty little boor," said Petereater. "Lucky for me I don't take orders from you."

"But you are under my orders."

"Professor," said Petereater.

"Professor," repeated Amadis.

"No," said Petereater.

"What do you mean, no?" asked Amadis. "You just asked me to say 'professor' and now you tell me not to say what I just said."

"No, I am not under your orders," replied Petereater.

"Yes, you are."

"Yes, professor," said Petereater, and Amadis repeated.

"I've got a contract," said Petereater. "I follow nobody's orders. What's more, as far as health issues are concerned, I give the orders."

"They didn't inform me of this, doctor," said Amadis, suddenly a bit less Amadisian.

"Now all of the sudden you're obsequious," said the professor.

Amadis wiped off his forehead. It was getting hot. Professor Petereater walked over to his car.

"Come and help me," he said.

"I can't," said Amadis. "The archaeologist planted me here and I can't uproot myself."

"Ridiculous!" said the professor. "That's just some writer's wordplay."

"You think so?" said Amadis anxiously.

"Arrghh!...." Petereater bluntly shouted into the young man's face. A frightened Amadis took off running.

"There, you see!" cried Petereater.

Amadis made his way back, looking quite annoyed.

"Can I help you professor?" he proposed.

"At last!" said Petereater. "You've finally come to your senses. Take this."

He tossed a huge case into his arms. Amadis wobbled as he caught it, letting it drop onto his right foot. Afterwards, hobbling around on his one good hoof, he provided the professor with a truly convincing imitation of a Flemish hipster.

"Good," said Petereater as he got back behind the wheel. "Take that stuff to the hotel. You'll find me there."

He gave a little nudge to the intern who had just dozed off.

"Hey, you!... We're here."

"Ah!...." sighed the intern. He had a blissful expression on his face.

The car then flew down the side of the dune in a whirlwind and the intern quickly plunged his head back into his disgusting sponge cloth. As the car sped off, Amadis stared at the doctor's case and with limp and all, attempted to hoist it upon his back. Unfortunately for him he had rounded shoulders.

VIII

Athanagore was heading out to meet the convoy, plod-ding through the sand with tiny little steps that perfectly suited his pointed boots, whose dignified air of antiquity was accented by the beige cloth material around the ankles. His shorts, made of a sort of chamfery fabric, were in fact quite short and left more than ample space for his bony knees to pass through unhindered. His khaki shirt, discol-ored by wear and tear, was tucked loosely under his belt. There was also a colonial helmet hanging in his tent and such being the case, he never wore it. He thought about the insolence of Amadis and how the young man should be taught a lesson, or maybe several lessons because one sure-ly wouldn't be enough. He looked down at the ground, as archaeologists are in the habit of doing. One mustn't neg-lect anything; quite often a discovery is lurking just under our noses, something to be happened upon by chance, as the writings of the monk Orthopompe - a second century figure who lived in a community of bearded priests and occupied a superior position because of his talent in callig-raphy - have demonstrated. Athanagore remembered the day when Lardier informed him of the presence of master Amadis Dudu and how a spark of hope was born in his mind - granted one is there - which was later kept alive by the subsequent discovery of the restaurant and brought back from the verge of extinction thanks to his recent con-versation with Amadis.

The convoy was now starting to stir up the dusty earth of Exopotamie. Another change, maybe some friendly people. Athanagore was having a truly terrible time trying to concentrate, for this is a habit one quickly loses in the desert. That must be why his thoughts were taking on a rather pompous air, an air filled with little rays of hope and all the rest of the crap washed out with the enema's fleet.

Then, while haphazardly surveying the edges of the ground and thinking of the monk Orthopompe, he noticed a piece of a stone half-covered with sand. Half-covered, he soon realized, was a premature judgement, for as he kneeled down and struggled to dislodge it he found that there was no end in sight. He struck the smooth granite with a sharp blow from his hammer and placed his ear almost immediately against the surface that had been made warm by the sun, whose rays had just fallen on that very spot. He heard the sound dance about and wander through the vast forays of the stone and realized that there were great things to be found there. In order to be sure that he could relocate the stone, he determined his position in relation to the convoy and then carefully covered the weathered portion of the monument with sand. He had barely finished when the first truck passed him by, loaded with cases. The second, which was carrying more baggage than material, was following closely. They were huge trucks, dozens of footstools in length, and they made a jovial sound. The rails and tools were jostling about between the tarp-covered sides of the vehicle and ragged red cloth from the tail-end frolicked before the eyes of the archaeologist. Further back there followed a third truck with people and baggage, and finally a yellow and black taxi whose lowered flag served as a warning to the imprudent. Athanagore waved at the pretty girl he saw in the car. The taxi stopped a bit further on and seemed to be waiting for him. He hurried towards it.

Angel, who was sitting next to the driver, got out and approached Athanagore.

"Were you waiting for us?" he asked.

"I've come to meet you," said Athanagore. "Did you have a nice trip?"

"Not too bad," said Angel, "except for when the captain tried to continue on shore on his own."

"That I have no trouble believing," said Athanagore.

"Are you Mr. Dudu?"

"Absolutely not! I wouldn't be Mr. Dudu for all the Exopotomian pottery in the *Britiche Muséomme*."

"Excuse me," said Angel. "I had no way of knowing."

"Don't worry about it," said Athanagore. "I'm an archaeologist. I work around here."

"Pleased to meet you," said Angel. "Me, I'm an engineer. The name's Angel. Rochelle and Anne are inside."

He pointed to the taxi.

"I'm here too," muttered the driver.

"Of course," said Angel. "We're not forgetting you."

"I feel sorry for you," said Athanagore.

"Why?" asked Angel.

"I don't think you're going to like Amadis Dudu."

"That's too bad," murmured Angel.

Anne and Rochelle were kissing in the taxi. The sour look on Angel's face betrayed his awareness of this fact.

"Do you want to come with me on foot?" proposed Athanagore. "I'll explain things."

"Sure," said Angel.

"Can I take off now?" said the driver.

"Go ahead."

After glancing down with satisfaction at his meter the driver put the vehicle into gear. It had been a good day.

In spite of himself, Angel looked through the rear window of the taxi as it departed. One could see from Anne's profile that he had but one thing on his mind. Angel lowered his head.

Athanagore looked at him with astonishment. Angel's face bore the marks of sleeplessness as well as daily torment and his slender back seemed to be slumping a bit.

"Isn't that odd?" said Athanagore. "And you're a good-looking guy."

"It's Anne that she likes," said Angel.

"But he's dense!" remarked Athanagore.

"He's my friend," said Angel.

"Yeah..."

Athanagore passed his arm under that of the young man.

"You're in for a scolding."

"From who?" asked Angel.

"From that shit, Dudu. He'll claim that you're late."

"I really don't care about that," said Angel. "Are you excavating?"

"At the moment, I'm letting my workers dig," explained Athanagore. "I'm sure we're well on the road to something big. I can feel it. So, I let them continue. My factotum, Lardier, takes care of everything. I give him little chores, because otherwise he bothers Dupont. Dupont's my cook. I'm just telling you all this so you'll be in the know. As a rather strange and disagreeable phenomenon might have it, Martin is in love with Dupont. And what's more, Dudu has taken to Dupont as well."

"Who's Martin?"

"Martin Lardier, my factotum."

"And Dupont?"

"Dupont doesn't care. He likes Martin, I suppose, but in the end he's a whore just like the rest of them. Excuse me... At my age, I shouldn't talk like that, but today I'm feeling young. Anyway, me alone with those three pigs, well, what's a man to do?"

"Nothing at all," said Angel.

"And that's exactly what I do."

"Where are we going to live?" asked Angel.

"There's a hotel. Don't worry."

"About what?"

"About Anne..."

"Oh, there's nothing to worry about," said Angel. "Rochelle prefers Anne to me. That's easy to see."

"Easy to see? How? It's no more evident than anything else. She kisses him. That's all."

"No," said Angel, "That's not all. She kisses him and then he kisses her and everywhere he touches her, afterwards, her skin is no longer the same. It's not easy to believe at first, when you see her leave his arms and she's all fresh, her lips plump and red and her hair all aglow. But she's being used up. With every kiss she's a bit more used up. Her breasts become less firm and her skin less smooth and fine. Her eyes grow dim and her walk gets heavy, and as the days pass it's no longer the same Rochelle. I know. When you see it, you believe it. Myself, in the beginning, I believed it without really being aware of any of it."

"You're just imagining things," said Athanagore.

"No. It's not just my imagination and you know it. I see it now and I can take note of it from day to day, and every time I look she's sunken a bit further. She's using herself up. He's using her. There's nothing I can do. Nor you."

"So you don't love her anymore?"

"Yes," said Angel. "As much as before. But it's a love that's bad for me, one that's mixed with hate because she's using herself up."

Athanagore had no response.

"I came here to work," Angel continued. "And I think I'll be able to do a good job. I had hoped that Anne and I would go alone and leave Rochelle behind. But since that hasn't happened I no longer hope for it. He stayed by her side during the entire voyage. Nevertheless, I'm still his friend. In the beginning he would tease me when I would tell him that she was pretty."

Angel's words were stirring up something profound in Athanagore: long, thin ideas that had been flattened out under a layer of more recent events, ideas so flat that looking at them in sections, as at this very moment, he was unable to distinguish or differentiate their form and color. He could only sense them moving underneath, sinewy and reptilian. He shook his head and the movement stopped; the frightened thoughts retracted and became still again.

He searched for something to say to Angel but had no ideas. He tried desperately. They walked side by side, the green grass tickling Athanagore's legs and brushing up against the fabric of Angel's pants. Beneath their feet the empty shells left by little yellow snails exploded into particles of dust, accompanied by a clean, pure sound, like a drop of water falling on a heart-shaped blade of crystal, which is quite silly, really.

From the top of the dune they had just scaled, one could see Barrizone's lonely restaurant and the huge trucks that were parked in front of it. It looked like a scene from a war. Athanagore's tent and the path that led to it were out of view, for he had chosen his site quite cleverly. The sun was never far off but they avoided looking at it because of a very disagreeable peculiarity: it sent out uneven rays. It was surrounded by alternate, radiant layers that were either clear or obscure, and the parts of the ground that were struck by the obscure layers always remained cold and somber. Angel hadn't yet noticed this curious aspect of the country because upon entering the desert the taxi driver had managed to follow a strip of clear rays. On top of the dune, however, he could see the black and immobile frontier of the obscure light and a shiver went up his spine. Athanagore was used to it, but he saw that Angel, ill at ease, was observing this spectacle of discontinuity with great concern. Atha tapped him on the shoulder.

"It's kind of shocking at first," he said, "but you'll learn to live with it."

It occurred to Angel that the archaeologist's remarks could equally apply to Anne and Rochelle.

"I doubt it," he responded.

They descended the smooth slope. They could now

hear the cries of the men who were beginning to unload the trucks as well as the sharp, metallic sound of the rails slapping up against one another. All around the restaurant their shadows raced back and forth like the confused activity of so many insects. They could see Amadis Dudu, bustling about all busy and self-important.

Athanagore sighed.

"I have no idea why I'm interested in all this. I'm an old man, after all."

"Well," said Angel, "I don't want to bore you with my stories."

"It doesn't bore me," said Athanagore. "I understand. I feel sorry for you. You see, I thought that I was too old."

He stopped for a moment, scratched his head, and started walking once more.

"It's the desert," he concluded. "It must have a preserving effect."

He placed his hand on Angel's shoulder.

"I'm going to leave you here," he said. "I have no desire to see that individual again."

"Amadis?"

"Yes. He..."

The archaeologist stopped to search for just the right word.

"He's a pain in the ass. That's what he is."

He blushed and shook Angel's hand.

"I know that I shouldn't talk that way but this Dudu character is intolerable. I'll see you later. We're sure to run into each other at the restaurant."

"So long," said Angel. "I'd like to come see your excavations."

Athanagore nodded his head.

"All you'll see is little boxes. Still, it's a nice little display. I've got to run. Come when you like."

"So long," repeated Angel.

The archaeologist turned off to the right and disappeared into a fold of sand. Angel stood there, waiting for the moment when his white head would reappear. He soon saw the whole body again. His stockings hung out over the sides of his boots, making his legs look like the dotted, white hoofs of a horse. He then vanished behind a lump of yellow sand, becoming smaller and smaller while the straight path of his footprints formed a gossamer thread.

Angel glanced once more at the white restaurant and the brightly colored flowers which freckled its facade, then hurried off to join his friends. Crouching next to the monstrous truck was the black and yellow taxi, as sorry looking as an old wheelbarrow placed next to a "dynamic new model" created by an inventor known only by a select few.

Not far from there, Rochelle's bright green dress was flapping in the sun, tossed about by the ascending winds and casting a splendid shadow in spite of the irregularity of the earth.

IX

"I'm telling you it's true," repeated Martin Lardier.

His plump, pink face was shining excitedly and a small blue aigrette shot out from atop each one of his hairs.

"I don't believe you, Lardier," responded the archaeologist. "I could believe anything, but not that. To be honest, I suppose there are a good number of things I wouldn't believe."

"Oh, drats!" said Lardier.

"Lardier, I want you to copy the third *Chant de Maldoror*, turning the words end on end and changing the spelling."

"Yes, master," said Lardier.

Furious with rage, he added:

"Why don't you just come and see for yourself!"

Athanagore stared at him carefully and shook his head.

"You're incorrigible. Still, I won't add to your punishment."

"But Master, I'm begging you!"

"O.K., I'll go," groaned Atha, finally giving in to this insistence.

"I'm sure it's there. I remember the description from William Bugle's book. It's exactly like it says."

"You're insane, Martin. A fiducial line just isn't found that way. Because you're an idiot, I'll pardon your impish behavior, but you shouldn't make a habit of getting carried away like this. You're too old for that."

"But for Pete's sake! I'm telling you it's not a joke..."

Athanagore had a good feeling. This was the first time since his factotum had started giving him daily briefings that he sensed they were truly on the verge of something.

"O.K. Let's see," he said.

He got up and left.

The vacillating rays of light from the gas lamp lit up the ground and the sides of the tent, cutting a somewhat cone-like space of light into the opaque night. Athanagore's head was lost in the darkness, while the rest of his body received the diluted rays emanating from the incandescent lantern. Martin ran along at his side, shaking his short little legs and round bottom. In the pitch-black darkness, Martin's lamp guided them towards the deep and narrow orifice which served as an entry shaft and led to the front of the tunnels. Martin went first. He was breathing heavily as he grabbed hold of the nielloed silver bars which Athanagore, prompted by his immodest yet excusable sense of refinement, had installed to help access his site of operation.

Athanagore looked towards the skies. The Astrolabe was twinkling as it usually did: three black sparkles, one green, two red, then two times it gave off no light at all. The Big Dipper, all limp and sallow, emitted a light that pulsed with feeble amperage and Orion had just turned itself off. The archaeologist shrugged his shoulders, put his feet together, and jumped into the hole. He was counting on the thick layer of fat around his assistant's body to ease the landing, but Martin was already in the horizontal tunnel. He returned to help his boss out of the plutonic-cylindrical hole that his slender body had dug into the ground.

After a short distance the gallery broke off into branches leading in all directions. It represented a considerable amount of work. Each tunnel was marked with a reference number scrawled across a white sign. Electrical wires, fastened to the ceiling of the gallery, ran silently along the dry stone. There were light bulbs shining here and there, pushing themselves fast and furiously towards a certain death. One could hear the hoarse breathing of the group and their emulsifying aerosol compression pump, which helped Athanagore get rid of a mixture of sand, earth, and crushed pinpinaquanguous rock that was extracted daily by the heavy machinery.

The two men made their way through gallery number 7. Athanagore had a hard time not losing sight of the overexcited Martin, who was moving rather quickly. The gallery formed a straight line: a single branch at the end of which they could start to make out the work crew that handled the heavier and more complex machinery which helped Athanagore to stockpile the marvelous findings in which his collection, when she found herself alone with her objects, would take great pride.

While traversing the residual distance, Atha was able to distinguish a characteristic odor that made all of his doubts instantly disappear. There was no question about it: his assistants had discovered a fiducial line. It was that mysterious and composite odor of chambers dug out of rock - the dry odor of pure emptiness that is preserved by the earth

115

when it discovers the ruins of one of its lost monuments. He ran. Small objects jingled in his pockets and the leather sheath of his hammer slapped up against the side of his thigh. Things grew lighter as he advanced, and when he arrived, he was panting impatiently. The group was at work in front of him. The shriek of the turbine, half-muffled by a soundproof cover, filled the narrow cul-de-sac as air roared in the huge annulated pipe of the emulsifier.

Martin's eyes were avidly following the progress of the cutting wheel while next to him, two men and a woman, naked from the waist up, looked on as well. Occasionally, one of the three would maneuver a control lever with a sure and steady hand.

The instant he saw it, Athanagore recognized the find. The sharp teeth of the tools dug into the dense material that covered the entrance to a hippostal chamber, which judging from the thickness of the wall was of considerable dimensions. The crew had adeptly unearthed the frame, and the wall, still lightly covered with a few millimeters of hardened silt, was starting to show itself in certain places. Odd shaped bits of compact earth broke loose from time to time as the stone started to breathe again.

Athanagore, who was having a hard time swallowing, pressed a button and the machine came to a halt with the soft sound of a fading siren. The two men and the woman turned around, saw Athanagore, and walked towards him. The cul-de-sac was now filled with a rich silence.

"You've found it," said Athanagore.

One after the other, the men shook hands. Atha pulled the young woman to his side.

"Copper, are you happy?"

A smile was her only response. She had black hair and black eyes and her skin was a rather curious shade of deep ochre. The tips of her breasts were almost violet, and rested firmly on the two hard and polished globes.

"It's over," she said. "After all this, we really found it."

"You three will be able to take a break now," said Athanagore as he caressed her hot, bare shoulders.

"Not a chance," said the man on the right.

"Why, Bertil?" asked Athanagore. "I'm sure your brother would like to get out of here."

"No," replied Brice. "We want to keep digging."

"You haven't found anything else?" asked Lardier.

"Over in the corner," said Copper. "Some pots, lamps, and a pernuclet."

"We'll see to that later," said Athanagore. "Come on, you," he said to Copper.

"Sure. This is one time I can't refuse," she said.

"Your brothers are nuts. They should get some air."

"There's plenty of air. Anyway, we want to see what's here."

He laid his hand on the machine and looked for the ignition switch. He pushed the black button and the machine made a soft, uncertain grinding noise that soon affirmed itself as a high squeal when the unit hit full-force.

"Don't suffocate in there," cried Athanagore over the tumult.

The teeth of the tools started once more to kick up a heavy dust that was immediately sucked up by the absorbers.

Brice and Bertil shook their heads and smiled at one another.

"We're fine," said Brice.

"Goodbye," shouted the archaeologist one last time.

He turned around and left. Copper joined arms with Athanagore and followed him. Her step was light and muscular and in the passage the electric lamps made her orange skin glimmer. Behind them walked Martin Lardier, who despite his usual tendencies was excited by the shapely curves of the young woman.

They made their way in silence to the circular room where all the galleries joined. She unhitched herself from

117

Athanagore's arm and walked up to a sort of hole dug into the rock's surface from which she drew some clothing. She took off her work skirt and slipped on a pair of white shorts and a silk blouse. Athanagore and Martin turned away, the first out of respect and the second because he didn't want to be unfaithful to Dupont, even in intention, for Copper wore nothing underneath her skirt. There was, in fact, no need for anything.

As soon as she was ready, they assumed their rapid pace and started up the entry shaft in the opposite direction. Martin went first and Athanagore brought up the rear.

Outside, Copper stretched her limbs. Through the sheer silk they could see the darkest spots of her torso. That is until Athanagore asked Martin to shine the light elsewhere.

"It's nice," she murmured. "Everything is so calm outside."

There was a metallic blast that came from far off and echoed for a long time in the dunes.

"What's that?" she asked.

"A bunch of newcomers," said Athanagore. "A whole load of newcomers, come to build a railroad."

They approached the tent.

"What are they like?" asked Copper.

"Two men," said the archaeologist. "Two men and a woman. And also some workers, some kids, and Amadis Dudu."

"What's he like?"

"He's a lousy homo," said Athanagore.

He stopped himself. He'd forgotten about the presence of Martin. But Martin had just left them to join Dupont in the kitchen. Athanagore took a breath.

"I don't want to be rude to Martin, you understand," he explained.

"And the two men?"

"One's real nice," said Athanagore. "The other, well, the woman is in love with that one. But the first one, he's in love with the woman too. He's called Angel. Handsome guy."

"Handsome..." she said slowly.

"Yeah," replied the archaeologist. "But this Amadis..."

A shiver ran through him.

"Let's go have something. You're going to get cold."

"I'm fine," murmured Copper. "Angel...that's a strange name."

"Yeah," said the archaeologist. "They all have strange names."

The phosphorescent lamp shone on the table and the entrance to the tent hung open, warm and welcoming.

"Go ahead," he said to Copper, nudging her ahead as she entered.

"Hello," said the abbot, who rose from his seat at the table when he saw her.

X

"How many cannonballs does it take to demolish the city of Lyon?" continued the abbot, shouting out his question point-blank at the archaeologist as he penetrated the tent behind Copper.

"Eleven!" replied Athanagore.

"Damn! That's too many. Say three."

"Three," repeated Athanagore.

The abbot grabbed his rosary and quickly said it three times. Then he placed it back down. Copper was seated on Atha's bed, while Atha stared at the priest, dumbfounded.

"What are you doing in my tent?"

"I just got here," explained the abbot. "Do you know how to play insult your neighbor?"

119

"Oh, wow!" said Copper, clapping her hands. "I love insult your neighbor!"

"I shouldn't even speak to you," said the abbot, "wanton creature that you are. But you've got such damn fine breasts."

"Thank you," said Copper. "I know."

"I'm looking for Claude Leon," said the abbot. "He should have arrived about fifteen days ago. I'm the regional inspector. Let me show you my card. There are a lot of hermits in this country, but quite far from here. Claude Leon, on the other hand, should be rather close by."

"I haven't seen him," said Athanagore.

"Well I hope not," said the abbot. "A hermit, according to the rules, should never leave his hermitage unless he's been formally authorized to do so with special permission from the appropriate inspector general."

He saluted.

"That's me," he said. "Two, four, six, eight..."

"Slap that sausage on the plate," added Copper, remembering her catechism.

"Thank you," said the abbot. "I was just saying that Claude Leon is probably not far off. Would you like to come along and see him?"

"We'd better have something before we go," said Athanagore. "Copper, you haven't eaten a thing. That's not sensible."

"I could go for a sandwich," said Copper.

"Care for a Cointreau, abbot?"

"Cointreau? Must say no," said the abbot. "My religion prohibits it. But I could sign a special waiver if there are no objections."

"Please do," said Athanagore. "I'll get Dupont. Would you like a pen and some paper?"

"I have some forms already printed," said the abbot. "In a loose-leaf binder. That way, I can keep track."

Athanagore went out and turned to his left. Dupont's kitchen stood close by. He opened the door without knock-

ing and sparked up his lighter. In the flickering light he saw
Dupont's bed, where Lardier lay sleeping. One could see
where the tracks of tears had dried on his cheeks and as he
sobbed he heaved a great sigh, as they say... Athanagore
leaned over him.

"Where's Dupont?" he asked.

Lardier woke up and began crying again. In his semi-
slumber he had vaguely understood Atha's question.

"He's left," he said. "He wasn't here."

"Oh," said the archaeologist. "You have no idea where
he is?"

"With that whore Amadis, I'm sure," cried Lardier.
"She'll pay this time, that bitch."

"Come on, Lardier," said Atha, taking a firm tone. "It's
not like you're married to Dupont."

"Yes it is," replied Lardier, quite curt.

He was no longer crying.

"When we came here, we broke a pot," he continued,
"like in *Notre-Dame-de-Paris*. It broke into eleven pieces.
He's married to me for six more years."

"First of all, you shouldn't be reading *Notre-Dame-de-
Paris* because it's outdated. Furthermore, it's a marriage
only in a manner of speaking. Besides that, I've been kind
enough to sit and listen to your whining. Copy the first
chapter of this book for me using your left hand, writing
from right to left. Now, where's the Cointreau?"

"In the cabinet," said Lardier, calmly.

"Now back to sleep," said Athanagore.

He approached the bed and ran his hands over
Lardier's hair.

"Maybe he just went to run an errand."

Lardier simply sniffled and said nothing. He seemed a
bit more tranquil.

The archaeologist opened the cabinet and easily located the bottle of Cointreau, which was sitting next to a jar
of grasshoppers in tomato sauce. He took three dainty lit-

tle glasses that he had found a few weeks earlier in one of his more fruitful sites. He had deduced that several thousand years ago queen Nefourpitonh had used them for calming eyebaths. He made a big sandwich for Copper, placed everything on the tray, and headed back to the tent.

The priest was seated on the bed with Copper. He had unbuttoned her blouse and was staring inside with devoted attention.

"This is a very interesting young woman," he said to Athanagore when he saw him enter.

"Oh, yeah?" said the archaeologist. "In what way, exactly?"

"Exactly," said the abbot. "My god, I don't know. The whole package, I guess. Not to say that certain diverse parts don't also have their charm."

"Did you also sign a waiver for this examination you're giving?" asked Atha.

"For that I have a permanent card," said the priest. "It's necessary in my profession."

Copper laughed, not at all embarrassed. She hadn't rebuttoned her blouse. Athanagore couldn't help smiling. He put the plate down on the table and handed the sandwich to Copper.

"What tiny glasses!..." cried the abbot. "It's a pity to have wasted a waiver for this. Tanquam adeo fluctuat nec mergitur."

"Et cum spiritu tuo," replied Copper.

"Raise the hammer and smash the piggy banks," concluded the abbot and Athanagore in concert.

"Well, on my honor as a Littlejohn!" he instantly exclaimed. "It's a real pleasure to meet people as religious as you."

"Our profession," explained Athanagore, "obliges us to be in the know about these things. But we're nonbelievers, more or less."

"Thanks for the reassurance," said Littlejohn. "I was

starting to feel a state of volatile sin creeping up on me, but it's passed. Let's see if this Cointreau has a kick."

Athanagore opened the bottle and filled the glasses. The abbot stood and took one. He looked at it, sniffed, and swallowed.

"Hmmm..." he said.

He held out his glass for another.

"How is it?" asked Athanagore as he refilled the glass.

The abbot drank the second shot and reflected.

"Vile," he said. "It smells like kerosene."

"Then I must have grabbed the wrong bottle," said the archaeologist. "They looked similar."

"Don't worry about it," said the priest. "It was drinkable, anyway."

"Well it is fine kerosene," the archaeologist assured him.

"Would you excuse me while I step outside to vomit?" said Littlejohn.

"Please do... I'll get the other bottle."

"Hurry up," said the abbot. "The worst part about it is that it has to come back out my mouth. Too bad. I'll close my eyes."

He was off like a whirlwind. Copper was stretched out on the bed, laughing, her hands crossed behind her head. Glimmers of light bounced off her black eyes and healthy teeth. Athanagore was still hesitating, but he heard Littlejohn hiccupping outside and his withered old face finally brightened up.

"He's nice," he said.

"He's an idiot," said Copper. "What does he take us for, a couple of clerics? Well, at least he's funny. And adept with his hands."

"All the better for you," said the archaeologist. "I'll go get the Cointreau. But you should at least wait until you've seen Angel."

"Of course," said Copper.

The priest reappeared.

"Can I come in?" he asked.

"Certainly," said Athanagore, who moved aside to let him pass and then left with the bottle of kerosene.

The abbot came back and sat down in a canvas chair.

"I'm not sitting next to you," he explained, "because I smell like vomit. I even got it into my buckled shoes. Shameful. How old are you?"

"Twenty," replied Copper.

"Too much," said the abbot. "Say three."

"Three."

Once more, Littlejohn's hands worked their way through three of the rosary beads with the speed of a pea-shelling machine. Athanagore reappeared just as the priest finished.

"Ah!" cried the abbot. "Let's see if this Cointreau stays put."

"That's not so witty," judged Copper.

"Excuse me," said the abbot. "But one can't be inspired twenty-four hours a day, especially when one's busy making amens in one's spare time."

"That's for sure," said Copper.

"Point well taken," said Athanagore.

"So, let's drink," said the abbot. "Then I'll go locate Claude Leon."

"Can we come along with you?" proposed the archaeologist.

"But..." said the abbot, "aren't you going to sleep tonight?"

"We rarely sleep," explained Athanagore. "It's a stupid waste of time, sleeping."

"You're right," said the abbot. "I don't know why I asked you that, because I never sleep either. I'm probably upset because I thought I was the only one."

He stopped to reflect.

"In fact, I'm quite upset. But I can live with it. Give me another Cointreau."

"Here you are," said Athanagore.

"Ah!" sighed the abbot, holding his glass up to the light. "That's much better."

He tasted it.

"This one's drinkable, at least. But after that kerosene everything tastes like donkey piss."

He finished the rest, then sniffled.

"Disgusting," he concluded. "That'll teach me to waste my dispensation forms."

"It's no good?" asked Athanagore, astonished.

"Sure, it's fine," said Littlejohn. "But after all, it's only forty-three per cent. I'll take a 190 proof Arquebuse or good old rubbing alcohol any time. When I was at Saint-Philippe-du-Roule, that's all I used for mass. And those masses were some real barnburners, I'm telling you."

"Why didn't you stay there?" asked Copper.

"They sent me packing," said the abbot. "They made me an inspector, called it a dismissal. I guess I'm no longer Littlejohn."

"But now you have the chance to travel," said Athanagore.

"Sure," said the abbot. "I'm quite content. Let's go find Claude Leon."

"Let's go," said Athanagore.

Copper stood up. The archaeologist extended his hand toward the flame of the phosphorescent lamp and lightly flattened it out so that it took on the form of a night light, then the three of them left the dark tent.

XI

"We've been walking quite a long time," said Athanagore.

"Really?" said Littlejohn. "I hadn't noticed. I was lost in meditation, contemplating the classic notion, as it were, of the greatness of God and the insignificance of man in the desert."

"Oh yeah," said Copper. "That's not so original."

"Generally speaking," said Littlejohn, "I don't think along the same lines as my colleagues, and that lends a certain charm to my meditations, a little personal touch. In this meditation, I inserted a bicycle."

"I wonder," said Athanagore, "...how are you able to do it?"

"At first..." said the abbot, "...I was also surprised. But now I realize it's a trick I play on myself that permits me to accomplish this feat. I just have to think of a bicycle and 'voila' - there it is."

"When you explain it like that," said Athanagore, "it sounds simple."

"Sure," said the abbot. "But don't be misled. What's that, up ahead?"

"I don't see anything," said Athanagore, staring with eyes wide-open.

"It's a man," said Copper.

"Ah!..." said Littlejohn. "It could be Leon."

"I don't think so," said Athanagore. "I didn't see anyone here this morning."

They approached the object while continuing their debate, but their progress was thwarted because the figure was also moving in the same direction.

"Ho!" cried Athanagore.

"Ho!" responded the voice of Angel.

The figure halted. It was indeed Angel. They caught up with him in a matter of moments.

"Hello," said Athanagore. "Let me introduce you to Copper and Abbot Littlejohn."

"Hello," said Angel.

They shook hands.

"Just out walking?" asked Littlejohn. "Meditating, no doubt."

"No," said Angel. "I was just leaving."

"Where are you headed?" asked the archaeologist.

"Anywhere," said Angel. "They're making too much noise at the hotel."

"Who?" asked the abbot. "You know, you can trust my discretion."

"Oh, I can tell you," said Angel. "It's no secret. It's Rochelle and Anne."

"Oh!" said the abbot. "They're... doing it?"

"And she can't manage without all the moaning," said Angel. "It's terrible. I'm in the room next door. I just can't put up with it."

Copper approached Angel. She put her arms around his neck and kissed him.

"Come on," she said. "Come along while we go find Claude Leon. The abbot here, he's a riot."

The night was like yellow ink, sliced open by luminous and slender brush strokes that fell from the stars at various angles. Angel tried to make out the face of the young woman.

"You're nice," he said.

Athanagore and the abbot were walking ahead of them.

"Not really," she said. "Not especially so. Would you like to see what I look like?"

"I'd like to," said Angel.

"Use your lighter."

"I don't have a lighter."

"Then touch me with your hands," she said, drawing back from him a bit.

Angel put his hands on her square shoulders and worked his way up. His fingers moved over her cheeks and then her eyelids, finally losing themselves in Copper's black hair.

"You smell like a strange perfume," he said.

"What?"

"The desert."

He let his arms fall back to his sides.

"But you only know my face..." she protested.

Angel was silent and motionless. She moved close to him once more and put her naked arms around his neck. She whispered in his ear while her cheek pressed up against that of the boy.

"You've been crying."

"Yes," murmured Angel.

He remained still.

"You shouldn't cry over a girl. They're not worth it."

"I'm not crying over her," he said. "It's the idea of what she once was and what she's going to become that makes me cry."

He seemed to be waking from a deep sleep and he placed his hands on the young woman's hips.

"You're nice," she repeated. "Come on, let's catch up with the others."

She loosened her embrace and took him by the hand. Copper laughed as they tripped and tumbled down the sand dunes in the dark.

The Abbot Littlejohn had just finished explaining to Athanagore why Claude Leon had been made a hermit.

"You see," he said, "this boy really didn't deserve to go to prison."

"Certainly not," said Athanagore.

"That's right," said Littlejohn. "He should have been guillotined. But the Bishop has a lot of influence."

"Good thing for Leon."

"But that really doesn't change anything. Being a hermit can be fun, if you want it to be. Anyway, it gives him a breather for a few more years."

"How's that?" asked Copper, who had heard the last part of the phrase.

"Well, after three or four years of hermitage," said the abbot, "most everyone goes nuts. They take off and kill the first little girl that comes their way and then they rape her."

"Always?" said a flabbergasted Angel.

"Always," affirmed the abbot. "There has only been one exception."

"Who was it?" said Athanagore.

"Real nice guy," said Littlejohn. "A saint. It's a long story, but damned edifying."

"Tell us..." begged Copper in a persuasive voice.

"No," said the abbot. "Impossible. It's too long. I'll just tell you the end. He took off, and the first little girl he came across..."

"Stop it!" said Athanagore. "This is disgusting..."

"She killed him," said Littlejohn. "She was a maniac."

"Oh," sighed Copper, "how atrocious. The poor boy. What was his name?"

"Littlejohn," said the abbot. "Excuse me, that's wrong. I was thinking of something else. Leverrier was his name."

"That's amazing," said Angel. "I know another Leverrier who had an entirely different experience."

"Must be someone else," said the abbot. "Or maybe I'm just a liar."

"More likely..." said Athanagore.

"Look," said Copper, "there's a light ahead."

"We must be there," proclaimed Littlejohn. "Pardon me, but I'd better go alone first. You can follow later. Those are the rules."

"It's not like we're being observed," said Angel. "We could accompany you."

"I have my conscience," said Littlejohn. "Comely Curtis, king butterfly..."

"Did a little fencing and took one in the eye," exclaimed the others in unison.

"O.K." said Littlejohn. "Since you know the ritual as well as I do you can come along. Anyhow, it's better that way. I get bored stiff when I'm alone."

He leaped into in the air and came somersaulting back down, landing in a crouched position on his heels. His cassock was spread around him, a huge black flower barely visible against the night sand.

"Is that part of the ritual?" asked the archaeologist.

"No!" said the priest. "It's just something my grandmother used to do when she wanted to pee at the beach without anyone noticing. I should tell you that I'm not wearing my apostolic underwear. It's too hot. I signed a waiver."

"All these exemptions are going to weigh you down," said Athanagore.

"I copy them onto microfilm," said Littlejohn. "That way, it's just a tiny little roll."

He stood back up.

"Let's go."

Claude Leon was tucked away in a little white shack that was smartly decorated. A bed of stones in the corner was the only item that occupied any space in the main room.

A door led to the kitchen. Through the windowpane they could see Claude on his knees, head in hands, meditating in front of his bed. The abbot entered.

"Kookoo," he said.

The hermit lifted his head.

"But I'm not ready yet," he said. "I've only counted to fifty."

"Are you playing hide and seek, my son?" said Littlejohn.

"Yes father," said Claude Leon. "With Lavender."

"Really," said the abbot. "Can we join you?"

"Of course," said Claude.

He stood up.

"I'll go get Lavender and tell her. She'll be very happy."

He passed into the kitchen. Angel, Copper, and the

archaeologist entered after the abbot.

"You have no special prayers to say when you encounter a hermit?" asked Copper, astonished.

"Oh, no," said the abbot. "He's used to this. It's good for the uninitiated, the special stuff. But with most of them, we just follow the ordinary rules."

Leon returned, followed by a ravishing negress. She had an oval face with a thin, straight nose, big blue eyes, and an extraordinary head of red hair. She was wearing a black bra.

"This is Lavender," explained Claude Leon. "Oh," he added, seeing the three other visitors. "Hello. How do you do?"

"My name is Athanagore," said the archaeologist. "This is Angel and this is Copper."

"Would you like to play hide and seek?" proposed the hermit.

"Let's be serious, my child," said the abbot. "I need to proceed with my inspection. I have some questions that you must answer for my report."

"We'll leave you alone," said Athanagore.

"Not necessary," said Littlejohn. "It'll be no more than five minutes."

"Have a seat," said Lavender. "Come into the kitchen while they work."

Her skin was exactly the same color as Copper's hair and vice-versa. Angel tried imagining the two women joined together and was struck with vertigo.

"Was this done on purpose?" he said to Copper.

"Not at all," responded Copper. "I don't even know her."

"I can assure you," said Lavender, "it's pure coincidence."

They went into the kitchen and the abbot stayed with Leon.

"So," said Littlejohn.

"Nothing new," said Leon.

"You like it here?"

"It's O.K."

"And as far as the question of grace is concerned?"

"It comes and it goes."

"Ideas?"

"Black ones," said Leon. "But with Lavender, that's excusable. They're black but not sorrowful. Black and fiery."

"That's the color of hell."

"Yes," said Claude Leon, "but inside of her, it's pink velvet."

"Really?"

"Honest to God."

"A little scotch, a little gin, drop the pants and jump right in."

"Amen!" responded the hermit.

The Abbot Littlejohn stopped to reflect.

"Everything seems to be in order here," he said. "I think you'll make an acceptable hermit. You'll have to put up a sign. People would come and see you on Sundays."

"I'd like that," said Claude Leon.

"Have you chosen your saintly deed?"

"What?..."

"They should have explained it to you," said the abbot. "Standing up on a column, or giving yourself five lashes a day, or wearing a hair shirt, eating gravel, praying for twenty-four hours straight, etcetera."

"They didn't tell me about that," said Claude Leon. "Isn't there something else I can choose? That stuff doesn't seem so saintly. And what's more, it's been done already."

"Don't put too much stock in originality, my son," said the abbot.

"Yes, father," replied the hermit.

He meditated for a moment.

"I could fuck Lavender..." he proposed.

"Personally, I don't see anything wrong with that. But you do understand that you'll have to do it every time there's a visitor?"

"It would be a pleasure," responded Claude.

"It's settled then. Pink velvet... You're not kidding?"

"It's true."

The abbot trembled and the hair on the back of his neck stood up. He passed his hand over his stomach.

"Frightening," he said. "Well, I've said what I have to say. I'll have Hermit Aid bring you a supply of canned goods."

"But I have supplies," said Claude.

"You're going to need a lot. You'll have plenty of visitors. They're building a railroad over there."

"Fantastic," said Claude Leon.

He was pale, but thoroughly delighted.

"I certainly do hope they visit often."

"I have to say again that you've frightened me," said Abbot Littlejohn. "And I'm one tough customer. Pick, nick, ice-cream scoop..."

"You're the one who's a nincompoop," the hermit added.

"Let's join the others," proposed Littlejohn. "As for your saintly deed, then, it's understood. I'll make out my report accordingly."

"Thank you," said Claude.

PASSAGE

Amadis Dudu is, beyond any shadow of a doubt, a horrible fellow. He annoys everyone and will perhaps have to be done away with simply because he is dishonest, haughty, insolent, and pretentious. Furthermore, he's a homosexual. Almost all the characters are in place now and a variety of events will start to take shape. First of all, the construction of the railroad represents a challenge because they have forgotten the roadbed. The gravel is essential and can't be substituted - as by the way no one has proposed - with little yellow snail shells. For now, they will simply leave the assembled rails propped up against the crosspieces and then add the roadbed when it arrives. Naturally, one can construct a track in this manner. However, when I said that I would talk about the pebbles in the desert, I wasn't predicting the drama that would arise around the roadbed. It served, I suppose, as a rather crudely symbolic and faintly intellectual means of representation. Anyhow, it goes without saying that the atmosphere of a desert like this becomes, over a period of time, rather depressing, especially because of this sun and its black rays. Finally, I draw your attention to the arrival of another incidental character: Alfredo Jabes, authority on scale models. But it's too late for that now. Crock's boat will be shipwrecked and when he arrives it will all be over. I won't speak about this again until the next passage, or perhaps not at all.

SECOND MOVEMENT

I

It was cool and stormy, without a trace of wind. The green blades of grass stood firm, as usual, while the indefatigable sun bleached their pointed tips and overwhelmed hepatrols closed their petals. There was a growing vibration over the restaurant, where Joseph Barrizone had just closed all the blinds. In front, the yellow and black taxi waited, ready for business. The trucks had just left in search of roadbed and the engineers worked in their rooms while the laborers started sanding down the ends of the rails that were unevenly cut. The atmosphere resonated with the melodic grinding of the new files and from his window, Angel could see Olive and Didiche, walking hand in hand and filling their little brown basket with sandpeepers. Next to him, the ink was drying on the drafting table. In the neighboring room, Anne was making calculations, while down the hall, Amadis dictated letters to Rochelle. That bastard Arland was drinking in the downstairs bar, waiting for the moment when he could return to harass Marin and Carlo. Above him, Angel could hear the steps of Professor Petereater, who had transformed the attic into a model infirmary. Seeing as nobody was ill, he used the operating table to construct his little planes. Every now and then Angel would hear him jump for joy, and then on other occasions the professor's ranting voice would bounce off the ceiling in a terrible wail when he howled at his intern, whose whining drone would then continue on for several moments.

Angel leaned back over his drafting table. If they continued to follow the data supplied by Amadis Dudu there would be no doubt about it. He shook his head and put down his drafting pen. He stretched his limbs and headed wearily for the door.

"Can I come in?"

It was Angel's voice. Anne lifted his head and told him yes.

"Hey, pal."

"Hello," said Angel. "Making any headway?"

"Yeah," said Anne. "It's almost finished."

"I found something troubling."

"What?"

"We're going to have to evict Barrizone."

"You're kidding," said Anne. "Are you sure?"

"Positive. I've looked it over twice."

Anne verified the calculations and the blueprints.

"You're right," he said. "The track'll pass right through the center of the hotel."

"What are we going to do?" said Angel. "We'll have to divert it."

"Amadis'll never accept that."

"Why not ask him?"

"Let's go," said Anne.

He hoisted up his massive frame and pushed back his chair.

"This is the shits," he said.

"Yeah," said Angel.

Anne walked out. Angel followed and closed the door. Anne made his way to Amadis' door, behind which could be heard the sound of voices and the sharp explosions of the typewriter. He knocked twice.

"Enter!" cried Amadis.

The machine came to a halt. Anne entered, followed by Angel, who closed the door.

"What is it?" asked Amadis. "I don't like being disturbed."

137

"It's not going to work," said Anne. "According to your specifications, the track will intersect the hotel."

"What hotel?"

"This one. Hotel Barrizone."

"So?" said Amadis. "What's the worry? We'll just evict him."

"Couldn't we divert it?"

"Are you insane, my friend?" said Amadis. "First of all, what right did Barrizone have to settle smack in the middle of the desert without finding out whether or not he would be bothering anybody?"

"He wasn't bothering a soul," observed Angel.

"Well it's clear to see that he is now," said Amadis. "And you gentlemen are paid to make plans. Are they ready?"

"We're working on them," said Anne.

"So, if they're not finished, finish them! I'll take this matter up with the Senior Administrative Council, but I'm sure that the original plans will have to be adhered to."

He turned toward Rochelle.

"Let's continue, miss."

Angel looked at Rochelle. With the blinds closed, her face appeared sweet and simple, maybe a bit fatigued under the eyes. She smiled at Anne. The two boys left Amadis' office.

"So?" said Angel.

"So, we continue," said Anne, shrugging his shoulders. "What difference does it make anyway, when all's said and done?"

"None, I guess," murmured Angel.

He wanted to go into Amadis' office. He wanted to kill him and then kiss Rochelle. The floor of the crude wooden hallway smelled a little like detergent and yellow sand filled its cracks. At the end of the hallway, a light breeze was tossing about the weighty bough of a hepatrol in front of the window. Angel once again felt the sensation of awakening, as he had that night at Claude Leon's.

"I'm sick of this," he said. "Let's take a walk."

"What?"

"Put away your plans and come take a walk."

"We'll still have to finish them sometime," said Anne.

"Later," said Angel.

"I'm wiped out," said Anne.

"It's you own fault."

Anne smiled complacently.

"Not completely my fault," said Anne. "It takes two to tango."

"You could have just left her behind," said Angel.

"Then I wouldn't have been so tired."

"Well you're not obliged to bed down with her every evening."

"She likes it," said Anne.

Angel hesitated before saying what he had to say.

"She'd like it with anybody."

"I don't think so," Anne replied.

He stopped to reflect and then spoke without any conceit.

"Personally, I'd prefer it if she slept around a little, that is if I could manage not to care about it. But she only wants to do it with me. And what's more, it happens that I still do care a bit."

"Then why not marry her?"

"Because," said Anne, "I know that moment will come when I really do stop caring. That's what I'm waiting for."

"And if that moment doesn't come?"

"That might well happen," he said. "If she'd been my first woman. But there's always a kind of degradation. With the first one, you really do love her, for maybe two years. Then you realize that she no longer has the same effect on you."

"But why?" said Angel. "If you love her."

"I can assure you," said Anne. "That's how is works. It takes about two years, maybe less if you make a poor choice. Then you realize that someone else now moves you the way the first one did. But this new fling only lasts about a year, and the cycle continues like this. Sure, you can still see your first love. You might even like her and still sleep with her. But it's not the same thing; it just becomes a reflex."

"Well I don't buy that spiel," said Angel. "I don't believe I'm like that."

"We're all like that," said Anne. "Nothing you can do. The fact is we don't especially need women."

"Perhaps physically," said Angel.

"No," said Anne. "Not only physically, but intellectually. They're too square. No woman is indispensable."

Angel said nothing. They had stopped in the hall and Anne was leaning up against the doorpost of his office. Angel looked at him. His breathing became more labored as he began to speak.

"That's what you think, Anne... that's what you think..."

"Yeah," said Anne. "That's what I know."

"If I was given Rochelle," said Angel, "and if she loved me, I would never need the love of any other woman."

"Sure you would. In two, three, four years. And if she still loved you like before, you'd do something to yourself to change things."

"Why?"

"So that she wouldn't love you any longer."

"I'm not like you," said Angel.

"Women don't have any imagination," said Anne. "They think that they, women, are all a man needs to make life complete. But there are so many other things."

"I thought like that too, before I met Rochelle," said Angel. "But it's not true."

"Nothing's changed. It hasn't stopped being true just because you met Rochelle. Life has so many things. Just this green, pointy grass for example. Just to touch it: to run your fingers over this dry sand and break one of these little, yellow snail shells; to marvel at the tiny, brilliant brown pieces mixed with the dry sand and to feel it in your hands. And to see a brand new rail, cold and blue, resonating so clearly. To see the vapor rise out of a ventilation pipe, or whatever... I don't know..."

"That's what you think, Anne."

"Or this sun and its black zones...who knows what lies beyond that?... Or Professor Petereater's planes, or a cloud, or digging a hole in the ground and finding things. Or listening to music."

Angel closed his eyes.

"Let me have Rochelle." he begged. "You don't love her."

"I love her," said Anne. "But it's nothing more than that. I can't pretend that nothing else exists. You can take her, if you want, but she wouldn't have it. She wants me to think about her all the time, to live my life for her and only her."

"Tell me more," said Angel. "What else does she want?"

"She wants the rest of the world to shrivel up and die. She wants everything to crumble, leaving just us two. She wants me to take the place of Amadis Dudu, so she can be my secretary."

"You're destroying her," murmured Angel.

"You want to take my place?"

"I wouldn't destroy her," said Angel. "I wouldn't even touch her. I'd just kiss her, and drape her naked body in white."

"They aren't like that," said Anne. "Women don't understand that there are other things. Or at least there are only a few who understand. It's not their fault, but they don't risk anything. They don't realize that life is full of things to do."

"But what are these things?"

"Lying down on the earth," said Anne. "Just lying down on this sand, empty-headed, with the wind blowing over you. Just walking along, seeing and doing things, building stone houses for people, bringing them cars and light and all that the world has to offer... simply to enable them to do absolutely nothing but empty their heads, have sex with women, and lie stretched-out on the sand, in the sun."

"First you don't want them," said Angel, "then you do?"

"I want them all the time," said Anne. "But I also need my rest."

"Don't ruin Rochelle," said Angel.

His voice trembled as he pleaded. Anne wiped his hand across his forehead.

"She's ruining herself," he said. "You can't stop her. After I will have left her, she'll look really devastated. But if she falls in love with you, she'll get better. Almost like before. Nevertheless, she'll deteriorate twice as fast the next time and you won't be able to stand it."

"So?..."

"So I don't know what you'll be able to do," said Anne. "Little by little, she'll fall apart with a rapidity that'll grow exponentially."

"Try to be mean to her," Angel said.

Anne laughed.

"I can't. Not yet. I still like her. And I like sleeping with her."

"Shut up," said Angel.

"I'm going to finish my calculations," said Anne. "You're insane. They're pretty girls everywhere."

"They bore me," said Angel. "It's too much trouble."

Anne patted him on the shoulders.

"Take a walk," he said. "Get some air and try to think of something else."

"I wanted to walk," said Angel. "It's you who demurred. And I can't think of anything else. She's changed so much."

"Not at all," said Anne. "She just knows a few more tricks in bed."

Angel sniffled and left. Anne was laughing. He opened his door and returned to his desk.

II

Angel's feet slid along the hot sand and through openings of his Spartan-style sandals he could feel the tiny grains enter and fall through his toes. His ears were still filled with the words and the voice of Anne, but his eyes saw only the sweet, fresh face and radiant mouth of Rochelle, and the distinct arc of her eyebrows shouted out to him from Amadis Dudu's office, where she sat in front of her typewriter.

Before him, in the distance, the first black strip fell without a wrinkle, cutting a somber line into the earth that tightly hugged the rigid and inflexible lines of the dunes. He was walking as quickly as the unstable terrain would permit, getting bogged down a bit while he ascended, then hurling himself down the contoured slopes at great speeds, happy, at least physically, that his prints were the first to mark the yellow trail. Bit by bit, his pain subsided, insidiously dried out by the porous purity of everything that surrounded him, by the absorbing presence of the desert.

The threshold of the shadow grew nearer, giving way indefinitely to a naked, lifeless wall, which was more attractive than a true shadow because it was more like an absence of light, a compact emptiness, a final solution in which nothing disrupted the utter harshness.

Just a few more steps and Angel would enter the blackness. He faced the wall and timidly stuck out his hand. It disappeared before his eyes and he felt the coldness of the other zone. Without any hesitation he entered, and the black shroud enveloped his entire being.

He walked slowly. He was cold and his heart was beating more rapidly. He looked through his pockets, found some matches, and lit one. He had the impression that the match was burning but things remained pitch black. A bit frightened, he dropped the match and rubbed his eyes.

143

Once more, he carefully scratched the little phosphorous tip against the rough surface of the box. He heard the hissing sound as the match caught fire. He put the box into his left pocket, and groping, was able to bring his index finger to the tip of the slender stick. He pulled back his finger as soon as he felt the burn and then dropped the second match.

He carefully turned around and tried to get back to his point of departure. He felt that it was taking longer that it had when he entered and he was still surrounded by the impenetrable night. He stopped a second time. His blood was pounding through his veins more quickly and his hands were cold. He sat down. He had to calm himself. He put his hands under his armpits to warm them up.

He waited. The beats of his heart became less intense. His limbs held onto the memory of the movements he had executed since he entered the blackness. Calmly and coolly, he reoriented himself, and with a sure and steady step, walked towards the sun. A few seconds later, he could feel the hot sand of the desert, immobile and yellow, all ablaze in front of his glistening eyes. In the distance, he could see the vibration above the flat roof of the Hotel Barrizone.

He stepped back from the wall and dropped onto the shifting sands. Before his eyes, a sandpeeper slid lazily over a long, curving blade of grass, covering it with an iridescent film. He stretched out and made a place for each one of his limbs, completely relaxing his muscles and his brain. He sat breathing, calm and sad.

III

MEETING

1.

Ursus de Janpolent, the president, wrinkled up his eyebrows when he arrived and saw that the usher was not at his post. He continued along, nevertheless, and entered the conference room. His eyebrows frowned once again; no one was at the table. With his index finger and thumb he reached for the winding mechanism of his gold watch, which lay beneath a chain of the same material. He pulled on it. Oddly enough, this irreproachable mechanism showed the same time that had caused him, just a short while ago, to quicken his pace. This explained, undoubtedly, what he now suspected were the mere innocent absences of the usher and the members of the council. He ran back to his limousine and beckoned to his zealous chauffeur to take him somewhere else. He'd be damned if anyone was going to see the president of the administrative council arrive first!

2.

The usher, with a sour smile on his lips, emerged from the buen-retiro and without any dillydallying made his way to the huge cabinet that housed the pornographic cards. His lips formed a weary rictus. His hands were shaking and, because today was the day, it was damp around his fly. Still dripping a bit, it lit up the spine of his discordant, descend-

ing zipper and constricted his old, gluteal muscles, which
were worn out from all the years spent in a chair.

3.

As he swept the remains into a sewage ditch, the city
sanitation worker noticed the peculiar green color of the
lungs of the little dog that had been crushed by Agathe
Marion who, as usual, was driving recklessly. Soon after, the
sewer began vomiting things up and traffic had to be
rerouted for several days.

4.

After some diverse mishaps, brought on as much by the
malice of human beings and other things as by the inex-
orable laws of probability, almost all the called upon members convened at the doors of the meeting room, which they
entered into after the usual rubbing together of hands and
salivary ejaculations that typify civilized gatherings and
which are replaced, in military society, by salutes to the chief
and by the friendly fire of clicking boot heels, and in certain
cases by brief interjections shouted from afar, which on the
whole might lead one to conclude that the military was
quite sanitary, although one may be forced to reconsider this
opinion after seeing their latrines, with the exception, of
course, of those belonging to the yanks, who crap in order
of rank and keep their little shithouses constantly clean and
smelling of disinfectant, just as they do in certain countries
that take great care in their propaganda and where one is
fortunate enough to have a populace easily persuaded by
such tactics, given that such careful propaganda is not
arrived at capriciously, but rather by taking into account the
desires reflected by the bureaus of polling and research, as
well as by the results of referenda that are generously offered

up by content governments in order to further accentuate the happiness of the people they administer.

Thus, the council began. They were missing only one member, who was held up and able to make it only two days later. He excused himself, but the usher was quite severe with him.

5.

"Gentlemen, I give the floor to our devoted secretary."

"Gentlemen, before conveying the preliminary results of our first few weeks of labor, and because the correspondent himself is absent, I'd like to read you myself a report received from Exopotamie that, happily, has arrived on time. We should all praise this dedication to punctuality and foresightedness, considering how easy it is for anyone to fall prey to complications."

"You're absolutely right!"

"What's this about?"

"I'm sure you know."

"Yes! I remember."

"Here, gentlemen, is the letter in question:

"In spite of an array of difficulties, the efforts and ingenuity of director Amadis Dudu have succeeded in the procurement of all necessary material, and there is no need to question the devotion, abnegation, courage, or professional ability of technical director Dudu, for the enormous difficulties encountered and the underhanded trickery of the construction workers and the engineering faction in general - with the exception of Arland, the foreman - are such that this almost impossible task could be handled only by him."

"I'm in complete agreement."

"An excellent report."

"I don't understand. What's this all about?"

"Come on, of course you understand!"

"Oh, sure. Pass me your cards."

"Sirs, a situation has arisen for which it has been impossible to find any preventive or modifying remedy: the existence of Hotel Barrizone in the path of the future track. Director Dudu proposes that we expropriate the hotel and, by some convenient means, partially destroy it."

"Do you know what a sandpeeper is?"

"This is a staggering proposal."

"I believe that we must approve it."

"Gentlemen, we'll proceed by a vote of hands."

"It's useless."

"Everyone is in complete agreement."

"Absolutely. We must expropriate Barrizone."

"Gentlemen, Barrizone will be expropriated. Our secretary will handle the procedures. Given that this is an enterprise of some public interest, it will no doubt be a matter of little formality."

"Gentlemen, I propose that congratulations are in order for the author of this report we've read, none other than our technical director, Amadis Dudu."

"I believe, gentlemen, that we are all in agreement that a letter of felicitation be sent to Dudu, as our eminent colleague Mr. Marion has suggested."

"According to the letter, gentlemen, the attitude of Dudu's subordinates is troublesome. I believe it wise to diminish their salary by twenty per cent."

"We could deposit the difference into the account of Mr. Dudu, as an increase in his relocation compensation."

"He will undoubtedly, gentlemen, refuse to accept any such benefit."

"I agree wholeheartedly."

"Which means all the more savings."

"And no raise for Arland, either?"

"That would be useless. These men have a conscience."

"But we cut the pay of the others, naturally."

"Gentlemen, all decisions will be recorded in the minutes by the secretary. Are there no other matters to be raised?"

"What do you think about this decision?"

"It's staggering!"

"Gentlemen, the meeting is adjourned."

IV

Copper and Athanagore, arm in arm, followed the path toward Hotel Barrizone. They had left in the galleries both Brice and Bertil, who didn't want to leave until completely clearing the immense chamber discovered a few days earlier. The machines were digging away nonstop in new corridors and new rooms, linked together by avenues lined with columns and overflowing with precious objects such as hairpins, broaches made of aluminum silicate and pliable bronze, votive statuettes with and without urns, and mounds of pots. Atha wasn't ready to retire his hammer, but the archaeologist needed to get some rest and clear his head. Copper accompanied him.

They scaled and then descended the rounded slopes and the sun enveloped them in gold. From the top of the dune, they saw the facade of the hotel with its red flowers, as well as the entire construction site of the railroad. The workers were moving around the huge rails and crosspieces and Copper recognized the spindly outlines of Didiche and Olive, who were playing on the woodpiles. They walked without pausing and reached the hotel bar.

"Hello, La Pipe," said Athanagore.

"Bon giorno," said Pippo. "Faccè la barba à six houres c'to matteïgno?"

"No," said Athanagore.

"Putain de nocce cheigno Bendetto!..." exclaimed Pippo. "You're not ashamed of yourself, boss?"

"No," said Athanagore. "How's business?"

"It's utterly miserable," said Pippo. "It's misery, you know, that drives us all mad. When I was a prep-cook at Spa, well, you should have seen that... But here! Just a bunch of poorks...

"What?"

"Poorks... Pigs, for God's sake!"

"Give us a drink," said the archaeologist.

"I should shove this diplomatic bullshit right up their ass, send 'em packin all the way back to Warsaw," said Pippo.

He illustrated this threat with an apropos gesture, which consisted of holding out his right hand and curling his thumb up under the palm.

Athanagore smiled.

"Give us a couple of Turins."

"Here you go, boss," said Pippo.

"So what have they done to you?" asked Copper

"They wanna take my joint and plow it down," said Pippo. "Finito. It's over."

He started to sing:

"When he see Guillermo,
Vitto he a-say
You go a-Roma
Geet a job with lousy pay..."

"Nice tune," said the archaeologist.

"Give him Trento and Trieste
It's nothing, Vitto say
And in da aeroplano
Annunzio sing all da way.
Chi va piano sano..."

"I've heard that before somewhere," said the archaeologist.

"Chi va sano va lontano

150

Chi va forte a la morte
Evviva la liberta!"

Copper applauded. Pippo sang out with what was left of his voice, passable but hoarse. They heard heavy blows coming from the ceiling.

"What's that?" asked the archaeologist.

"It's that other lousy poork!" said Pippo.

As always, he seemed at once furious and joyful. He responded:

"Amopolis Dudu. He doesn't like me to sing."

"Amadis," said Copper, correcting him.

"Amadis, Amopolis, Amaodou...What the hell difference does it make?"

"So what's the story with your joint?" said Atha.

"Amopolis and his diplomatic bullshit," said Pippo. "He wants to 'exteriorize' me... Those are the only kinds of words that come out of the mouth of that poork, that goddamn whore! He says that he didn't foresee it."

"Your expropriation?"

"I suppose that's it, in lay terms," said Pippo.

"You won't have to work any longer," said Atha.

"What the hell do I need with a vacation?" said Pippo.

"Come on, have a drink with us," said Atha.

"Thanks, boss."

"So the hotel is obstructing the railroad?" asked Copper.

"Yeah," said Pippo. "It's their fucking railroad. Cheers."

"Cheers," repeated Copper as they all emptied their glasses.

"Is Angel here?" asked Atha.

"I believe he's in his room," said Pippo. "I'm not sure, mind you, I just believe so. He's still drafting."

He pressed on the buzzer behind the bar.

"He'll come down if he's there."

"Thanks," said the archaeologist.

"That Amopolis," concluded Pippo, "is a real poork."

He started to hum again and polish his glass.

151

"How much do I owe you?" said the archaeologist, seeing that Angel wasn't coming down.

"Thirty francs," said Pippo. "This is utter misery."

"Here," said the archaeologist. "Do you want to come along and see the work site? It doesn't look like Angel is here."

"But I can't!" said Pippo. "With all these people buzzing around like flies? If I go they'll drink me dry."

"Well then, I'll see you later," said the archaeologist.

"See you later, boss."

Copper shot him a pretty smile and Pippo began stumbling on his words. She followed Atha and the two of them headed for the work site.

The air smelled like flowers and resin. Coarsely cut green grass was piled up in big heaps on both sides of a sort of track made by the graders and the stiff stems of the weeds slowly dripped large and aromatic drops which rolled onto the sand and coated the yellow granules. The railroad followed the traces of this machine-made path that had been devised according to Amadis' specifications. Athanagore and Copper looked sadly upon the clumps of stiff grass, scattered about tastelessly here and there, and they beheld the destruction that had ravaged the smooth faces of the dunes. They continued up, then down, then up once more before they finally saw the work site.

Their bare torsos slouching in the heat of an indifferent sun, Carlo and Marin gripped with both hands their large-caliber pneumatic hammers. The air was filled with the grumbling noise of a nearby compressor and the back-firing of the engines. They worked incessantly, half-blinded by the stream of sand that blew from an exhaust pipe and stuck to their sweaty skin. A part of the tracks was already level and the two sides of the excavation rose up clean and sharp. They had cut into the dune and stabilized themselves at a level equal to the desert's average elevation, which was calculated by Anne and Angel from early topographic reports and which was quite inferior to the surfaces that

152

they were accustomed to treading over. They would have to move a lot of earth to construct this section of track and heaps of sand were accumulating on both sides.

Athanagore wrinkled his brow.

"This is going to be nice..." he murmured.

Copper made no reply. They approached the two men.

"Hi," said the archaeologist.

Carlo raised his head. He was big and blond, and his blue eyes, shot through with blood, seemed not to see their interlocutor.

"Hello!..." he murmured.

"It's really coming along," admired Copper.

"It's hard," said Carlo. "Hard like stone. It's only that outer layer that's sand."

"Of course," said Athanagore. "There's never any wind. The sand is petrified."

"Then why is the surface like that?" asked Carlo.

"Petrification will only begin," explained the archaeologist, "where the heat of the sun stops penetrating."

"Ah!" said Carlo.

Marin also stopped working.

"If we stop," he said, "we're going to have that bastard Arland on our backs."

Carlo turned his pneumatic hammer back on.

"It's just you two alone on this job?" asked Athanagore.

He was forced to cry out in order to overpower the infernal blare of the jackhammer. The long steel blade of the machine attacked the sand, stirring up a bluish dust as the hardened hands of Carlo constricted themselves despairingly around the two horizontal grips.

"All alone..." said Marin. "The others are looking for roadbed."

"The three trucks?" screamed Athanagore.

"Yeah," responded Marin with a similar shriek.

His head was covered with tousled, brown locks. He had a hairy throat and the face of a ravaged child. Breaking

153

eye contact with the archaeologist, he fixed his gaze on the young woman.

"Who's this?" he asked the archaeologist as he turned off his hammer.

"My name's Copper," she said as she held out her hand. "We do the same job as you, only underground."

Marin smiled and gently shook her nervous fingers in his dry and crusty hand.

"Hi," he replied.

Carlo continued to work. Marin looked at Copper with an air of regret.

"We really can't take a break because of Arland. Otherwise we could have gone for a drink."

"What about your wife?..." cried Carlo.

Copper laughed.

"Is she really that jealous?"

"Not at all," said Marin. "She knows very well that I'm trustworthy."

"It would be hard not to be," observed Carlo. "Not much opportunity round these parts."

"We'll see each other Sunday," promised Copper.

"Sure... After mass," joked Marin.

"Around here, we don't go to mass."

"There's a hermit," said Athanagore. "Theoretically speaking, we're supposed to visit the hermit on Sundays."

"Whose idea was that?" protested Marin. "I'd much rather have a drink with the little lady."

"The abbot will come and explain it all," said the archaeologist.

"Shit," said Marin. "I don't like priests."

"You have something better to do?" Carlo pointed out. "You want to traipse around all day with your wife and kids?"

"I don't like priests myself," said Athanagore, "but this one's not like the others."

"Yeah," said Marin, "I bet he wears a cassock, all the same."

154

"He's a real comedian," said Copper.

"Those are the most dangerous ones."

"Get a move on, Marin," said Carlo. "That bastard Arland is going to be all over us like a cheap suit."

"Let's go..." murmured the other.

The pneumatic hammers resumed their brutal percussion and once again dust filled the air.

"We'll see you boys later," said Athanagore. "Have a drink at Barrizone's, and put it on my tab."

He departed. Copper waved goodbye at Carlo and Marin.

"See you Sunday!" said Marin.

"Why don't you shut up!" said Carlo. "You're just making fun of him."

"He's a stupid old man," said Marin.

"I think he's nice enough," said Carlo.

"O.K. then, he 's a nice, stupid old man," said Marin. "And there are plenty of those to go around."

"You're a real pain in the ass," said Carlo.

He moved the back of his arm across his face to wipe away the sweat. They were weightless atop the huge masses. Compact blocks fell and crumbled before their eyes and the sand burned their throats. Their ears were accustomed to the constant noise of the hammers, so much so that they could communicate with just murmurs. They spoke while working, just out of habit, in order to alleviate the endless misery of the task. Here is what Carlo said as he dreamt out loud:

"When we'll have finished..."

"We'll never finish..."

"The desert can't go on forever..."

"There are other jobs."

"We'll have the right to a little rest..."

"We could stop working..."

"We'd have some peace of mind..."

"There'd be land, water, trees, beautiful girls."

"To just stop digging..."

"We'll never stop."

"Then there's that bastard, Arland."

"He doesn't do a thing and he makes more than us."

"It'll never happen."

"Maybe the desert does go on forever."

Their hardened fingers gripped the handles, the blood dried in their veins, and their voices became imperceptible: a murmur, a constant moaning covered by the vibration of the dancing hammers whose buzz surrounded their sweaty faces and the corners of their sunburned lips. Knotted muscles, rounded lumps that stirred like beasts working in unison, were busy at play in the compact tissue of their brown skin.

Carlo's eyes were half-closed. He felt in his arms the movement of the metal spike and he guided it instinctively, not even looking.

Behind them, a large slice of shadow shot out from the mass that was already cut away and crudely leveled out. They dug further and further into the petrified dune. Their heads sprouted out just above the level of the current incision, and far away on the other dune they saw for a moment the shrinking silhouettes of the archaeologist and the orange girl. Then some chunks tore loose and rolled off behind them. They would have to stop soon in order to clear away the enormous build-up of debris, but the trucks hadn't returned yet. The repetitive shock of the metal piston against the stem of the hammer blade as well as the whistling of the air in the exhaust tube bounced off the sides of the trench with intolerable force. But Carlo and Marin could no longer hear it. They beheld before them vast stretches of fresh green land and robust girls waiting naked in the grass.

V

Amadis Dudu reread the message that he had just received, which bore the heading of the main office and the signatures of two members of the administrative council, including the president's. His eyes lingered over certain words with a greedy satisfaction as he began to prepare in his head the phrases that would stun the listeners. He'd have to get them together in Hotel Barrizone, the sooner the better. Preferably after work, in any case. And see in advance if Barrizone had a platform. A clause in the letter concerned Barrizone himself and his hotel. Things moved quickly when a powerful company was involved. The plans for the railroad were practically completed, but still no ballast. The drivers searched night and day. Sometimes they had a bit of news, and other times they would come unexpectedly in their trucks and take right off again. Amadis was a bit exasperated with the ballast situation but the tracks were getting built all the same, above the ground on blocks. Carlo and Marin had a lot of free time, and fortunately, Arland was able to take full advantage of this. Together, the two managed to lay thirty meters of track a day. Forty-eight hours from now they would start cutting the hotel in two.

Someone knocked at the door.

"Enter!" said Amadis curtly.

"Bon giorno," said La Pipe as he entered.

"Hello, Barrizone," said Amadis. "You want to talk with me?"

"Yeah" said Pippo. "What's up with these goddamn railroad tracks? They've planted themselves right in front of my hotel. What the fuck do I want with a railroad?"

"The minister has just signed an eviction notice that concerns you," said Amadis. "I was going to tell you tonight."

"That's a bunch of diplomatic, big-word bullshit," said Pippo. "When are you gonna take that stuff away?"

"We are going to be obliged to demolish the hotel so that the train can pass through the middle," said Amadis. "It was necessary for me to inform you."

"What?" said Pippo. "Demolish the grand Hotel Barrizone? Those who taste my spaghetti à la Bolognese are Pippo's faithful customers for life!"

"That's regrettable," said Amadis. "The decree is already signed. Consider the hotel requisitioned for the good of the state."

"And what about me?" said Pippo. "What the hell am I gonna do? Go back to being a prep-cook?"

"You'll be compensated," said Amadis. "Not immediately, of course."

"Those poorks!" murmured Pippo.

He turned his back to Amadis and left without closing the door. Amadis called him back.

"Close your door!"

"It's not my door anymore," said La Pipe, furious. "Close it yourself!"

He took off cursing under his breath with the resonance of a typical southerner.

Amadis thought that Pippo should have been requisitioned along with the hotel, but the process was more complex and the formalities too time consuming. He got up and walked around his office. He found himself nose to nose with Angel, who entered without knocking, and for a very good reason.

"Hello, sir," said Angel.

"Hello," said Amadis, without offering to shake hands. He finished walking around and sat back down.

"Close your door, please," he said. "You want to talk to me?"

"Yes," said Angel. "When are we going to be paid?"

"You're in quite a hurry."

"I need money and we were supposed to be paid three days ago."

"Do you realize that we're in a desert?"

"No," said Angel. "In a real desert there isn't any railroad."

"That's sophistry," remarked Amadis.

"It's whatever you want it to be," said Angel. "The 975 passes regularly."

"Sure," said Amadis. "But we can't entrust the dispatching to an insane conductor."

"The porter isn't crazy."

"I've traveled with him," said Amadis. "I can assure you he's not normal."

"Well this is too long," said Angel.

"You're a nice boy," said Amadis... "Physically, I mean. You have such fine skin. What's more, I'm going to tell you something that you won't know until tonight."

"Well that's not so," said Angel, "since you're telling me now."

"I'll tell you if you're a really good little boy. Come closer."

"I'd suggest that you don't touch me," said Angel.

"Well look at him. Isn't he in a huff!" exclaimed Amadis. "Come on, don't be so uptight!"

"I don't go for that."

"You're young. You have time to change."

"Are you going to tell me what you had to tell me or should I go?" said Angel.

"O.K. You're getting a twenty per-cent salary cut."

"Who?"

"You, Anne, the construction workers, and Rochelle. Everyone but Arland."

"Arland. What a bastard!" murmured Angel.

"If you'd show a little good will," said Amadis, "I might be able to spare you."

159

"I'm full of good will," said Angel. "I finished my work three days earlier than you asked me to and I've almost finished the specifications for the main train station."

"I won't harp on about what I consider to be good will," said Amadis. "If you need more information, talk to Dupont."

"Who's Dupont?"

"The archaeologist's cook," said Amadis. "A nice lad, Dupont. But a real bitch."

"Oh! Now I see what you mean."

"No," said Amadis. "You're confusing him with Lardier. He's disgusting, Lardier."

"Even so..." said Angel.

"No, really, Lardier is repugnant. What's more, he's married."

"I know."

"So I give you the creeps, do I?"

Angel didn't respond.

"It bothers you, I know. I'm not in the habit of sharing confidences with just anyone, you understand, but I'll tell you up-front that I'm perfectly aware of how you all feel about me."

"So?"

"So I don't give a damn," said Amadis. "I'm a homosexual. Why would you want to change that?"

"I don't want to change anything," said Angel. "In a way, I prefer it like that."

"Because of Rochelle."

"Yes," said Angel. "Because of Rochelle. I like the fact that you ignore her."

"Because I'm sexy?" asked Amadis.

"No," said Angel. "You're hideous, but you're the boss."

"You've got a strange way of showing your love," said Amadis.

"I know how she is. The fact that I don't see her more often has nothing to do with whether or not I love her."

160

"How can you love a woman?" said Amadis.

He seemed to be talking to himself.

"It's inconceivable. Those soft masses they have all over. Those humid folds..."

He shuddered.

"Horrible..."

Angel started laughing.

"Well, anyway," said Amadis, "don't tell Anne that you've received a pay cut. I'm telling you this confidentially. Woman to man."

"Thanks," said Angel. "Do you know when the money's arriving?"

"No idea. I'm just waiting."

"O.K."

Angel lowered his head and looked at his feet. Finding nothing special, he looked back up.

"Good-bye," he said.

"Good-bye," said Amadis. "And don't think about Rochelle."

Angel walked out and then quickly returned.

"Where is she?"

"I sent her to the 975 bus stop to get the mail."

"O.K.," said Angel.

He left the room and closed the door.

VI

Why did this type of invariance escape
ordinary tensorial calculations?

G. Whitrow, *La structure de l'Univers,*
Gallimard, p. 144.

"Ready!" said the intern.

"Turn," said Petereater.

With an energetic gesture, the intern launched the hard wooden propeller. The motor sneezed and let out a nasty little belch, then there was a backfire. The intern yelped and held his left hand in his right.

"There you go," said Petereater. "I told you to be careful."

"Jesus Christ!" said the intern. "Fucking Jesus Christ almighty. This is just great!"

"Can I see?"

The intern held out his hand. The nail of his index finger was all black.

"It's nothing," said Petereater. "You still have your finger. Guess you'll lose that next time."

"No."

"Sure," said Petereater. "Either that or start paying attention."

"But I am paying attention," said the intern. "It's this stinking shitty motor that always flies off into my hands. I've had enough. That's it."

"If you hadn't done what you did..." said the professor, sententiously.

"Just shut up about that chair, would you..."

"O.K."

Petereater pulled back, gathered his force, and smashed

the intern with a blow to the jaw.

"Ow!..." groaned the intern.

"I bet your hand's not hurting now, huh?"

"Grrr..." growled the intern.

He seemed almost ready to bite.

"Turn!" said Petereater.

The intern stood still and started to cry.

"Oh, no!" screamed Petereater. "Enough! You always end up crying. It's getting to be a habit. Just shut your mouth and turn the propeller. That sobbing routine doesn't work anymore."

"But it's never worked," said the intern, miffed.

"Precisely. I don't understand why you have the nerve to keep trying it."

"Alright," said the intern. "I won't harp."

He dug into his pocket and found a disgusting handkerchief. Petereater was losing patience.

"You O.K. now, or what?"

The intern blew his nose and put the handkerchief back in his pocket. He moved up to the motor and with a reticent air prepared to launch the propeller.

"Go!" commanded Petereater.

After two turns of the propeller the motor sputtered and started up and the blades were enveloped by swirls of grey smoke.

"Increase the compression," said Petereater.

"I'll burn myself," protested the intern.

"Oh!" said the professor, beside himself. "You're such a..."

"Thank you," said the intern.

He adjusted the lever.

"Stop there!" said Petereater.

The intern cut the gas flow by turning the needle and the motor stopped, its propeller swaying in an unsteady manner.

"Good," said the professor. "We'll try it outside."

The intern remained sullen.

"Let's go," said Petereater. "And show a little spirit, for

God's sake! It's not a burial."

"Not yet," the intern clarified, "but it soon will be."

"Grab the plane and come along," said the professor.

"Are we going to let it fly free or with a cord?"

"Free, of course. What other reason is there to be in the desert?"

"Never have I ever felt less alone than in this desert."

"Enough of your whining," said Petereater. "There's a beautiful girl in the neighborhood, you know. Her skin's a strange color but she's got one hell of a body."

"Yeah?" asked the intern.

He seemed a bit more indulgent.

"You bet," said Petereater.

The intern gathered up the various parts of the plane which they would have to assemble outside. The professor examined the room with satisfaction.

"Nice little infirmary we have here," he said.

"Yeah," said the intern. "Considering what we do. Nobody is sick around this place. I'm forgetting everything I learned."

"You'll be less dangerous," Petereater assured him.

"I'm not dangerous."

"I know a few chairs who don't share that opinion."

The intern turned royal blue and the veins at his temples started to pulse spasmodically.

"Listen," he said. "One more word about that chair and I'll..."

"I'll what?" jeered Petereater.

"I'll kill another one."

"Whenever you want," said Petereater. "What the hell do I care, after all? Let's go."

He left, with his yellow shirt projecting enough light to keep him from stumbling on the uneven steps of the attic staircase. Such was not the case for the intern, who fell, luckily enough for the welfare of the plane, flat on his ass. He arrived downstairs about the same time as the professor.

"Very clever," he remarked. "Couldn't you have used your feet?"

The intern rubbed his buttocks with one hand while the other held together the wings and the fuselage of the Ping 903.

They kept descending until they were at the first floor. Behind the counter, Pippo was methodically emptying a bottle of Turin.

"Hi!" said the professor.

"Hello, boss," said Pippo.

"Business going well?"

"Amopolis is kicking me out."

"You're kidding?"

"I'm being exteriorized. More big words. It's for real."

"He's expropriating you?"

"Yeah, that's how he put it," said La Pipe. "I'm being exteriorized."

"What are you going to do?"

"I have no idea. I suppose I'll just be swept under the rug. It's finished. She's gone."

"The man's an idiot," said Petereater.

The intern was impatient.

"Are we going to fly the plane?"

"Want to come along, La Pipe?" said Petereater.

"I don't give a shit about that pig of an airplane!"

"Well, see you later," said Petereater.

"Goodbye, boss. And hey, your plane... it's pretty as a cherry."

Petereater left, followed by the intern.

"When can we see her?" asked the latter.

"Who?"

"The beautiful girl."

"You really annoy me," said Petereater. "We're going to fly the plane, and that's all."

"Oh, swell," said the intern. "You dangle something in front of my eyes and then poof ... it's gone. You're heartless."

"And you?"

"Alright, so am I. I understand that," said the intern. "But I've been here three weeks and I haven't done it one time."

"Oh, yeah?" said Petereater. "Not even with one of the construction workers' wives? What do you do in the infirmary in the morning, when I sleep?"

"I ..." said the intern.

Petereater looked at him, not understanding, and then broke out into laughter.

"Good God!" he said. "You.. You...That's hilarious!... That's why you're in such a bad mood!..."

"You think so?" asked the intern, a bit worried.

"Certainly. It's unwholesome."

"Oh, and you've never done it?" said the intern.

"Never alone," said Petereater.

The intern stopped talking because they were climbing a dune and he needed his breath. Petereater started laughing again.

"What is it?"

"Nothing. I was just thinking of the faces you must make."

He was laughing so hard that he collapsed onto the sand. Huge tears gushed forth from his eyes as he choked on his lighthearted laughter. The intern turned his petulant face and placed the pieces of the plane on the ground, where, on his knees, he haphazardly started to assemble it. Petereater began to calm down.

"Anyway, you haven't been looking so well."

"Are you sure?"

The intern was feeling more and more worried.

"Perfectly sure. You're not the first, you know."

"I thought..." murmured the intern.

He examined the wings and the cabin.

"So you think others have done it, before me?

"Naturally."

166

"Of course. I was thinking the same thing," said the intern. "But in the same conditions? In the desert, because there were no women?"

"Without a doubt," said, Petereater. "What else do you think it means, that symbol of Saint Simeon Stylite? That pillar? That guy perpetually busy with his pillar? It's obvious, after all! I suppose you've studied Freud?"

"Of course not," said the intern. "He's outdated. Come on! Only backward fools still believe in that stuff."

"That's one thing," said Petereater, "and the pillar is another. Representation and transfer, as the philosophers call it, exist nonetheless, as do complexes, and repression, and in your particular case, onanism."

"You're obviously going to tell me, once again, that I'm a moron," said the intern.

"Not at all," said Petereater. "You're simply not too intelligent. And that's forgivable."

The intern had assembled the fuselage and the wings and tastefully arranged the stabilizer. He stopped for a moment to reflect upon Petereater's remarks.

"But you," he asked him. "How do you do it?"

"How do I do what?"

"I dunno..."

"That's a vague question. So vague, in fact, that I would call it indiscreet."

"I didn't want to get you mad," said the intern.

"Oh, I know. But you have a gift for getting into business that doesn't concern you."

"I was better back home," said the intern.

"Me too," said Petereater.

"I'm down in the dumps."

"That'll pass. It's the sand."

"It's not the sand. We've got no interns, nurses, patients..."

"No chairs either, huh?" said Petereater.

The intern shook his head and a look of bitterness

sprouted up in blotches all over his face.

"So for the rest of my life I'm going to hear your reproaches about this chair, eh?"

"And that won't be too long," said Petereater. "You're not going to get real old. You have too many bad habits."

The intern hesitated, opened his mouth, and then closed it again without saying anything. He started fiddling with the cylinder and the motor and then Petereater saw him jump back and stare at his hand as he had done a half-hour earlier. He was bleeding from a large cut to the palm. He turned towards Petereater. He wasn't crying, but he was very pale and his lips were green.

"It bit me..." he mumbled.

"What did you do to it this time?" asked Petereater.

"Nothing..." said the intern.

He placed the plane on the table.

"It hurts."

"Let me see."

He held out his hand.

"Pass me your handkerchief," said Petereater.

The intern handed him his disgusting tissue and Petereater haphazardly bandaged the hand, giving every indication that he was quite repulsed.

"O.K.?"

"O.K." said the intern.

"I'll launch it myself," said the professor.

He seized the plane and aptly started the motor.

"Grab me around the waist!..." he shouted to the intern, trying to overpower the noise of the motor.

The intern held on to him with both arms. The professor adjusted the points and the propeller began to turn so quickly that the extremities of the blades started to turn a dark red. The intern hung on to the vacillating Petereater, who was shaken by the ferocious wind from the model plane.

"I'm letting go," said Petereater.

The Ping 903 took off like a bullet and vanished in a

few seconds. Seeing this, the intern let loose his grip and stretched out. He remained seated and looked on, expressionless, towards the spot where the plane had just disappeared. Petereater snorted.

"My hand hurts," said the intern.

"Take off that ragged bandage," said the professor.

It was a gaping wound and greenish folds of flesh rose all around it. The blackish-red center was already spilling over with little bubbles.

"Hey!..." said Petereater.

He grabbed the intern by the arm.

"Let's go fix this!..."

The intern got up and galloped along on his feeble legs. They made their way towards Hotel Barrizone.

"And the plane?" asked the intern.

"Seems to work fine," said Petereater.

"Will it return?"

"I think so. I adjusted it for that."

"It's flying very fast..."

"Yeah."

"How will it stop?"

"I don't know..." said Petereater. "I hadn't thought about that at all."

"It's this sand..." said the intern.

They heard a sharp noise and something whisked by about a meter above their heads. Then there was a sort of explosion and the windows of the first floor shattered into a million pieces, leaving a hole in the shape of the Ping. They heard bottles falling inside, one after another, smashing against the floor.

"I'm going on ahead," said Petereater.

The intern stopped and saw the black silhouette of the professor hurl down the slope in a whirlwind. His bright yellow collar glistened above his old-fashioned frock coat. He opened the door and disappeared into the hotel. The intern looked down at his hand and galloped off again with

169

heavy and uncertain steps.

VII

Hoping to find Rochelle and walk her back to Amadis'
office, Angel hurried over the dunes, marching quickly
uphill and then running with long strides as he descended.
As he did so his feet dug into the sand with a flat and muffled sound. From time to time he would land on a clump
of grass and sense the crackling of tough stems and the odor
of fresh resin.

The stop for the 975 was a couple of kilometers from
the hotel. At the pace Angel was keeping, it wouldn't be
long. Rochelle was coming back and Angel noticed her figure as she stood out from on top of the dune. Angel was in
the hollow. He wanted to run up the slope but was unable,
so he met her halfway.

"Hello," said Rochelle.

"I came to get you."

"Is Anne working?"

"I believe so."

There was a silence. Things were getting off to a bad
start. Fortunately, Rochelle twisted her ankle and took
Angel's hand to help stabilize her step.

"These dunes are inconvenient," said Angel.

"Especially with high heels."

"Do you always wear them when you go out?"

"Oh, I don't go out so often. I usually stay at the hotel
with Anne."

"You really love him, don't you?" asked Angel.

"Yes," said Rochelle. "He's very neat, very healthy, and

he's got a great build. I really enjoy sleeping with him."

"But intellectually..."

He was trying hard not to think about Rochelle's words. She laughed.

"Intellectually, I get my fill. After I finish working with Dudu I have no desire for any intellectual conversations."

"He's an idiot."

"In any case, he knows his business," said Rochelle. "And I can assure you, as far as work is concerned, he's nobody you'd want to screw with."

"He's a rotten bastard."

"Women get along fine with his type."

"He disgusts me."

"You've just got a hang-up about the sexual thing."

"That's not true," said Angel. "Except with you, maybe."

"You're boring me," said Rochelle. "I like working with Amadis. Just like I like sleeping with Anne and talking with you. But I couldn't imagine sleeping with you. It seems obscene."

"Why?" said Angel.

"You attach so much importance to that..."

"No. I attach importance to it when it concerns you."

"Don't say that. It... bothers me... it disgusts me a little."

"But I love you," said Angel.

"Certainly. Of course you love me. And I'm happy with that. I love you, too, like a brother. I've told you that. But I can't sleep with you."

"Why?"

She let out a little laugh.

"After Anne," she said, "the only thing you really want is sleep."

Angel didn't respond. It was difficult to pull her along because her shoes made it hard for her to walk. She wore a sweater made of thinly knit material, through which the tips of her breasts protruded, a bit saggy but still quite nice. Her chin had a vulgar curve to it. Angel loved her

171

more than anyone.

"What does he make you do, Amadis?"

"He dictates letters or reports. He's always got some work for me. Notes on the roadbed, the construction workers, on archaeology, on everything."

"I wouldn't want you to..."

He stopped himself.

"Want me to what?"

"Nothing... If Anne left, would you go with him?"

"Why would Anne leave? The work is far from finished."

"Oh, I don't want Anne to leave," said Angel. "But say he didn't love you any more?"

She laughed.

"You wouldn't say that if you saw him..."

"I don't want to see that," said Angel.

"Of course not," said Rochelle. "It would be disgusting. We don't always perform that well."

"Shut up!" said Angel.

"You're annoying. And you're always depressed. It's tedious."

"But I love you!..." said Angel.

"Right. And it's tedious. When Anne's had his fill, you give me a holler."

She laughed again.

"You're going to be single for a long time!"

Angel didn't respond. They were approaching the hotel when suddenly they heard a violent hiss and the blast of an explosion.

"What's that?" said Rochelle, distracted.

"I don't know..." said Angel.

They stopped to listen. There was a rich and majestic silence, followed by the rattling of glass.

"Something's happened..." said Angel. "Let's hurry."

This was a pretext to hold her even more closely.

"Leave me here..." said Rochelle. "Go and check it out. I'll just hold you up."

172

Angel sighed and left without looking back. Rochelle progressed cautiously on her all too high heels. One could now hear the sound of voices.

He saw the precision-shaped hole in the glass surface. Shards of the glass were strewn about the ground and people were scurrying around the room. Angel pushed open the door and entered. Inside were Amadis, the intern, Anne and Doctor Petereater. The corpse of Joseph Barrizone lay in front of the counter, the top half of his head missing.

Angel lifted his eyes and saw the Ping 903 stuck into the wall opposite the glass entryway; only its landing gear had stopped it from penetrating further into the construction. On the upper left-hand side were the remains of Pippo's skull, which gently slid towards the frayed extremity of the wing and fell to the earth with a dull thud, cushioned by La Pipe's curly, black hair.

"What happened?" asked Angel.

"It's the airplane," explained the intern.

"I was counting," said Amadis "on telling him that the construction workers were going to start cutting into his hotel tomorrow. There were some arrangements to make. This is outrageous."

He seemed to be talking to Petereater, who was nervously fiddling with his goatee.

"We have to move him," said Anne. "Help me."

He grabbed the cadaver by the armpits and the intern took hold of the feet. Walking backwards, Anne made his way toward the staircase. He slowly ascended, keeping Pippo's bloody head at a distance. The curved body, inert and flimsy, was almost dragging against the steps. The intern was in a good deal of pain because of his hand.

Amadis observed the room. He looked at Doctor Petereater. He looked at Angel. Rochelle, arriving quietly on the scene, entered the room.

"Ah ha!" said Amadis. "There you are. I had some mail."

"Yes," said Rochelle. "What happened?"

"Nothing," said Amadis. "An accident. Come on, I've got some urgent letters to dictate to you. They'll explain this later."

He moved rapidly toward the staircase, Rochelle behind him. Angel followed her with his eyes for as long as she was visible, then he moved his gaze in the direction of the black spot in front of the counter. One of the white leather seats was all splattered with irregular little drops in lazy little rows.

"Come on," said Professor Petereater.

They left the door open.

"The scale model?" said Angel.

"Yes," responded Petereater. "It was working well."

"Too well."

"No. Not too well. When I left my office I thought I would find a desert. How was I supposed to know that there would be a restaurant right in the middle?"

"It's just bad luck," said Angel. "No one blames you."

"You think so?" said Petereater. "Let me explain. One figures, when one has never built a scale model, that such a thing is a childish pastime. But that's inaccurate. There's something more. You've never built one?"

"No."

"Well then, you can't understand. There's a certain drunkenness that comes from model planes. Running behind a scale model that dashes off straight in front of you, while it climbs slowly or while it turns around your head, quivering, all stiff and awkward in the air as it flies... I thought the Ping was flying fast, but not that fast. It's the motor."

He stopped suddenly.

"I forgot about the intern."

"Another accident?" asked Angel.

"The motor chewed him up," said Petereater. "I left him to take Pippo's body upstairs. He was moving like a zombie."

They made their way back.

"I've got to go take care of him. Do you want to wait

here? I won't be long."

"I'll wait," said Angel.

Professor Petereater jogged off and Angel watched as he penetrated into the hotel.

The petals of the hepatrols, glittering and lively, spread wide open to receive the layers of yellow light which were striking the desert. Angel sat down on a table. He felt as if he were living in slow-motion. He regretted not having helped the intern carry Pippo.

From his seat, he heard the dull and heavy blows of Carlo and Marin's hammers driving into the crosspieces of the round-headed spikes that were destined to hold the rails firm. Now and then, one of the iron masses would crash against the steel of the rail, letting loose a long, vibrating shriek that pierced his chest. Further off still, he could distinguish the laughter of Didiche and Olive, who, for a change of pace, were chasing after sandpeepers.

Rochelle was a lousy bitch, anyway you cut it. And her breasts... sagging lower and lower... Anne is going to ravage her... completely. He'll pull on her, stretch her out, soften her up, and squeeze her dry. A used-up lemon. She still has nice legs. The first thing that one...

He stopped himself and turned his thoughts forty-five degrees to the left. It's completely useless to formulate these obscene commentaries about a girl who's nothing more, give or take, than a hole with a little hair around it, and who... That's not far enough. Another forty-five degrees. You have to seize her and rip off this thing that's on her back, dig your nails in and disfigure it. But even once out of the reach of Anne, there's not much left for one to do when she's already this devastated, this withered: wrinkles, blotches, muscles gone soft, dirtied, lax, all broken in. The bell and its clapper. A space has been created, where nothing fresh, nothing new remains. To have had her before Anne... the first time. Her fresh odor. It could have happened, for example, after having lounged about in the little

175

dance club, after the drive back home, with your arm around her waist. An accident. She's afraid. They just ran over Cornelius Onte who's squirming on the sidewalk. He's happy. He's not going to Exopotamie. And if you want to see, ladies and gentlemen, the man kiss the woman, you have only to turn around. Or just come to the train, at the moment when the man kisses the woman, because the man is always kissing her and grabbing her body with his hands and looking for the woman's scent all over the body of the woman...

But it isn't the right man. From whence comes, in effect, the feeling that there is a possibility, and that it is enough just to end your days lying flat on your belly, hanging your head and drooling and dreaming that it is possible to lie drooling for the rest of your life. Perhaps it's an unreasonable dream, seeing that there isn't enough drool available for that. Hanging your head and drooling is nevertheless a soothing action, and something which people don't do enough of. But one must say, in their defense...

It's absolutely useless to formulate obscene commentaries about a girl who...

Angel was shaken by Professor Petereater, who had just tapped him on the head.

"And the intern?" he asked.

"Uh..." said Petereater.

"What?"

"I'll wait till tomorrow evening, then we'll amputate his hand."

"It's come to that?"

"You can live with one hand," said Petereater.

"You mean without one," said Angel.

"Yes," said Petereater. "Taking into account certain basic hypotheses and pushing this reasoning to the extreme, one could undoubtedly reach the point of living with no body at all."

"Those aren't admissible hypotheses," said Angel.

176

"In any case," said the professor, "they're going to lock me up pretty soon."

Angel stood back up. For the third time, he started walking away from the hotel.

"Why?"

Professor Petereater reached for a little notepad inside his left pocket. He opened it to the last page. There were names arranged into two columns, the left column exceeding the right by one name.

"Look," said the professor.

"Your record of patients?" said Angel.

"Yes. The ones on the left, I've healed. The ones one the right are dead. I can continue as long as the left side exceeds the right."

"How's that?"

"It means that I can kill people up to and equal with the number I heal."

"Kill them? Just like that?"

"Yes. Naturally. I've just killed Pippo and now things are perfectly equal."

"You mean you weren't more ahead of the game than that?"

"After the death of one of my patients," said Petereater, "a couple of years ago, I had a bout of depression and killed quite a few people. Foolishly, I might add. I didn't really gain anything from it."

"But you could start healing people again," said Angel, "and live a peaceful little life."

"No one's sick here," said the professor. "And I can't just con people. Anyway, I don't like medicine."

"But the intern?"

"That's my fault, too. If I heal him, it's invalid. If he dies..."

"The hand at least, that must count?"

"Of course not!" said the professor. "I mean it's just a hand. It's nothing!"

"I see," said Angel, and then added, "So why are they going to lock you up?"

"It's the law. You should know that."

"You know," said Angel, "generally speaking, we know nothing. And the people who should know, I mean those who know how to manipulate ideas, who labor over their concepts so that they imagine they've come up with some original thought, these people never question or bring new life into their original ideas, and so their means of expression is always twenty years ahead of the substance of this expression. The result is that one can learn nothing from them because they're happy to make do with words."

"It's useless to lose yourself in philosophical discourse just to explain to me that you don't understand the law," said the professor.

"Sure," said Angel, "but there is a place for these types of reflections. So much as one might call them reflections. Myself, I'm inclined to treat them as simple reflexes of a sound individual who is open to criticism."

"What kind of criticism?"

"An objective kind, without prejudice."

"You might add, *without bourgeois prejudice*," said the professor. "That's very popular."

"I'd be happy to add that," said Angel. "Thus the individuals in question have dedicated so much time and thoroughness to studying the forms of thought that the form conceals from them the thought itself. You can put something right in front of their nose and they'll just obscure your perception with another construct. They've enhanced the form with numerous parts and ingenious mechanical devices and they do their best to confuse this with the idea in question, whose purely visceral, reflex-like, emotional, and sensory nature completely escapes them."

"I don't follow you at all," said Petereater.

"It's like in jazz," said Angel. "A trance."

"I'm starting to glimpse it," said Petereater. "You're saying, in other words, that certain individuals are sensitive and others are not."

"Yes," said Angel. "It's strange, when one's in a trance, to see people who are still able to speak and maneuver their forms. I mean, when one feels one's thought. The material thing."

"You're vague," said Petereater.

"I'm not looking to be precise," said Angel, "because I truly detest trying to express something that I feel so clearly. What's more, I don't give a damn about being able or not being able to convey my point of view to others."

"One just can't debate with you," said Petereater.

"No, I don't think it's possible," said Angel. "Granted this extenuating circumstance represents the first time, since the beginning, that I've ventured into something of this sort."

"You don't know what you want," said Petereater.

"When I'm satisfied in my arms and in my legs," said Angel, "and when I can remain relaxed and limp like a sack of wheat, that's when I know what I want, because it's then that I can think of how I'd like things to be."

"I'm completely stupefied," said Petereater. "The impending, implicit, and implacable menace of which I am currently the object, pardon the alliteration, must be akin to the nauseous and neighboring state of coma in which my bearded, forty-year-old carcass finds itself. You'd be better off talking to me about something else."

"If I talk about something else," said Angel, "I'm going to talk about Rochelle, and that would tear to the ground this construct that I have painstakingly labored over for the last few minutes. Because I want to fuck Rochelle."

"Sure you do," said Petereater. "So do I. I plan on doing so after you. That is, if you don't mind and if the police leave me enough time."

"I love Rochelle," said Angel. "And because of that, I'll probably make a fool of myself. I'm starting to get tired of it all. My system is too perfect to ever be realized.

Furthermore it's incommunicable; I'd be forced to implement it on my own and people wouldn't take to it. Consequently, any foolish blunder I might commit would be of no importance."

"What system?" said Petereater. "I am literally stupefied by you today."

"My system of solutions to all problems," said Angel. "I've really found solutions for everything. They're excellent and efficient, but I'm the only one who knows about them and I haven't had the time to tell others because I'm too busy. I do my work and I'm in love with Rochelle. You understand?"

"There are people who do a lot more," said the professor.

"Yes," said Angel, "but I still need more time to lie on the ground, on my belly, and just drool. I'll do it soon. I'm really looking forward to it."

"If this guy comes to arrest me tomorrow," said Petereater, "I'll ask you to look after the intern. I'm going to cut off his hand before I go."

"They can't arrest you yet," said Angel. "You have the right to one more cadaver."

"Sometimes they arrest you in advance," said the professor. "The law's all askew at the moment."

VIII

The Abbot Littlejohn paced down the trail with large steps. He carried a heavily charged knapsack and, just like a high school student playing with his ink-well, was carelessly swinging his breviary which hung on a piece of string. Furthermore, to amuse his ears (and also as an act of self-sanctification) he sang an old hymn:

> *A rat all green-oh*
> *Running through the weeds-oh*
> *Grabbed him by the tail-oh*
> *Showed him to some gentlemen*
> *These gentlemen they say-oh*
> *Dip it in the oil-oh*
> *Dip it in the water-oh*
> *That'll make an escar-goh*
> *Faster than you knoh*
> *Rue Lazare Carneau*
> *Numero Zee-roh*

With a vigorous kick of his heel, he chanted the traditional strains of the piece and the physical state resulting from this set of activities seemed to him satisfactory. From time to time there were little tufts of pointed grass right in the middle of the road, and here and there, prickly and harmful spinifex scrub which scratched his calves underneath his robe. What on earth are these things? Nothing much. The Abbot Littlejohn had seen plenty others, for God is great.

He noticed a cat pass by from left to right and figured he must be getting close. All of the sudden, he found himself in the middle of Athanagore's camp and soon was standing right in the center of the very tent that housed Athanagore. The aforementioned was busy working with one of his standard boxes that was refusing to open.

"Hi!" said the archaeologist.

"Hi!" said the abbot. "What are you doing?"

"I'm trying to open this box," said Athanagore, "but I can't seem to get it."

"Then don't open it," said the abbot. "Never strain yourself with what's beyond your ability to accomplish."

"This box is made of fasin," said Athanagore.

"What's fasin?"

"It's a mixture," said the Archaeologist. "It'd take a long time to explain."

"Please, say no more," said the abbot. "What's new?"

"Barrizone died this morning," said Athanagore.

"Magni nominis umbra..." said the abbot.

"Jam proximus ardet Ucalegon..."

"Oh!" reckoned Littlejohn, "One shouldn't believe in omens. When do they commit his body to the sands?"

"This evening or tomorrow."

"We'll be sure to go," said the abbot. "See you later."

"I'll come with you," said the archaeologist. "Just a second."

"Shall we have a drink first?" proposed Littlejohn.

"Some Cointreau?"

"No!... I brought something with me."

"I've also got some zythum," suggested the archaeologist.

"Thanks, but no thanks."

Littlejohn detached the straps from his knapsack, and after searching a while produced a gourd.

"Here," he said. "Taste it."

"After you..."

Littlejohn complied and drank a big gulp. Then he handed the device to the archaeologist, who held the opening to his lips, tipped back his head, and then promptly straightened up.

"There's no more," he said.

"That doesn't astonish me... I never change," said the abbot. "An indiscreet drunkard... and a pig to boot."

"I'm not too keen on the stuff," said the archaeologist. "I wouldn't have really drunk any."

"That doesn't matter," said the abbot. "I deserve to be punished. How many prunes are there in a case of secret-agent prunes?"

"What's a secret-agent prune?" asked the archaeologist.

"Yes," said Littlejohn, "you do have the right to ask me

that question. It's an imagistic expression of my own that I use to refer to 7.65 mm cartridges, the ones that the agents use in their equalizers."

"That coincides with the attempt at an explanation that I was forcing myself to work out," said the archaeologist. "Let's say twenty-five."

"Damn! That's too many," said the abbot. "Make it three."

"Three, then."

Littlejohn pulled out his rosary and said it three times, so quickly that the polished beads started smoking between his fingers. He put it back in his pocket and waved his hands in the air.

"That burns!..." he said. "Well it's over with. And the hell with what anyone thinks."

"Oh," said Athanagore, "No one holds it against you."

"You're well-spoken," said Littlejohn. "You have breeding. It's a pleasure to meet someone of your stature in a desert full of sand and slimy sandpeepers."

"And elymes," said the archaeologist.

"Oh, yes," said the abbot. "Those little yellow snails. By the way, what's happened to that young friend of yours, the woman with the nice breasts?"

"She hardly ever goes out," said the archaeologist. "She digs with her brothers. Things are progressing. But elymes aren't snails. They're weeds."

"So we won't see her?" asked the abbot.

"Not today."

"But why did she come here?" said Littlejohn. "A beautiful girl, extraordinary skin, superb hair, a chest worthy of excommunication, intelligent and strong as a beast, and we never see her. She doesn't sleep with her brothers, does she?"

"No," said the archaeologist. "I think it's Angel she likes."

"Well I can marry them if you like."

"He's only interested in Rochelle," said the archaeologist. "I'm not so nuts about her. She's rather full of herself."

"Yes," said Athanagore. "But he likes her."

"Does he love her?"

"Determining that would be an interesting little task."

"Can he still love her when he sees her sleeping with his best friend?" said Littlejohn. "In speaking to you about all this I hope you don't judge it to be simply the sexual curiosity of a repressed man. Even I have been known to sport a bit of wood when I've got some free time on my hands."

"I'm sure that's true," said Athanagore. "No need for excuses. In all reality, I believe he really loves her. I mean to the point where he'll keep chasing after her with no hope. To the point where he'll even lose interest in Copper, who asks for so little."

"Good god!" said Littlejohn. "It must be clawing at him."

"What?"

"Clawing. Excuse me. That was a little sacristy slang."

"I... ah, yes!" said Athanagore. "I understand. But no, I don't think it's clawing at him."

"Under these conditions," said Littlejohn, "we should be able to get him to sleep with Copper."

"I'd like him to," said Athanagore. "They make a pleasant couple."

"We'll have to take them to see the hermit," said the abbot. "Really, he has this saintly act that just takes the cake. Oh shit! Again! Too bad. Remind me to do my rosary later."

"What is it?" asked the archaeologist.

"I can't stop blaspheming," said Littlejohn. "But that's not really important. I'll recapitulate later. Getting back to the matter at hand, I was telling you that the hermit's little show is quite interesting."

"I haven't been yet," said the archaeologist.

"It might not do anything for you," said the abbot. "You're old."

"Yeah," said the archaeologist, "I'm more interested in objects. And memories from the past. But the sight of two young, well-built bodies in simple and natural positions doesn't bother me in the least."

"The negress..." said Littlejohn.

He didn't finish his phrase.

"What's with her?"

"She's... very gifted. Very supple, I mean. Would you mind talking to me about something else?"

"Not at all," said the archaeologist.

"I'm starting to get excited," said Littlejohn. "And I don't want to bother your young lady friend. Talk to me about a cold glass of water tossed on my neck, or torture with a mallet."

"What's that? Torture with a mallet?"

"Very common among certain Indian tribes," said the abbot. "It consists of gently pressing the scrotum of the patient on a wooden block, in such a way as so the glands protrude outward to be crushed with a swift blow of the mallet. Ouch! Ooooo..." he added, squirming where he stood. "That must really hurt!"

"It's well-conceived," said the archaeologist, "it reminds me of another."

"Don't insist," said the abbot, all doubled over. "I've completely calmed down."

"Perfect," said Athanagore. "So we can leave?"

"What?" The abbot was astonished. "We haven't left yet? I'm stunned! You sure are a chatterbox."

The archaeologist started to laugh. He took off his colonial helmet and hung it on a nail.

"I'll follow you," he said.

"One goose, two geese, three geese, four geese, five geese, six geese!..." said the abbot.

"Seven geese," said the archaeologist.

"Amen!" said Littlejohn.

He crossed himself and was the first one out of the tent.

```

IX

*These eccentrics are adjustable...*

*La mécanique de l'exposition de 1900,*
Dunod, vol. 2, page 204.

"You were saying that these are elymes?" asked Abbot Littlejohn, pointing to the grass.

"Not those there," observed the archaeologist. "But there are elymes here."

"That's of no interest," remarked the abbot. "What good does it do to know the name of a thing when we know the thing itself."

"It's useful for conversation."

"You could just give the thing another name."

"Naturally," said the archaeologist, "but we wouldn't be designating the same thing with the same name, in accordance with the interlocutor with whom one would be in the process of conversing."

"That's a solecism," said the abbot. "The interlocutor that one would be in the process of converting."

"No, no..." said the archaeologist. "In the first place, it would be called a barbarism. Furthermore, that's not at all what I was trying to say."

They moved towards the Hotel Barrizone. The abbot had nonchalantly joined arms with Athanagore.

"I'd like to believe you..." said the abbot. "But it astounds me."

"A prejudice brought on by your confessional profession."

"Apart from that, how are the digs coming?"

"We're advancing rapidly. We're following a fiducial line."
```

"Is it connected to something, more or less?"

"Oh..." said the archaeologist... "I don't know... We'll see..."

He seemed to be searching.

"Approximately speaking, it should pass rather close to the hotel."

"Have you found any mummies?"

"We eat them with every meal. It's not bad. Generally speaking, they're very well prepared. Sometimes a bit too much seasoning."

"I've tasted them before, in the Valley of the Kings," said the abbot. "It's a specialty of the region."

"Those are fakes. Ours are authentic."

"Mummy meat repulses me," said the abbot. "I think I'd even prefer your gasoline."

He took leave of Athanagore's arm.

"Excuse me for a second."

The archaeologist watched him as he gathered his strength and performed a double flip in mid-air. He fell on his hands and started doing cartwheels. His cassock, draped all around him, hugged his legs and accentuated his large calves. He wheeled off a dozen of them and stopped on his hands, then swiftly stood back up.

"I was raised by the Eudists," he explained to the archaeologist. "It's a harsh upbringing, but beneficial for the mind and the body."

"I regret," said Athanagore, "not having pursued a religious career. Seeing you makes me realize what I've missed."

"You've been pretty successful," said the abbot.

"Discovering a fiducial line at my age..." said the archaeologist. "It's too late now..."

"The young will profit from it."

"Undoubtedly."

From atop the hill they had just scaled the two could make out the hotel. In front of them lay the tracks of the train line, brilliant and new, sparkling in the sun on the slipway. Two high sand embankments arose on the left and the right and the extremities disappeared behind another dune. The construction workers were finishing pounding the last spikes into the crosspieces and before hearing the clang, they would see the glare from each blow of the hammer on the head of the spikes.

"But they're going to cut into the hotel!..." said Littlejohn.

"Yes... The calculations showed that it was necessary."

"That's idiotic!" said the abbot. "We don't have that many hotels around here."

"That's what I thought," said the archaeologist. "But it's Dudu's idea."

"It'd be easy to make some nice little wordplay with that name, Dudu," said the abbot, "but one would think that there was some forethought involved in his choice. And I'm in the position to say that this isn't the case."

They ceased to speak because the noise became intolerable. The yellow and black taxi had moved a bit in order to let the tracks pass and the hepatrols continued to flourish with the same exuberance. The hotel, as usual, let off a strong trembling which rose above its flat roof, and the sand remained the sand, which is to say yellow, pulverulent, and enticing. As for the sun, it shone without modification, and the building concealed from the two men the boundary of the cold, black zone which stretched out behind it to the right and left, in all its dead flatness.

Carlo and Marin stopped, first in order to let Athanagore and the abbot pass and also because they were finished for now. They had to demolish an entire piece of the hotel before continuing, and prior to that they would have to extract Barrizone's body.

They relaxed their massive frames and with slow steps walked towards the pile of crosspieces and rails to prepare, in the meantime, the assembly of the next section. The spindly profile of the lightweight steel lifting machines stood out above the mounds of material, cutting dark,

188

black triangles into the sky.

They scaled the embankment, helping each other hand-in-hand because of the steepness of the slope, and then hurtled down the other side, escaping the gazes of the abbot and his companion.

The latter two entered the main room and Athanagore closed the glass door behind him. It was hot inside and a medical odor came swooping down from the stairway onto the floor, leveling off in the room at about the height of a sheep and infiltrating the available concave nooks. There was nobody there.

They lifted their heads and heard someone walking upstairs. The abbot moved toward the staircase and headed up, followed by the archaeologist. The odor made them nauseous. Athanagore had to force himself not to breath. They arrived at the hallway of the upper floor and the sound of voices guided them to the room where the body was resting. They knocked and were told to enter.

They had placed what remained of Barrizone in a large case, into which he just fit because the accident had shortened him a bit. What remained of his skull covered the head; instead of a face one could only make out a mass of fuzzy, black hair. In the room there was Angel, all alone and speaking to himself. He stopped when he saw them.

"Hello," said the abbot. "How are you?"

"So-so..." said Angel.

He shook the archaeologist's hand.

"It looked like you were talking," said the abbot.

"I'm afraid he's lonely," said Angel. "I was trying to tell him some things. I don't think he understands, but it can only calm him. He was a really great guy."

"It was a nasty accident," said Athanagore. "It's disheartening, this business."

"Yes," said Angel. "Petereater is of the same opinion. He's burned his scale model."

"Shoot!" said the abbot. "I was hoping to see it fly."

"It appears to be quite a frightening sight," said Angel.
"What do you mean?"

"Because you don't see anything. It flies too fast. You just hear the noise."

"Where's the professor?" asked Athanagore.

"Up above," said Angel. "He's waiting for them to come and arrest him."

"Why?"

"His logbook for the sick has equaled out," explained Angel. "He's afraid the intern won't make it. He must be cutting the hand off."

"The scale model again?" asked Littlejohn.

"The motor chewed up the intern's hand," said Angel. "Infection set in right away, so they have to cut it off."

"This is no good, all this," said the abbot. "None of you have been to see the hermit, I bet."

"No" admitted Angel.

"How can you live in such conditions?" said the abbot. "We're offering you a saintly deed of the highest order, truly fortifying, and no one goes to see it..."

"We no longer have the faith," said Angel. "Me personally, I think about Rochelle above all."

"She's revolting," said the abbot. "When you've got Athanagore's little friend to turn to!... You're atrocious, you and your feeble woman."

The archaeologist was looking out the window, not taking part in the conversation.

"I want so much to sleep with Rochelle," said Angel. "I love her with intensity, perseverance, and despair. It makes you laugh, maybe, but it's that and nothing else."

"She doesn't give a damn about you," said the abbot. "For Pete's sake! If I was in your place!..."

"I'd really like to kiss Copper," said Angel, "and take her in my arms. But I wouldn't be any less unhappy."

"You really make me sick!" said the abbot. "Go see the hermit, for the love of God!... That'll make you change your mind!..."

"I want Rochelle," said Angel. "It's time that I have her. She's sinking farther and farther. Her arms have taken the shape of my dead friend here and her eyes no longer speak to me. Her chin is disappearing and her hair is oily. She's feeble, that's true; she's soft like a half-rotten piece of fruit with the same odor as the flesh of that rotten fruit and just about as attractive."

"Don't try and be poetic," said Littlejohn. "Rotten fruit? That's disgusting. It's slimy. All mashed up."

"It's simply very ripe..." said Angel. "It's more than ripe. In a way, it's better."

"You're too young."

"It's not a matter of age. I would prefer the face she had before. But it just doesn't look the same."

"Open your eyes!" said the abbot.

"I have opened my eyes and I see her every morning coming out of Anne's room. Still all bare, all humid from everything, all hot and clinging, and I want it. I want to drape her over me. She must bend like putty."

"This is nauseating," said the abbot. "It's Sodom and Gomorrah, only less normal. You're a real sinner."

"She must smell like seaweed that's simmered in seawater under the sun," said Angel. "When it starts to decompose. And to have her must be like making it with a mare, with plenty of room and nooks and crannies and a sweaty, unwashed odor. I'd like her not to wash for a month, for her to sleep with Anne every day, once a day, until he's sick of it, and then take her right after she walks out. Still full."

"That's enough of this..." said the abbot. "You're a pig."

Angel looked at Littlejohn.

"You don't understand," he said. "You haven't understood anything. She's damned."

"I understand that she is!" said the abbot.

"Yes," said Angel. "In that sense, too. But it's over for

me."

"If I could kick your ass," said Littlejohn, "things would be different."

The archaeologist turned around.

"Come with us, Angel," he said. "Come see the hermit. We'll get Copper and we'll go together. You've got to change your mind and get away from Pippo. Things are finished here, but not for you."

Angel wiped his hand across his forehead and seemed to calm down a bit.

"I'd like that," he said. "We'll bring the doctor."

"Let's go and get him together," said the abbot. "How many steps do we have to climb to get to the loft?"

"Sixteen," said Angel.

"Too many," said Littlejohn. "Three's enough. Let's say four."

He pulled the rosary from his pocket.

"I'm catching up on my backlog," he said. "Excuse me. I'll follow you."

X

When you make the rounds at the tables, it would be ridiculous to perform with the largest slates.

Bruce Elliot, *Précis de Prestidigitation*, Payot, p.223.

Angel entered first. In the infirmary there were only the intern, stretched out from head to toe on the operating table, and Doctor Petereater in a white veterinarian's smock, sterilizing over the blue flame of an alcohol lamp a scalpel that he would later dip into a bottle of nitric acid. A square, nickel-plated box, half-full of water and shiny instruments, boiled atop an electric burner while a turbulent vapor escaped from a glass bottle that was filled with a red liquid. His eyes closed, the naked intern shivered on the table, attached by solid straps which dug deep into a flesh that had been softened by inactivity and bad habits. He remained silent as Petereater whistled that same passage from "Black, Brown, and Beige." It was always the same part because he could never remember the rest. He turned around when he heard Angel's footsteps. Athanagore and Littlejohn arrived at the same moment.

"Hello, doctor," said Angel.

"Hi," said Petereater. "How's things?"

"Alright."

The professor greeted the archaeologist and the abbot.

"Can we help you?" asked Angel.

"No," said the professor. "I'm just about finished."

"Did you put him to sleep?"

"You must be joking..." said Petereater. "Not for a tiny thing like this."

He looked uneasy and kept glancing suspiciously over his shoulder.

"I rendered him senseless by giving him a few blows on the head with a chair," he said. "You didn't see a police inspector when you came?"

"No," said Athanagore. "There wasn't anybody, professor."

"They must be coming to arrest me," said Petereater. "I've surpassed my number."

"Is that bothering you?" asked the abbot.

"No," said Petereater. "But I loathe inspectors. I just have to cut off this imbecile's hand and then I'll leave."

"Is it serious?" asked Angel.

"Look for yourself."

Angel and the abbot approached the table. Athanagore remained a few steps behind. The hand was a hideous sight. For his operation, the professor had laid it out alongside the body of the intern. The bright green wound stood gaping and an abundant quantity of foam spewed nonstop from the center to the edges, which were now completely burned and shredded. Liquid secretions flowed between the intern's fingers and soiled the thick linens where his body lay agitated and trembling rapidly. Now and then, a large bubble would come to the surface of the wound and explode, bombarding the area around the patient's hand with an infinity of small, irregular spots.

Littlejohn turned away first, seemingly bored. Angel observed the flaccid body of the intern, his grey skin and slackened muscles, and a few shabby little black hairs he had on his chest. He saw his knobby knees, rather crooked tibias, and dirty feet. He closed his fists and turned toward Athanagore, who put his hand on his shoulder.

"He wasn't like that when he first came..." murmured Angel. "Does the desert do this to everyone?"

"No," said Athanagore. "Don't torture yourself, my friend. An operation isn't a pleasant thing."

The Abbot Littlejohn went to one of the windows in the long room and looked outside.

"I think they've come for Barrizone's body," he said.

Carlo and Marin were walking towards the hotel, carrying a makeshift stretcher.

Professor Petereater took a few steps and looked out as well.

"Yeah," he said. "A couple of construction workers. I thought they were inspectors."

"Guess they don't need any help," said Angel.

"No," said Littlejohn. "We need to go and see the hermit. In fact, that's why we came to get you, professor."

"I'm almost done," said Petereater. "My instruments

are ready. Anyhow, I'm not coming with you. As soon as I've finished, I'm on my way."

He pulled up his sleeves.

"I'm going to cut off the hand. Don't look if it disgusts you. It's absolutely necessary. He'll probably kick the bucket. He's in a real sorry state."

"There's nothing we can do?" asked Angel.

"Nothing," said the professor.

Angel turned away. The abbot and the archaeologist followed suit. The professor decanted the red liquid of the bottle into a sort of crystallizing dish and grabbed a scalpel. The three others heard the sound of the blade grind into the bones of the wrist and it was finished instantly. The intern was no longer moving. The professor wiped up the blood with a handful of cotton and ether, then took the arm of the intern and dipped the bloody extremity into the liquid of the crystallizing dish, which congealed around the stump, forming a sort of scab.

"What are you doing?" asked Littlejohn, who was watching stealthily.

"It's bayou wax," said Petereater.

He delicately picked up the severed hand with a pair of nickel-plated tongs, set it on a glass plate, and sprinkled it with nitric acid. A red smoke rose up and the corrosive vapors made him cough.

"I've finished," he said. "We'll unstrap him and wake him up."

Angel took care of the straps on the feet and the abbot the one on the neck. The intern was still motionless.

"He's probably dead," said Petereater.

"How can that be?" asked the archaeologist.

"When I knocked him out... I must have hit him too hard."

He laughed.

"I'm joking. Look at him."

The eyelids of the intern shot open like two little rigid

195

shutters and he sat up.

"Why am I naked?" he asked.

"Don't know..." said Petereater, as he started unbutton-ing his smock. "I've always suspected that you had exhibi-tionist tendencies."

"Would it really bother you that much to stop needling me?" snapped the intern belligerently.

He looked at his stump.

"You call this a tidy job?" he said.

"Oh, shut your mouth!" said Petereater. "Why didn't you just do it yourself?"

"The next time I will," the intern assured him. "Where are my clothes?"

"I burned them..." said Petereater. "No need to con-taminate everybody."

"So I suppose I'll just have to stay naked?" said the intern. "Shit!"

"That's enough," said Petereater. "You're annoying me."

"It's nothing to fight over," said Athanagore. "I'm sure there are other clothes."

"You... old man," said the intern, "give me your hand."

"That's it!" said Petereater. "Are you going to pipe down?"

"What's wrong with you?" asked the abbot. "Stiff-lip, catnip..."

"What crap," said the intern. "You're driving me nuts with your bullshit. Go get fucked. And that goes for the whole lot of you!"

"That's not the response," said the abbot. "You must say: All aboard the battleship."

"Don't talk to him," said Petereater. "He's an ill-man-nered brute."

"Better than being an assassin..." said the intern.

"Certainly not," said Petereater. "I'm going to give you a shot."

He moved over to the table and nimbly refastened the straps. The now one-armed patient was in no position to

AUTUMN IN PEKING

defend himself, fearful of ruining his beautiful new waxy stump.

"Don't let him do it..." said the intern. "He's going to do me in, that rotten old scumbag."

"Just quiet down," said Angel. "We have nothing against you. Let yourself be helped."

"By this old assassin?" said the intern. "Hasn't he given me enough shit about that chair? And who's laughing now?"

"I am," said Petereater.

He quickly forced the needle into the cheek. The intern let out a sharp cry, then his body went limp and he stopped moving.

"There," said Petereater. "Now I'm getting the hell out."

"Will he calm down and sleep?" asked the abbot.

"He has all eternity for that!" said Petereater. "That was Karpathian cyanide."

"The active variety?" asked the archaeologist.

"Yes," responded the professor.

Angel looked on, baffled.

"What?..." he murmured. "He's dead?"

Athanagore took him towards the door. The Abbot Littlejohn followed. Professor Petereater took off his shirt. He leaned over the intern and put a finger in his eye. The body remained motionless.

"There was nothing anyone could do," said the professor. "Look."

Angel turned around. On the side where the stump was, the intern's biceps had just cracked and split open. The flesh around the tear popped up in greenish folds and millions of little bubbles arose, swirling about in the deep obscurity of the gaping wound.

"Good-bye, my children," said Petereater. "I'm sorry about all this. I didn't think things would turn out this way. In fact, if Dudu had really disappeared, like we thought he would, none of this would have happened, and the intern and Barrizone would still be alive. But no use trying to

197

swim upstream. It's too steep a climb, and what's more..."

He looked at the time.

"And what's more, we're too old."

"Good-bye, Doctor," said Athanagore.

The professor wore a sad smile.

"Good-bye," said Angel.

"Don't worry," said the abbot. "The inspectors are usually morons. Would you like to be a hermit?"

"No," said Petereater. "I'm tired. It's better this way. Good-bye, Angel. Don't be a knucklehead. I'll leave you my yellow shirts."

"I'll wear them," said Angel.

They walked back and shook the hand of Professor Petereater. Then, with Abbot Littlejohn leading the way, they descended the noisy staircase. Angel was the third one down. He turned around one last time. Professor Petereater bid him farewell. The corners of his mouth betrayed his emotion.

XI

Athanagore was in the middle. On his left walked Angel, whom he held by the shoulder, and on the right was the abbot, clinging onto his arm. They walked towards Athanagore's camp to look for Copper and to take her to see Claude Leon.

They were silent at first, but Abbot Littlejohn couldn't take too much of that.

"I wonder why Professor Petereater refused a place as a hermit," he said.

"I think he's had his fill," said Athanagore. "Taking care of people all your life, just to have it come to this..."

"But it's that way with all doctors," said the abbot.

"Still, all of them aren't arrested," said Athanagore. "Generally speaking, they cover things up. Professor Petereater never wanted to result to that kind of trickery."

"But how do they hide things?" asked the abbot.

"They unload their sick onto other doctors, to younger colleagues just when the patient's ready to die, and so on."

"But I'm missing something. If the patient dies at just that moment, there's still a doctor who takes the rap?"

"Often, in this case, the patient gets better."

"In what case?" said the abbot. "Excuse me, but I'm not really following you."

"When an old doctor pawns one of his patients off to a younger colleague," said Athanagore.

"But doctor Petereater wasn't so old..." said Angel.

"Forty, forty-five..." the abbot estimated.

"Yeah," said Athanagore. "He's had some hard luck."

"Listen," said the abbot, "we all kill people. It happens every day. I don't understand why he refused the hermit's post. Religion was invented to find places for criminals. What's the problem?"

"You were right to have proposed," said the archaeologist, "but he's too honorable to have accepted."

"He's nuts," said the abbot. "Nobody's asking him to be honorable. What's he going to do now?"

"I couldn't say..." murmured Athanagore.

"He'll go away," said Angel. "He doesn't want to get arrested. He'll go and find some hell-hole, intentionally."

"Let's talk about something else," proposed the archaeologist.

"That's a good idea," said Abbot Littlejohn.

Angel said nothing. The three of them continued to walk in silence. From time to time, they would crush some snails and the yellow sand would fly up in the air. Their shadows followed, vertical and minuscule. As they spread their legs they could glimpse their silhouettes, but by a curious coincidence, the shadow of the abbot was in the place of that of the archaeologist.

XXIII

Louise: - Yes.

François de Curel, *The Lion's Feast*,
G. Grès, act 4, sc. 2, p. 175.

Professor Petereater cast a rectilinear stare around himself. Everything seemed to be in order. The body of the intern on the operating table continued to burst open here and there and bubble up. It was the only thing left to take care of. In the corner there was a large, lead-lined sink, and Petereater rolled the table over to it. He cut the straps with a scalpel and tipped the body into the basin. He came back to the shelf that housed demijohns and flasks, chose two, and spread their contents over the rotting flesh. Then he opened the window and departed.

In his room, he changed his shirt, combed his hair in front of the mirror, checked out his goatee, and brushed his shoes. He opened his closet, located the pile of yellow shirts, and with care, brought them to Angel's room. Then without retracing his steps, without turning around, without emotion, in short, he descended the staircase. He left by the back door. His car was there.

Anne was working in his room and director Dudu was dictating some letters to Rochelle. All three of them jumped at the sound of the motor and leaned towards the windows. It had come from the other side. Intrigued, they made their way down in turn. Anne almost immediately went back up because he was afraid of Dudu giving him a hassle about taking leave from his job in the middle of the workday. Professor Petereater made a half-turn before taking off for good but the clamor of the gears kept him from hearing what Amadis was shouting. He merely waved his hand, and at top speed, absorbed the first dune. The agile wheels danced over the sand and fine streams of powder flew everywhere. Against the sunlight, they formed the most gracious of rainbows. The professor reveled in this polychromaticism.

On top of the dune he just barely missed a sweaty cyclist who was clothed in a regulation cachou Safari outfit and sturdy spiked shoes from which grey wool socks emerged above the ankle area. A helmet completed the look of this velocipedist. It was the inspector in charge of arresting Petereater.

They crossed paths and Petereater, in an amicable gesture, waved to the cyclist while passing and then hurled down the slope.

He looked out at this country so apropos for the testing of scale models and he could almost feel the frenzied vibration that the Ping 903 made in his hands that time it left his grip for the one and only successful flight of its career.

The Ping was destroyed, Barrizone and the intern were in the process of decomposing and he, Petereater, was zipping past the inspector who was coming to arrest him, all because of that little notebook which had one too many names in the right-hand column. Or a name too few in the left-hand column.

He tried to avoid the tufts of shiny grass in order not to ravage the harmony of the desert and its flawless curves, which were without shadow because of this sun which was perpetually on the vertical, and still lukewarm somehow,

201

lukewarm and soft. Even at this speed, there was almost no wind and without the noise of the motor he would have rolled along in complete silence, climbing and descending. He liked to attack the dunes at an angle. The black zone was capriciously moving closer, at times with brusque jolts and then imperceptibly, in accordance with the direction that the professor transmitted to his mobile machine. He closed his eyes a while. He was almost there. At the last minute, he spun the steering wheel a quarter turn and moved away along a large curve whose convolutions followed precisely the ridge of his reflection.

Two small silhouettes grabbed his attention and the professor recognized Olive and Didiche. They were squatted in the sand, amusing themselves with a game. Petereater accelerated and stopped just beside them. He got out.

"Hello," he said. "What are you playing?"

"We're hunting sandpeepers..." said Olive. "We've got a million already."

"One million two hundred and twelve," specified Didiche.

"Marvelous!" said the professor. "You're not sick, are you?"

"No," said Olive.

"A little bit..." confirmed Didiche.

"What's the problem?" said Petereater.

"Didiche ate a sandpeeper."

"That's crazy," said the professor. "That must be disgusting. Why'd you do that?"

"Because," responded Didiche. "I just wanted to see. It's not so bad."

"He's nuts," assured Olive. "I don't want to marry him anymore."

"You're right..." said the professor. "What if he made you eat sandpeepers, huh?"

He caressed the blond head of the girl. Under the sun, the strands of her hair had changed color and her skin shone with a beautiful tint. The two children, kneeling in front of their basket of sandpeepers, watched him impatiently.

"Aren't you going to say good-bye to me?" proposed Petereater.

"You're leaving?" asked Olive. "Where are you going?"

"I don't know," said the professor. "Could I give you a little kiss?"

"No funny stuff, eh?" said the boy.

Petereater started to laugh.

"You're not afraid, are you? Seeing that she no longer wants to marry you, she could simply leave with me."

"No way!" protested Olive. "You're too old."

"She prefers that other guy. The one with the dog's name."

"No I don't," said Olive. "You're being stupid. That guy's name is Anne, the one with the dog's name."

"So you like Angel better?" said Petereater.

Olive blushed and lowered her nose.

"She's an idiot," affirmed Didiche. "He's way too old, too. What does she think, that he's interested in a little girl like her!"

"You're not much older than she is," said the professor.

"Six months older," said Didiche, proudly.

"Oh, well O.K..." said Petereater. "In that case..."

He leaned over and kissed Olive. He also kissed Didiche, who was a bit astonished.

"Goodbye, doctor," said Olive.

Professor Petereater climbed back into his car. Didiche got up to look at the instruments.

"Could you let me drive it?" he asked.

"Another time," said Petereater.

"Where are you going?" asked Olive.

"Out there..." said Petereater.

He pointed out the dark zone.

"Wow!" said the boy. "My father told me what would happen if I ever stepped inside."

"Mine too!" confirmed Olive.

"You haven't tried?" asked the professor.

"Well I guess we can tell you... We tried it and we didn't see anything..."

"How'd you get out?"

"Olive didn't go. She held on to me from the edge."

"Don't do it again!" said the professor.

"It's not any fun," said Olive. "You can't even see anything. Hey! What's coming?"

Didiche looked.

"Looks like a cyclist."

"I'm off," said Petereater. "Good-bye, children."

He kissed Olive one more time. She was always easily swayed by a gentle kiss.

The motor of the vehicle groaned at a high pitch and Petereater accelerated brutally. The car grumbled at the bottom of the hill and then gobbled it up. This time Petereater didn't change direction. He held his wheel with a steady hand and his foot crushed the accelerator pedal. He had the impression that he'd flung himself into a wall. The black zone grew and invaded his field of vision and the car disappeared brutally in the middle of the massive shadows. At the place where the vehicle penetrated into the night there remained a slight impression which disappeared little by little. Slowly, in the same way a plastic regains its form, the impenetrable surface became flat and smooth once more. A double groove in the sand still marked the point of entry of Professor Petereater.

The cyclist set foot just a few meters from the two children who watched as he approached. He moved closer, pushing his machine. The wheels dug in up to the rim and the friction of the sand had polished the nickel until it was perfectly dazzling.

"Hello, kids," said the inspector

"Hello, sir," responded Didiche.

Olive moved closer to Didiche. She didn't like the

helmet.

"You haven't seen a fellow called Petereater, have you?"

"Yeah," said the boy.

Olive nudged him with her elbow.

"We haven't seen him today," she said.

Didiche opened his mouth but Olive stopped him from continuing.

"He left yesterday, to take the bus."

"You're giving me the run-around," said the inspector. "There was a fellow in that car. He was with you, just a while ago."

"That was the dairyman," said Olive.

"You want to go to prison for telling lies?" said the inspector.

"I don't want to talk to you," said Olive. "And I don't tell lies."

"Who was it then?" the inspector asked Didiche. "Tell me and I'll let you try my bike."

Didiche looked at Olive. The bike was shining spectacularly.

"It was..." he began.

"It was one of the engineers," said Olive. "The one with the dog's name."

"Is that so?" said the inspector. "The one with a dog's name? Really?"

He moved towards Olive and took on a threatening pose.

"The one with the dog's name? I saw him at the hotel, you little brat!"

"That's not true," said Olive. "That was him."

The inspector raised his fist as if ready to strike her and she put her hand in front of her face as a defensive gesture. This made her little round breasts pop out and the inspector took notice.

"I'll try another approach," he proposed.

"You're annoying me," said Olive. "It was one of the engineers."

The inspector moved even closer.

"Hold my bike," he said to Didiche. "You can take it for a spin."

Didiche looked at Olive. She seemed afraid.

"Leave her alone," he said. "Don't you touch Olive."

He took the bike that the inspector had just shoved into his hands and let it drop.

"I don't want you touching Olive," he said. "Everyone's trying to touch her and kiss her. I've had enough, get it!... This is my friend. Mine! And if you bother me, I'm going to break your bike."

"Hey, now," said the inspector, "you don't want to go to prison too, do you?"

"It was the professor," said the boy. "Now I've told you. Leave Olive alone."

"I'll leave her alone... if I feel like it," said the inspector. "She deserves to go to jail."

He grabbed Olive by the arms. Didiche gathered his force and kicked the front wheel with all his force, right in the spokes. It made quite a noise.

"Leave her alone," he said. "Or I'll give you a kick too."

The inspector let Olive go and his face turned red with anger. He dug into his pocket and pulled out a huge equalizer.

"Keep it up and I'll fire on you."

"I don't care," said the boy.

Olive threw herself on Didiche.

"If you shoot Didiche," she cried, "I'll make so much noise that you'll be a dead man. Just leave us alone, you old crab. Take yourself and your stinking helmet and get out of here. You're hideous, and you're not going to touch me again. You do and I'll bite you."

"I know what I'm going to do," said the inspector. "I'll shoot you both and afterwards I can touch you as much as I want."

"You're a dirty, rotten cop," said Olive. "You're not

doing your job. Your wife and daughter won't be too proud of you. Shooting people - that's all cops are good for these days. But can you count on a cop to help old ladies and children across the street, huh? Fat chance! Or to get a wounded dog off the street? You have your equalizers and helmets and you can't even catch some poor man like Professor Petereater on your own."

The inspector reflected on this, put his equalizer back in his pocket, and turned away. He remained standing for a minute and then stood the bicycle back up on its wheels. The front one no longer turned. It was all twisted. He grabbed the handlebars and looked over the ground around him. One could distinctly see the trails of the professor's wheels. The inspector shook his head. He observed the children. He seemed to be ashamed. Then he left in the direction taken by Petereater.

Olive stayed with Didiche. They were afraid, the both of them. They saw the inspector moving away, climbing and descending the dunes and becoming more and more tiny as he dragged his useless bicycle. He walked at an uneven pace, without slowing down, right in the middle of the two ruts left by the professor's car. He then took a deep breath and penetrated the black zone. The last thing they saw was a piece of red glass attached to the fender, which closed up like an eye after a smack in the face.

Olive was the first to start running toward the hotel, with Didiche following behind her, calling. But she was crying and couldn't hear him. They had forgotten the little brown basket full of sandpeepers squirming at the bottom and Olive stumbled quite often because her eyes were thinking of something else.

XIII

Abbot Littlejohn and Angel were waiting under Athanagore's tent. The archaeologist had left them for a few moments to go and find the brown girl. The abbot was the first to break the silence.

"Are you always mixed up in such idiotic circumstances?" he asked. "Sexually speaking, I mean?"

"Oh, I suppose you were right," said Angel, "wanting to give me a good kick in the ass. Those things I felt like doing, they're repugnant. But I really wanted to do them because physically, I need a woman right now."

"That, I understand," said the abbot. "All in good time. The only thing you need to do is show some interest in this little filly who's on her way."

"I'm sure I will," said Angel. "At a certain time in my life, I couldn't have. I wanted to love the first woman with whom I would sleep."

"Did you succeed?"

"I succeeded," said Angel. "But I'm not completely convinced, because I've had that same feeling twice now that I'm in love with Rochelle."

"What feeling?" said Littlejohn.

"The feeling of knowing," said Angel. "Of being sure. Sure of what I have to do. Of knowing why I'm alive."

"So why is it?" said Littlejohn.

"Somehow I just can't say," said Angel. "It's enormously difficult trying to speak of it when one isn't accustomed to words."

"Let's go back to the beginning," proposed the abbot. "My word, you're confusing me! I've completely lost track. How strange. I am Littlejohn, after all? Right?"

"And so," said Angel, "I loved a woman. It was the first time for the both of us. As I said, it was a success. Now, I love Rochelle. There isn't a lot of time. She... She doesn't care about me."

"Don't use those melancholy clichés," said Littlejohn. "You don't know anything."

"She's sleeping with Anne," said Angel. "He's ruining her. Wrecking her. Demolishing her. What does it matter?"

"It matters," said Littlejohn. "And don't hold it against Anne."

"I don't," said Angel. "But I'm starting to like him less and less. He's just enjoying himself a bit too much. And he said in the beginning he didn't give a damn about her."

"I know," said the abbot. "Then afterwards, they get married."

"He won't marry her. And while she doesn't love me, I still love her. Even so, I can see that she's nearly done for."

"She's still alright. In spite of your repugnant descriptions."

"That's not enough. That doesn't matter much to me, you understand, that she was better once, back before I met her. It's enough that there's been this degradation, which was not caused by me, since I've known her."

"But she would have experienced this same degradation with you."

"No," said Angel. "I'm not a brute. I would have let her go long before having destroyed her. Not for my sake, but for hers. So she could find someone else. That's all they have for finding men. Their bodies."

"You really make me laugh," said the abbot. "Even the real hags end up finding a man."

"They don't count," said Angel. "I beg your pardon, but when I say women, I mean pretty women. The others, that's a whole different world."

"How do they find someone, then?"

"It's like products that are recommended by the medical establishment," said Angel. "There's no advertising involved, never. The doctors recommend them to their clients, and they're sold uniquely in this way. Word of mouth. These women, the ugly ones, marry men who know them. Or they ensnare them with their scent. Or they find lazy men. Things like that."

"This is frightful," said Littlejohn. "You're revealing to me a quantity of details that my chaste life and long meditations have kept me from learning. I must say that with priests, things are different. Women come and find you, and theoretically, you have only to choose. But they're all ugly, and so you're obliged to make no choice at all. That's one way of resolving the problem. Stop me, because I'm getting all mixed up myself this time."

"I say, then," continued Angel, "that we should leave or set free a pretty woman before having reduced her to nothing. That's always been the rule governing my behavior."

"But they don't always accept this separation," said Littlejohn.

"Sure. You do it in accordance with them, because there are those who understand what I've just explained to you and from that moment on you can live your entire life and not lose them. Or you can become voluntarily nasty with them to the point where they decide to leave for themselves. But that's the pitiful way, because you have to remember the moment you let them go, and leave them when you're still in love with them."

"Doubtless that's how you recognize that they're not completely ruined. By the fact that you still love them."

"Yes," said Angel. "That's why it's so difficult. You can't remain completely cold. You leave them voluntarily. You even find them another guy and you think that will work. Then you're jealous."

He remained silent. Abbot Littlejohn took his head in his hands and wrinkled up his brow in ardent reflection.

"Even to the point that you yourself would find them another," he said.

"No. Even when you yourself find someone new, you're

still jealous. But you have to save your jealousy for yourself. You can't not be jealous, since you haven't gone all the way with the one before. There's always that leftover, that part you'll never have. That's what jealousy is. You never try to take that last part, if you're a nice guy, I mean."

"Or rather a guy like you," the abbot clarified, somewhat off the topic.

"Anne's taking things all the way," said Angel. "He won't stop. There'll be nothing left if we let him continue."

"If we stop him," said the abbot, "will there be enough left?"

Angel didn't answer. His face was a bit pale, and the effort of having to explain one more time had exhausted him. The two were seated on the archaeologist's bed and Angel stretched out, his arms behind his head as he looked up at the tight, opaque canvas.

"This is the first time," said Littlejohn, "that I've gone so long without saying some load of rubbish that's more full of shit than I am myself. I wonder what's happening."

"Rest assured," said Angel. "You've just said it."

XIV

"What Claude Leon had told me," explained Abbot Littlejohn, "was that the insides of this negress were like pink velvet."

The archaeologist nodded his head. He and the abbot were in front, followed by Copper and Angel. He had his arm around her waist.

"You seem a lot better than the other day," she said to him.

211

"I don't know," responded Angel. "If you think so, I probably am. I have the impression that I'm close to something."

Abbot Littlejohn was obstinate.

"It's not that I'm nosey," he said, "but I'd like to know if he's right."

"He must have tried," said Athanagore.

Copper took Angel's hand in her rough fingers.

"I'd like to spend some time with you," she said. "I think that afterwards, you'd be just fine."

"I don't think that's enough," said Angel. "Naturally, you're quite pretty and it's something I'd have no trouble doing. That's the first condition."

"You think that I wouldn't satisfy you in the end?"

"I can't say," said Angel. "I have to get rid of this idea of Rochelle. It's impossible because I love her. Anyway, that's what's on my mind. Doubtless, you'd suffice. But at this moment I'm pretty hopeless and I can't be sure about anything. After Rochelle there'll be this dead period for me… and it's too bad you've come just at this moment."

"I'm not asking that there be any emotion," she said.

"Emotion or not, this thing is really out of your hands. It's up to me to get there. As you see, I haven't gotten there with Rochelle."

"You still haven't suffered enough."

"All this was confused inside my head," said Angel. "I started untangling the web just a short time ago. The catalytic influence of the desert is probably a big help. In the future, I'll also be counting on Professor Petereater's yellow shirts."

"He left them to you?"

"He promised to."

He looked at Littlejohn and the archaeologist. They advanced with large strides and Littlejohn was busy explaining with great gestures, on the top of the dune at the foot of which Copper and Angel had just arrived. Their heads started descending the other side and then they disappeared. The hollow of dry sand was inviting and Angel sighed.

Copper stopped and stretched out on the sand. She was still holding Angel's hand and she pulled the boy up against her. As usual, she was wearing only shorts and a light, little silk blouse.

XV

Amadis was finishing up his correspondence and Rochelle took it down in dictation, the action of which created a huge shadow that moved in the room. He lit a cigarette and leaned back in his armchair. A pile of letters, ready to be sent, was accumulating on the right corner of his desk, but the 975 hadn't come for several days and the mail would be late. Amadis was annoyed by this hindrance. Decisions had to be made: he had to complete progress reports, perhaps replace Petereater, try and resolve the problem with the roadbed, and attempt to reduce salaries -- except for Arland.

He jumped up because the building had just trembled in response to a violent impact. Then he looked at his watch and smiled. It was time. Carlo and Marin were starting to demolish the hotel. The part that housed Amadis' office would remain standing, as would the one in which Anne worked. Only the center, Barrizone's room, was going to come down. Some of Petereater's as well, and the intern's, too. Rochelle and Angel's rooms wouldn't be moved either. The construction workers lived on the bottom floor, or in the cellars.

The blows now rang out at irregular intervals, in series of threes, and one could hear the stony, crumbling noise of rubble and plaster and pieces of glass slamming down onto the floor of the restaurant.

"Type all of that for me," said Amadis, "and then we'll see where we stand with the mail. We have to find a solution."

"Very well, Sir," said Rochelle.

She put down her pencil and uncovered her typewriter, which was all hot underneath its sheath and shivered upon contact with the air. With a touch of her hand, she calmed it down and prepared her carbon paper.

Amadis stood up. He moved his legs quickly as he put his affairs in order, and then left the room. Rochelle heard his steps on the staircase. She stared out into space for a minute and then started her work.

Dust from the plaster filled the large room on the bottom floor and Amadis saw the silhouettes of the construction workers against the sunlight, their heavy hammers dropping and then raising again with effort.

He plugged his nose and left the hotel by the opposite door. Outside, he saw Anne, his hands in his pockets, smoking a cigarette.

"Hello!..." said Anne, without moving a muscle.

"Shouldn't you be working?" remarked Amadis.

"You think we can work in all this commotion?"

"That's not the question. You're paid to work in an office and not to stroll around with your hands in your pockets."

"I can't work with this noise."

"And Angel?"

"I don't know where he is," said Anne. "He's wandering around with the archaeologist and the priest, I think."

"Rochelle is the only one working," said Amadis. "You should be ashamed of yourself. And remember, I'll point out your attitude to the administrative council."

"She performs a mechanical task. She doesn't need to think."

"When you're paid for something you should at least pretend," said Amadis. "Go back up to your office."

"No."

Amadis was looking for something to say, but Anne had a strange expression on his face.

"You're not even working yourself," said Anne.

"I'm the director. I supervise the work of others, in particular, and watch over their performance."

"Come off it," said Anne. "We all know what you are. A homosexual."

Amadis snickered.

"Go ahead, continue. It doesn't bother me."

"In that case I won't continue," said Anne.

"What's gotten into you? You're usually more compliant, you and Angel. All of you. What's wrong with you? Have you gone berserk?"

"You can't understand it," said Anne. "Remember that you are normally, that's to say ordinarily abnormal. That should comfort you. But us, we're more or less normal, and so from time to time we need these breakdowns."

"What do you mean by breakdowns? What you're doing right now?"

"Let me explain. In my opinion..."

He stopped.

"I can only give you my opinion. I think that the others... those that are normal, would tell you the same. But maybe not."

Amadis Dudu agreed and seemed to be a bit impatient. Anne leaned against the wall of the hotel, which still trembled under the brutal impact of iron masses. He looked above Amadis' head. He didn't rush his words.

"In a sense," he said, "you certainly do have a horribly monotonous and ordinary existence."

"How's that?"

Amadis snickered again.

"I think, on the contrary, that it's proof of one's originality, being a homosexual."

"Not at all," said Anne. "That's idiotic. It limits you.

215

Enormously. You're no longer anything but that. A normal man or woman can do so many more things, and take on a vast array of personalities. Perhaps it's in this way that you're more narrow."

"A homosexual is narrow-minded, according to you?"

"Yes," said Anne. "A homosexual or a dyke. All of those types. They're all horribly narrow-minded. I don't think it's their fault. Still generally speaking, they revel in it, while it's just an unimportant weakness."

"It is, without any doubt, a social weakness," said Amadis. "We're always being marginalized by people who lead a normal life. I mean men who sleep with women or who have children."

"You're talking rubbish," said Anne. "I wasn't thinking at all about people's disgust with homosexuals or their laughter. Normal people don't feel so superior; that's not what's keeping you down. It's the boundaries of life, and the individuals whose existences are reduced to these boundaries. That's what's burdening you. But that doesn't matter. It's not because you group together, with your odd habits, your affectations, your conventions. That's not why I pity you. It's truly because you're so limited. Because of some slight glandular or mental anomaly, you receive a label. Already things are dismal. But then, you force yourselves to correspond to the markings on the label. So that the label speaks the truth. People make fun of you in the same way a child makes fun of a cripple, without thinking. If they thought, they'd pity you. Still, it is an infirmity less serious than blindness. What's more, the blind are the only handicapped whom we can really poke fun at because they don't see it, and that's why no one makes fun of them."

"Why, then, do you call me a homosexual and make fun of me?"

"Because at the moment I'm letting myself go. Because you're my boss and because you have ideas about work that I can no longer put up with. So I use all available means, even the unfair."

"But you've always worked so consistently," said
Amadis. "Then all of the sudden, bang!... You're continual-
ly screwing off."

"That's what I call being normal," said Anne. "To be
able to react, even if it comes after a period of mindlessness
or fatigue."

"You claim to be normal," insisted Amadis, "and you
sleep with my secretary until you become vanquished by
this idiotic senselessness."

"I've almost reached the end," said Anne. "I think I'll
be finished with her pretty soon. I feel like going to see that
negress..."

Amadis shivered with disgust.

"Do what you want, after working hours," he said.
"But first of all, don't speak to me about it. And second, get
back to work."

"No," Anne said, steadily.

Amadis scowled and passed a nervous hand through his
tow-colored hair.

"It's incredible," said Anne, "when you start to think
about all these guys working for nothing. Who spend eight
hours a day in their offices. Who are actually able to stay
there for eight hours a day."

"But you were like that, until now," said Amadis.

"You're boring me to death with this 'he who was' crap.
Don't we have the right to understand anymore, even after
having been an ass for a while?"

"Don't use those words," observed Amadis. "Even if
you weren't aiming them at me personally, which I doubt,
they have an unpleasant effect."

"I'm aiming at you as a boss," said Anne. "It's too bad
if the means I employ happen to strike another target. But
do you see to what point you're limited, to what point
you're stuck with your label? You're as limited as some guy
who's a member of a political party."

"You're a real bastard," said Amadis. "And you're physically unappealing to me. And a slacker."

"Plenty of those in offices," said Anne. "Masses of them. They're bored all morning, all evening. At noon they go and chow down some disfigured looking garbage from an alpax lunch box, then they have the rest of the afternoon to get through. They sit around poking holes into sheets of paper, writing personal letters, telephoning their friends. From time to time you'll see another type, the useful kind. One who's productive. He writes a letter and it arrives at an office. It's about some business deal. It would have been enough to just say 'yes' or 'no' and conclude things. But no, it just isn't done that way."

"You've got some imagination," said Amadis. "And a poetic soul. Epic and all. Now for the last time, get to your office."

"For just about every living man, there exists one of these office types, a parasite man. That's the justification of the parasite man, this letter that'll straighten out the business of the living man. So he drags it out to prolong his existence, and the living man doesn't know about it."

"Enough!" said Amadis. "I can swear to you that this is idiotic. I guarantee you that there are people who respond immediately to letters. That it's possible to work like this, and be useful."

"If every living man," pursued Anne, "got up, searched the offices for his own personal parasite, and killed him..."

"You're really pestering me. I should get rid of you. Replace you. But I sincerely believe that it's the sun and this affectation of yours for sleeping with a woman."

"Then," said Anne, "all the offices would be coffins and in each little yellow or green-painted linoleum-lined cube, there would be a skeleton of a parasite. And we'd put away all those alpax lunch boxes. So long. I'm going to see the hermit."

Amadis Dudu remained mute. He saw Anne move away

with large and vigorous steps, effortlessly scaling the dune and stretching out his well-placed muscles. His alternating footprints formed a capricious line which ended atop the rounded sand. His body continued alone, then disappeared.

Director Dudu turned around and then went back into the hotel. The noise from the hammers had just ceased. Carlo and Marin were starting to clear away the pile of material amassed in front of them. On the second floor, one could hear the clicking of the machine and the shrill sound of the bell at the end of the lines, covered over by the scraping of the shovels. Blue-green mushrooms were already rising from the rubble.

PASSAGE

Professor Petereater is surely dead by now, making for an already quite sizeable tally. The inspector who left in pursuit, being younger and all fired up from his encounter with Olive, must have been able to hold out the longest. In spite of everything, it's impossible to know what's happened to them beyond the black zone. As is often said by the merchants of speaking parrots, there is a place for incertitude. Curiously enough, we haven't yet witnessed the fornication between the hermit and the negress, which seems rather unexplainable given the relatively considerable importance initially accorded the character of Claude Leon. It would be nice if they could finally do it in front of some impartial spectators, for the consequences of this repetitive act on the physiognomy of the hermit must be such that one could reasonably predict whether he'll be able to keep it up, or if he'll die from exhaustion. Without undue prejudice to the following events, one should be able to determine precisely what Angel is going to do. Anyone can see that the opinions and behavior of Anne, his pal (who has a name like a dog, although strictly speaking this factor doesn't come into play), have a rather strong influence on Angel, whose moments of awakening need only to start occurring at regular intervals, instead of sporadically and when rarely needed. Luckily, these moments almost always occur in the presence of a witness. The fate of the other characters is less predictable: either the irregular recording of their actions leads to a vagueness of different degrees of independence, or they have no real existence, in spite of the effort made along these lines. One must presume that their lack of usefulness will lead to their deletion. We've certainly noticed the weak presence of the main character, who's obviously Rochelle, and that of the Deus ex machina, who is *either the porter or the conductor of bus 975, or even the driver of the yellow and black taxi (whose color allows us all to recognize that the vehicle is surely condemned). These elements are furthermore only adjuvants in the reaction - they don't play a part in the actual process of it, nor in the final equilibrium that is attained.*

THIRD MOVEMENT

I

Amadis kept watch over the movements of Carlo and Marin. The breach made in the hotel had not yet reached the desired height because it was still limited to the first floor and should, in the end, completely sever the building. But the two construction workers were cleaning the area before continuing. Leaning against the wall near the staircase, Dudu, his hands in his pockets, was scratching himself, thinking about what Anne said and wondering if he couldn't do without his services. So he decided, while going up, to look in on the work of the engineers. If it was finished, or almost finished, this would be a good time to fire them.

He followed with his eyes the numerous lengths of track already constructed. Placed on the slipway as it was, it looked like a toy. The sand, leveled out beneath the crosspieces, awaited the roadbed. The locomotive and the cars, dismantled, were lying under tarps near piles of rails and crosspieces from the worksite.

Carlo stopped. His back was hurting. He stretched it out and rested his hands on the handle of his shovel, then wiped his forehead with his wrist. His hair was shiny with sweat and dirt clung to his humid body. His pants, hanging low on his waist, made huge, soft pockets at the knees and he looked at the ground while turning his head slowly from right to left. Marin continued to clean away the fragments of glass, which rang out against the metal of his shovel.

With a large heave, he tossed them back onto a mound of rubble behind him.

"Get back to work," Amadis said to Carlo.

"I'm tired," said Carlo.

"You're not paid to loaf around."

"I'm not loafing, sir. I'm catching my breath."

"If you don't have enough breath to do this job you shouldn't have accepted it."

"I didn't ask to do it, sir. I was forced to."

"Nobody forced you," said Amadis. "You signed a contract."

"I'm tired," said Carlo.

"I'm telling you to get back to work."

Now Marin had also stopped.

"We can't work like beasts without even stopping for a breather," he said.

"Yes, you can," said Amadis. "The foremen are here to make you respect this undebatable rule."

"This what?"

"This undebatable rule."

"You're a real pain in the ass," said Marin.

"Please do remain polite," said Amadis.

"For once, that bastard Arland has laid off us," said Marin. "Why don't you do the same?"

"I intend on reminding Arland about the rules," said Amadis.

"We're doing our job," said Marin. "And the way we do it is our business."

"For the last time," said Amadis, "I'm ordering you to get back to work."

Carlo let go of the handle of the spade that he held between his forearms and spat into his dry hands. Marin dropped his shovel.

"We're gonna pound your head in," he said.

"Don't do it, Marin..." murmured Carlo.

"You touch me and I'll scream," said Amadis.

Marin took two steps closer, looked him over, and advanced until he was almost touching him.

"I'm gonna pound your head in," he said. "We never should have done it. You stink like perfume. You're a lousy fairy and a pain in the ass."

"Leave him alone, Marin," said Carlo. "He's the boss."

"There is no boss in the desert."

"But this is no longer a desert, is it?" remarked Amadis, ironically. "Have you ever seen a railroad in the desert?"

Marin thought about it.

"Let's get back to work, Marin," said Carlo.

"He's pissing me off, him and his flowery language," said Marin. "If I start listening to what he says, he'll trick me. I know I shouldn't pound his head but I think I'm going to do it anyway, or else he'll trick me."

"Well, if you're set on doing it," said Carlo, "at least I can help."

Amadis stiffened up.

"I forbid you to touch me," he said.

"If we let you talk," said Carlo, "You'll dupe us for sure. You see how it works."

"You're imbeciles and brutes," said Amadis. "Pick up your shovels, or you won't be paid."

"We don't give a damn," said Marin. "You've got money up there and we still haven't been paid. We'll just take what you owe us."

"You're thieves," said Amadis.

Carlo's fist traced a sharp trajectory, rigid and lighting-fast, and Amadis' jaw cracked. He let out a moan.

"You take that back," said Marin. "Take it back or you're a dead man."

"Thieves," said Amadis. "Thieves, not workers."

Marin got ready to slug him.

"Back off," said Carlo. "No need for two. Let me handle it."

"You're too excited," said Marin. "You're going to kill

him."

"Yeah," said Carlo.

"I'm furious, too," said Marin. "But if we kill him, he's really the one who wins."

"If he was afraid," said Carlo, "it'd be a lot easier."

"Thieves," repeated Amadis.

Carlo's arm fell once more.

"You're a stinking nelly," he said. "Say whatever you want. You think any of that matters to us, you and all your faggot talk? You're scared shitless."

"I am not," said Amadis.

"Wait a minute," said Marin. "I'll get my wife to take a look at you."

"Enough," said Amadis. "Get back to work."

"What a bastard!" said Carlo.

"Thieves... imbeciles..." said Amadis.

Marin's foot struck him in the lower stomach. He let out a muffled cry and fell to the ground, doubled-over. His face was white and he panted like a running dog.

"You shouldn't have done it," said Carlo. "I'd calmed down."

"Oh, don't worry," said Marin. "I didn't kick him hard. He'll be able to walk in five minutes. He wanted it."

"I think so," said Carlo. "You're right."

They picked up their tools.

"We're going to be canned," said Carlo.

"Too bad," murmured his comrade. "We'll rest up. They have plenty of snails in this desert. That's what the kids say."

"Yeah," said Carlo. "We'll cook up something wild."

"When the railroad's finished."

"When it's finished."

They heard a far-off rumbling.

"Quiet," said Marin. "What's that?"

"Hey!" said Carlo. "It must be the trucks coming back."

"We're gonna have to place the roadbed," said Marin.

"Under all the track..." said Carlo.

Marin leaned over his shovel. The noise from the trucks grew, reaching maximum pitch, and then they heard the piercing clamor of the breaks and there was silence.

II

Abbot Littlejohn seized the arm of the archaeologist and pointed out the hermit's cabin.

"We're here," he said.

"Good. Let's wait for the kids..." said the archaeologist.

"Oh, I'm sure they can get along without us," said the abbot.

Athanagore smiled.

"I hope so, for Angel's sake."

"Lucky dog!" said Littlejohn. "I would have gladly used up a few waivers for that girl."

"Come on..." said the archaeologist.

"Under my frock," clarified Littlejohn, "beats a virile heart."

"And you're free to love her, with your heart..." said the archaeologist.

"Yeah... sure..." agreed Littlejohn.

They had stopped and were looking behind them, if one can say that. Behind the them of five seconds ago.

"There they are," said Athanagore. "Where's Copper?"

"That's not Angel," said the abbot. "That's his friend."

"You've got good eyes."

"No," said Littlejohn. "It's just that I don't think even Angel is nuts enough to do it so quickly with a girl like that."

"It's the other one all right," confirmed Athanagore. "You know him?"

226

"A little. He's always sleeping or working. Or busy getting exercise with that fag's secretary."

"He's running..." said the archaeologist.

Anne was moving quickly towards them.

"Good-looking guy," said Littlejohn.

"We never see him around... What's up with him?"

"Things are taking a rather unusual turn at the moment."

"You're right," said the archaeologist. "Poor Professor Petereater."

They stopped talking.

"Hello. I'm Anne."

"Hello," said Athanagore.

"How are you?" asked an interested Littlejohn.

"Better," said Anne. "I'm going to dump her."

"Your little tramp?"

"Yeah, my little tramp. She's annoying me."

"So you're going to find another?"

"Exactly, dear abbot," said Anne.

"Oh, please!" the abbot protested. "None of those pretentious terms. And furthermore..."

He took a few steps away and started circling the others, slapping his feet vigorously on the ground.

"Three little gentlemen went into the woods!" he sang.

"When they came back, they said in a hush..." continued the archaeologist.

"Hachou! hachou! hachou!..." said Anne, stepping to the beat.

Littlejohn stopped and scratched his nose.

"He knows all the phrases too!" he said to the archaeologist.

"Yes..." confirmed Athanagore.

"So should we take him?" said Littlejohn.

"Of course," said Anne. "I want to see the negress."

"You're a pig," said Littlejohn. "You've got to have them all, huh?"

"No, no," said Anne. "It's finished with Rochelle."

227

"Finished?"

"Finished. Absolutely."

Littlejohn reflected.

"Does she know?" he asked.

Anne seemed slightly tormented.

"I haven't told her yet..."

"From what I can see," said the abbot, "this is a sudden and unilateral decision."

"I decided while I was running to catch up with you," explained the engineer.

Athanagore seemed annoyed.

"You're a real bother," he said. "This is going to cause more complications with Angel."

"Not at all," said Anne. "He'll be very happy. She's free."

"But what's she going to think?"

"Oh, I don't know," said Anne. "She's not the cerebral type."

"This is all easier said than done..."

Anne scratched his cheek.

"Perhaps she'll be a bit unhappy about it," he admitted. "Personally, I have no feelings about the matter. What's more, I can't be preoccupied with it."

"You handle things quite quickly."

"I'm an engineer," explained Anne.

"Maybe you're the archbishop," said the abbot, "that doesn't give you the right to dump a girl without even warning her, especially after you slept with her just yesterday."

"Just this morning."

"You've taken advantage of this moment, when your friend Angel is beginning to find his road to appeasement," said Littlejohn, "in order to push him back into incertitude. It isn't at all certain that he'll want to leave this road to appeasement for this girl that you've ground up into rubble."

"What's this road to appeasement stuff?" said Anne. "What's Angel done?"

"He's getting laid, that's what. And with one hell of a

chick," said Littlejohn. "That pig!"

He clicked his tongue noisily and quickly crossed himself.

"I've said another forbidden word," he said, excusing himself.

"Say all you like..." responded Anne, with mechanical acquiescence. "What's this woman like? It's not the negress, is it?"

"Certainly not," said Littlejohn. "The negress is reserved for the hermit."

"Is there another?" said Anne. "A nice one?"

"Let's go," said Athanagore. "Leave your friend in peace."

"But he's very fond of me," said Anne. "He won't say anything if I give her a go."

"You say some unpleasant things," observed the archaeologist.

"But he'll be as happy as an entrepreneur to know that Rochelle is available."

"I don't think so," said the archaeologist. "It's too late."

"It's not too late. She's still in fine shape. And she knows a few more tricks than before."

"That's not a pleasant thing for a man. A boy like Angel wouldn't take kindly to receiving lessons of that sort."

"Oh?" said Anne.

"Strange," said Littlejohn. "You're probably, on occasion, capable of being a quite interesting fellow, but right now you're simply obnoxious."

"You know, as for myself," said Anne, "I do what's necessary with women. But things stop there. I like them just fine, but on a daily basis I prefer my friends. For talking, I might point out."

"Maybe Angel's not like you," said Athanagore.

"We have to help him out," said Anne. "He sleeps with Rochelle and he'll have his fill but quick."

"He's looking for something else," said Littlejohn. "What I'm looking for myself, in religion... well... in principle... because I make a few benign adjustments to the rules... But I'll say fifty recapitulative rosaries. What I mean by fifty is... let's say three."

"What you're offering he could have with any girl," said the archaeologist. "He's getting it right now."

"That pig!" said Anne. "He didn't tell me that. Well, get a load of Angel!"

"He's looking for something else," repeated Littlejohn. "It's not just about getting laid. It's..."

He searched.

"I don't know what it is," he said. "As far as women go I guess I'm of the same opinion as you. They're fine for fooling around with. But one can imagine other things."

"Of course," said Anne. "And I'm telling you that for those things, I prefer friends."

"What he's looking for," said Athanagore, "is difficult to say. You'd have to have had the notion yourself. I can't use words to tell you about something that doesn't correspond to anything inside of you."

"Give it a try," said Anne.

"I think he's looking for a witness," said Athanagore. "Someone who knows him and to whom he is interesting enough so that he's able to control himself without having to always check his own behavior."

"Why not this other girl?" said Anne.

"It's Rochelle he loved first and the fact that she doesn't love him seemed to him upon reflection to be proof of impartiality. He still had to become interesting to her, enough so that she could be this witness..."

"Angel is a good guy," said Anne. "I'm sorry he has ideas like that. He's always been a bit dull."

The archaeologist hesitated a moment.

"Maybe I'm just imagining things," he said. "I doubt it'll happen so easily."

"What do you mean, so easily?"

"I don't know that Angel will find himself happy

enough to be able to love Rochelle, in total liberty. I think she disgusts him now."

"Come on," said Anne. "That would be difficult."

"You've ruined her," said Littlejohn. "And as a matter of fact, maybe she has no desire to replace you with him."

"Oh, I'll explain it to her..." said Anne.

"Shall we continue walking?" said Littlejohn.

"I'll follow you," said Anne.

"I want to ask you something else," said the archaeologist.

The three of them started down the road again, Anne in front of his companions by about a head. His head, to be precise.

"I'm going to ask you not to tell Angel."

"What?"

"That Rochelle is available."

"But he'll be happy!"

"I'd prefer that Rochelle know before him."

"Why?"

"For the construction of the thing," said the archaeologist. "I don't think it will do any good to tell Angel about it right away."

"Oh, alright!" said Anne. "But I can tell him after?"

"Naturally," said the archaeologist.

"So I have to advise Rochelle first," said Anne, "and Angel only afterwards?"

"It's only normal," said Littlejohn. "Suppose you change your mind after having advised Angel and not having told Rochelle. No problem for you. But for Angel it's just another deception."

"Of course," said Anne.

"Naturally, that's not the real reason," explained the archaeologist. "But it's useless for you to know."

"It's reason enough for me," said Anne.

"Thanks," said the archaeologist. "I'm counting on you."

"Let's go see the negress."

III

*For example, the heading "BALLET"
includes all our records of ballet music and is
placed alphabetically under the word ballet in
our classical section.*

Phillips Catalogue, 1946, p. III

Rochelle saw Amadis enter. He held one hand against his stomach and used the other to lean up against the doorframe and the walls. He was hurting. He limped over to his armchair and fell into it, exhausted. He blinked his eyes and his forehead bunched up into successive wrinkles which deformed the soft surface.

Rochelle stopped working and stood up. She didn't like him.

"What can I do for you?" she said. "Are you in pain?"

"Don't touch me," said Amadis. "It was one of those laborers who hit me."

"Do you want to lie down?"

"Nothing anyone can do," said Amadis. "Physically. But as to the others, they won't get off lightly."

He was fidgeting slightly.

"I'd liked to have seen Dupont."

"Dupont who?"

"The archaeologist's cook."

"Do you want me to go find him?"

"He must still be with that slob Lardier..." murmured Amadis.

"Won't you have something?" said Rochelle. "I can make you some edreanthian tea."

"No," said Amadis. "Nothing."

232

"O.K."

"Thank you," said Amadis.

"Oh, I'm not doing it to be nice to you," said Rochelle. "I really don't like you at all."

"I know," said Amadis. "Still they say, usually, that women are fond of homosexuals."

"Women who don't like men," said Rochelle. "Or women who generalize."

"They say that they can trust them, that they don't have to be afraid of being harassed, etc..."

"When they're handsome," said Rochelle, "maybe. Myself, I'm not afraid of being harassed."

"Who's harassing you here, other than Anne?"

"You're indiscreet," said Rochelle.

"It's really of no importance," said Amadis. "Anne and Angel have become normal men again. I fired them."

"Anne isn't harassing me," said Rochelle. "I make love with him. He touches me. He massages me."

"Is Angel harassing you?"

"Yes," said Rochelle, "because that's how I want it. He hasn't got that big, strapping look like his friend. Anyway, in the beginning I preferred Anne because he's less complicated."

"Angel is complicated? I find him rather lazy and stupid. Yet as far as looks go he's better than Anne."

"No. Not my type," said Rochelle. "Still, he's not bad, I guess."

"Could you sleep with him?"

"Sure!" said Rochelle. "Now I can. There's not much left to do with Anne."

"I ask you that because your world is so foreign to me," said Amadis. "I'd like to understand."

"Did getting beat up make you remember that you're a man?" said Rochelle.

"I'm in considerable pain," said Amadis. "And impervious to irony."

"When will you stop thinking that everyone's making

BORIS VIAN

fun of you?" said Rochelle. "Don't you know I couldn't care less about that?"

"Let's move on," said Amadis. "You say that Angel is after you. Is that what's bothering you?"

"No," said Rochelle. "It's a kind of a security net."

"But he must be jealous of Anne."

"How could you know that?"

"I'm making an analogy," said Amadis. "I know very well what I'd like to do to Lardier."

"What?"

"Kill him," said Amadis. "Kick his guts in. Crush him to bits."

"Angel's not like you. He's not that passionate."

"I'm sure you're mistaken," said Amadis. "He's got it in for Anne."

Rochelle gave him a worried look.

"You really think so?"

"I do," said Amadis. "Things'll get worked out somehow. It makes no difference to me. I'm not telling you this to upset you."

"You're talking like you really know all about this," said Rochelle. "I think you're trying to influence me. The mysterious airs, and all. That stuff doesn't work with me."

"No mysterious airs here," said Amadis. "I suffer, and I understand things. By the way, how's your work coming?"

"It's finished," said Rochelle.

"I'm going to give you something else. Get your writing pad."

"You must be suffering a lot less," said Rochelle.

"The roadbed has arrived," said Amadis. "We have to prepare the truck drivers' paychecks and try to get them to work on the track."

"They'll refuse," said Rochelle.

"Take a memo," said Amadis. "We can arrange things so that they won't refuse."

Rochelle took three steps and grabbed her pad and

234

pencil. Amadis leaned his elbows on his desk for few moments, head in hands, and then started to dictate.

IV

"Really first-rate, that saintly deed," said Abbot Littlejohn.

Anne, the archaeologist, and the abbot were slowly making their way back.

"The negress..." said Anne. "Good God, what a woman!"

"Come on, let's go," said the archaeologist.

"You leave Claude Leon in peace," said the abbot. "He's getting along just fine."

"I'd be happy to give him a hand," said Anne.

"It's not exactly the hand that he employs," said Littlejohn. "You weren't paying attention to detail."

"Oh, enough already!" said Anne. "Change the subject. I can't walk anymore."

"It does have quite an effect," said the abbot. "I agree. But me, I have a cassock."

"What do you have to do to become a priest?" asked Anne.

"You?" said Littlejohn, "You don't know what you want. First this, then that. One minute you spout out a load of crap, the next you seem rather intelligent. One moment you're sensitive, the next you're filthier than the lowest pig farmer with a one-track mind. You'll have to excuse me. My language still remains greatly inferior to my thought."

"You've done just fine," said Anne. "I understand."

He took the abbot's arm and started to laugh.

"Littlejohn," he said, "You're a man's man!"

"Thank you," said Littlejohn.

"And you," continued Anne as he turned to the archae-ologist, "you're a lion. I'm pleased to know you."

"I'm an old lion," said Athanagore. "And the compari-son would have been more exact had you chosen a burrow-ing animal."

"Come off it..." said Anne. "Your digs are a hoax. You're always talking about them and we never get to see anything."

"Would you like to see them?"

"Sure!" said Anne. "Everything interests me."

"Everything interests you a bit," said Littlejohn.

"Everybody's that way," said Anne.

"What about specialists?" observed the archaeologist. "I may serve as only a modest example, but archaeology is all that matters to me."

"That's not true," said Anne. "That's just a put on."

"Absolutely not!" said Athanagore, indignant.

Anne laughed again.

"It was just a crack," he said. "Like the ones you give those poor little earthenware pots that never did a thing to you."

"Just pipe down, you superficial creature!" said Athanagore.

He wasn't angry.

"So," said Anne. "Are we going to go see the digs?"

"Let's go," said Littlejohn.

"Come on," said the archaeologist.

V

Angel was coming to meet them. He walked with an uncertain stride, still all hot from Copper's body. She'd taken off the other way to rejoin Brice and Bertil and help them with their work. She knew it was better not to stay with this boy that she'd just taken, in a hollow of sand, delicately and tenderly and with no intention of doing him harm. She laughed and ran. Her slender legs rose up like springs on top of the light soil and her shadow danced nearby, lending her a fourth dimension.

Once he'd gotten close, Angel looked at them intensely. He didn't excuse himself for having left them. Anne was there too, robust and gay, like before Rochelle. Hence, Rochelle was finished.

There was only a short path to walk before reaching Athanagore's camp. They just talked. Things were getting ready to come to a head.

For now Angel knew the essence of Copper, and in an instant he lost all that Anne had of Rochelle.

VI

"I go down first," said Athanagore. "Be careful. There's a pile of rocks down there that need to be picked up. "

His body slipped into the opening of the shaft and his feet settled solidly on the silver bars.

"Go ahead!" said Anne, leaving the way clear for Littlejohn.

"This is a ridiculous sport," said Littlejohn. "Hey, you down there! Don't you look up. That's a no-no!"

He gathered his cassock together in his hands and put his foot onto the first rung.

"It's alright," he said. "I'm going down anyway."

Anne stayed close to Angel.

"How far down do you think it goes?" he said.

"I don't know," Angel replied with a strained voice. "It's deep."

Anne leaned over the opening.

"You can't see much," he said. "Littlejohn must be there. It's time."

"Not yet," said Angel, despairingly.

"Yes it is," said Anne.

He had knelt down next to the orifice of the shaft and was peering into the dense obscurity.

"No," repeated Angel. "Not yet."

He spoke more quietly, with a frightened voice.

"We have to go," said Anne. "Come on! Are you afraid?"

"I'm not afraid..." murmured Angel.

With his hand pressing against his friend's back, he brusquely pushed him into the void. Angel's forehead was drenched with sweat. After a couple of seconds something cracked and Littlejohn's voice cried out from the bottom of the shaft.

Angel's legs were trembling and he hesitated before finding the first bar. His legs led him down and his body felt like cold mercury. Above him, the entry to the shaft cut a blue-black hole into the inkish background. The lower level became slightly brighter and he hastened his descent. He heard Littlejohn reciting some words in a monotone voice. He didn't look down.

VII

"It's my fault," the archaeologist told Littlejohn.

"No," said Littlejohn. "I'm guilty too."

"We should have let him tell Angel that Rochelle was available."

"Then it would have been Angel lying there," said Littlejohn.

"Why did we have to choose?"

"Because one has to choose," said Littlejohn. "It's a pain in the ass, but that's the way it is."

Anne had broken his neck and his body was lying on the rocks. His face was blank and there was a large scratch across his forehead, half hidden by his tousled hair. One of his legs was curled up under his body.

"We have to get him out of there," said Littlejohn, "and lay him down."

They saw Angel arrive, feet first then body. He slowly approached.

"I killed him," he said. "He's dead."

"I think he leaned over too far," said the archaeologist. "Don't stand there."

"It's me..." said Angel.

"Don't touch him," said Littlejohn. "It's no use. It was an accident."

"No," said Angel.

"Yes it was," said the archaeologist. "You can take his word for at least that much."

Angel was crying and his face was hot.

"Wait for us over there," said Athanagore. "Follow the corridor."

He moved towards Anne. Gently, he smoothed back his blond hair and looked at the murdered and pitiful corpse.

239

"He was young," he said.

"Yes," murmured Littlejohn. "They are young."

"They're all dying..." said Athanagore.

"Not all of them... some still remain. You and I, for example."

"We're made of stone," said the archaeologist. "That doesn't count."

"Help me," said Littlejohn.

It was difficult picking him up. The slackened corpse sunk and dragged against the floor. Littlejohn's feet slipped on the humid soil. They hoisted him from the pile of stones and stretched him out along the chamber wall.

"I'm overwhelmed," said Athanagore. "This is my fault."

"I'm telling you again that it's not," said Littlejohn. "There was nothing else we could have done."

"It's shameful that we were forced to take part in this," said Athanagore.

"In any case, we must have been deceived," said Littlejohn. "It happens that in our flesh, we are deceived. It's more difficult to live with, but things will get better."

"Maybe for you," said Athanagore. "He was handsome."

"They are handsome," said Littlejohn. "Those that remain."

"You're heartless," said the archaeologist.

"A priest can't have a heart," said Littlejohn.

"I'd like to fix his hair," said the archaeologist. "Have you got a comb?"

"No, I don't have one," said Littlejohn. "It's not worth the trouble. Come on."

"I can't leave him."

"Don't get carried away. The fact that he's dead has touched you because you happen to be old. But he is dead."

"And I'm old, but alive," said the archaeologist. "And Angel is all alone."

"He won't have much company now," said Littlejohn.

"We'll stay with him."

"No," said Littlejohn. "He'll go away. He'll leave all alone. Things aren't going to get straightened out so easily. We haven't yet come to the end."

"What can happen?..." sighed Athanagore with a tired and broken voice.

"It'll come," said Littlejohn. "One doesn't work in a desert without there being consequences. Things are all screwed-up. You can smell it."

"You're used to cadavers," said Athanagore. "Not me. Just mummies."

"You don't have the knack," said Littlejohn. "All you can do is suffer, and you don't even learn anything from it."

"You learn something?"

"Me?" said Littlejohn. "I simply don't suffer. Come on."

VIII

They found Angel in the gallery. His eyes were dry.

"Is there anything we can do?" he asked Littlejohn.

"Nothing," said Littlejohn. "We can only inform the others when we return."

"O.K." said Angel. "I'll tell them. Are we going to go see the digs?"

"Of course," said Littlejohn. "That's why we're here."

Athanagore refrained from speaking. His wrinkled chin was quivering. He passed between the two others and took the lead.

They followed the complicated path which led to the front of the dig. Angel paid close attention to the crossbeams and the roof of the galleries and seemed to be trying to determine the positioning of the terrain. They came to the principal gallery, at the very end of which they could make out, in the distance, the luminous dot created by the lighting fixtures. Angel stopped at the entrance.

"Is she there?" he said.

Athanagore looked at him, not understanding.

"Your friend," repeated Angel. "Is she over there?"

"Yes," said the archaeologist. "With Brice and Bertil. She's working."

"I don't want to see her," said Angel. "I can't see her. I've killed Anne."

"Stop it," said Littlejohn. "Say that nonsense just one more time and you'll have me to deal with."

"I killed him," said Angel.

"No," said Littlejohn. "You pushed him and he died when he hit the rocks. It was an accident."

"You're a Jesuit..." said Angel.

"I believe I've already said that I was brought up by the Eudidsts," said Littlejohn, calmly. "If you'd take the time to listen when I speak, things might be better. You seemed to be reacting in a proper fashion just a moment ago, and now you fall apart again. I'm warning you that I won't let that happen. Cox's orange pippin and a pippin ina..."

"Tree, tree, a big green tree..." said Angel and the archaeologist, automatically.

"I think that you know the rest," said Littlejohn. "I won't press the issue. Now, I'm not going to force you to go and see those three guys at the end of the corridor. I'm no sadist."

Athanagore coughed conspicuously.

"No, indeed," he said, turning towards him. "I am not a sadist."

"Certainly not," said Athanagore. "Your cassock would be red instead of black."

"And at night," said Littlejohn, "there would be no difference."

"Or to a blind man," said the archaeologist. "You con-

242

tinue in your enunciation of truisms..."

"You're very persistent," said Littlejohn. "I'm trying to lift your spirits, the both of you."

"It's working just swell," said Athanagore. "We're almost about ready to tear your head off."

"When you're finally ready," said Littlejohn, "I'll know I've succeeded."

Angel kept quiet and looked to the end of the gallery, then turned around and attentively inspected the other side.

"What direction did you dig in?" he asked the archaeologist.

He made an effort to speak naturally.

"I don't know," said the archaeologist. "More or less two degrees east of the meridian."

"Ah..." said Angel.

He remained motionless.

"We have to decide," said Littlejohn. "Do we go or not?"

"I'll have to look at the plans," said Angel.

"What is it?" asked the archaeologist.

"Nothing," said Angel. "A hunch. I don't want to go on."

"Fine," said Littlejohn. "Let's head back, then."

They turned around.

"Are you coming to the hotel?" Angel asked the abbot.

"I'll keep you company," said Littlejohn.

The archaeologist walked behind them this time and his shadow was small beside those of his two companions.

"I have to hurry," said Angel. "I want to see Rochelle. I want to tell her."

"I can tell her," said the abbot.

"Let's hurry," said Angel. "I have to see her. I have to see how she's doing."

"Hurry," said Littlejohn.

The archaeologist stopped.

"I'm staying here," he said.

Angel turned back. He was standing in front of Athanagore.

243

"I must ask your forgiveness," he said. "And say thank you."

"For what?" said Athanagore sadly.

"For everything..." said Angel.

"It's all my fault."

"Thanks..." said Angel. "See you soon."

"Maybe," said the archaeologist.

"Come on, move your ass. See you, Atha!" cried Littlejohn.

"See you, abbot," said Athanagore.

He let them go on ahead of him. They circled through the gallery and Atha continued walking behind them. Anne was waiting all alone, stretched out along the cold stones. Angel and Littlejohn passed by and went up the silver ladder and then Athanagore arrived, knelt down next to Anne, and looked at him. His head dropped to his chest. He thought of things ancient and sweet, things whose odor had nearly evaporated. Anne or Angel. Why was it necessary to choose?

IX

Loving an intelligent woman is the fancy of a homosexual.

Baudelaire, *Fusées.*

Amadis walked into Angel's room. The young man was seated on his bed, one of Professor Petereater's shirts exploding at his side. Amadis blinked his eyes, trying to get used to it, but was forced to looked elsewhere. Angel said nothing. He'd hardly turned his head at the noise from the door, and he didn't move when Amadis sat down in the chair.

"Do you know where my secretary is?" asked Amadis.

"No," said Angel. "I haven't seen her since yesterday."

"She took it badly," said Amadis, "and I've got letters that are late for the mail. You could have easily waited until today before telling her that Anne was dead."

"It was Littlejohn that told her. I had nothing to do with it."

"You should go to her, console her. Tell her that work alone can pull her out of it."

"How can you say that?" said Angel. "You know quite well it's a lie."

"It's plain as day," said Amadis. "Work, that powerful distraction, gives man the ability to temporarily cut himself off from the pressures and worries of a humdrum life."

"Nothing's as humdrum as work... quit putting me on," said Angel. "How can you say that without laughing?"

"I haven't been able to laugh for a long time," said Amadis. "What I'd like is for Rochelle to come and take the letters and for the 975 to come back."

"Send the taxi," said Angel.

"I've done that," said Amadis. "But you don't think that I'm expecting him to come back, do you?"

"You'd be an idiot."

"Next you'll tell me that I'm a stinking fairy, huh?"

"Oh, shut up!"

"Why don't you go and tell Rochelle that I have some work for her?"

"I can't face her now," said Angel. "Don't you understand! Anne just died yesterday afternoon."

"I understand fine," said Amadis. "And before being paid. I'd like you to go and tell Rochelle that the mail just can't wait."

"I can't disturb her."

"Sure you can," said Amadis. "She's in her room."

"Then why were you asking me where she was?"

"So that you'd worry," said Amadis.

"I know very well that she's in her room."

"So it didn't work," said Amadis. "That's all."

"I'll go look for her," said Angel. "She won't come."

"She will so."

"She loved Anne."

"Sleeping with you would suit her just fine. She told me so. Yesterday."

"You're a bastard," said Angel.

Amadis didn't respond. He seemed absolutely indifferent.

"She would have slept with me if Anne was still alive," said Angel.

"No way. Not even now."

"You're a bastard," repeated Angel. "A filthy homosexual."

"There it is," said Amadis. "You said it: the majority opinion. Pushing the generalization to fit the specific case. So that's where you're going."

"Right. I'm going."

He stood up and the springs creaked lightly.

"Her bed doesn't make any noise," said Amadis.

"That's enough..." murmured Angel.

"You had that coming."

"That's enough... I can't take anymore of you... Get out..."

"Listen," said Amadis. "Do you know what it is that you want, this very day?"

"Anne is dead..."

"And so that frees you from what?"

"From myself," said Angel. "I'm waking up."

"No you're not," said Amadis. "You know very well that you're going to kill yourself now."

"I thought about it," said Angel.

"First go and find Rochelle."

"I'll go get her."

"You can take your time," said Amadis. "If you want to console her... or whatever else. But don't wear her out. I've got a lot of mail."

Angel passed by Amadis without looking at him. The director remained in his chair and waited for the door to close.

To one side, the hotel's hallway now looked out directly into the emptiness and Angel, before going to Rochelle's room, approached the edge. The tracks shone between the two halves of the hotel and the other side the hallway continued towards the remaining rooms. Between the rails and the crosspieces the clean, grey roadbed drew bursts of light on to its mica-tinted particles.

The track disappeared out of sight on both sides of the facades and the piles of rails and crossbeams, invisible to Angel from where he was standing, had almost vanished. Two of the truck drivers were finishing assembling pieces of the cars and the locomotive that were already resting on the tracks and the soft hiss of the pulley from the lifting machine meshed with the beating of the grimy motor that powered it.

Angel turned around and passed by two doors. He stopped before the third one and knocked.

Rochelle told him to enter.

Her room had the same furnishing as the others, simple and bare. Rochelle was stretched out on the bed. She wore the same dress as yesterday and the covers were undisturbed.

"It's me..." said Angel.

Rochelle sat up and looked at him. Her eyes evaporated into her marked figure.

"How'd it happen?" she said.

"I couldn't face you last night," said Angel. "I thought Littlejohn had told you."

"He fell into the shaft," said Rochelle. "You couldn't hold him back because he was so heavy. I know how heavy he was. How could that happen to Anne?"

"It's my fault," said Angel.

247

"Of course not... You weren't strong enough to hold him."

"I loved you enormously," said Angel.

"I know," said Rochelle. "You still love me a great deal."

"That's why he fell," said Angel. "It seems. So that I might love you."

"It's too late," said Rochelle, a bit flirtatiously.

"It was too late even before."

"So, why did he fall?"

"He couldn't have fallen," said Angel. "Not Anne."

"Listen," said Rochelle. "It was an accident."

"You haven't slept?"

"I thought that I shouldn't sleep," she said, "because after all, the dead deserve some respect."

"And you still fell asleep?..." said Angel.

"Yes. Abbot Littlejohn gave me something and I took it." She showed him the full vial.

"I took five drops. I had a good rest."

"You're lucky," said Angel.

"Lamenting over people when they die just doesn't change things," said Rochelle. "You know, this really hurt me."

"Me too." said Angel. "I wonder how we'll be able to live after this."

"You think it's so bad?"

"I don't know," said Angel.

He looked at the vial.

"If you'd taken half of this bottle, you would never have woken up."

"I had nice dreams," said Rochelle. "There were two men in love with me, fighting over me. It was marvelous. Like in a storybook."

"I see that," said Angel.

"Maybe it's not all that late," said Rochelle.

"Have you seen Anne?"

"No!" said Rochelle. "Don't talk to me about it, it

bothers me. I don't want to think about it."

"He was handsome," said Angel.

Rochelle gave him a worried look.

"Why do you say those things to me?" she said. "I was calm and now you've upset me and made me afraid. I don't like you when you're like that. You're always sad. We shouldn't think about what happened."

"You can stop yourself?"

"Everybody can stop themselves," said Rochelle. "Me, I'm alive. And so are you."

"I'm ashamed to be alive..." said Angel.

"Really?" said Rochelle. "You loved me that much?"

"Yes," said Angel. "That much."

"I'll be over it soon," said Rochelle. "I can't dwell on something sad for too long. Of course I'll think of him often..."

"Not as often as me," said Angel.

"Listen, you're no fun," said Rochelle. "We're alive after all. The both of us!"

She stretched her limbs.

"Amadis wanted you to come for the mail," said Angel, and started to laugh bitterly.

"I don't want to," she said. "I'm wiped out from these drops. I'm going to go to sleep for good, I think."

Angel stood up.

"You can stay," she said. "I don't mind. Do you think that after something like this I'm going to worry about appearances?"

She started taking off her dress.

"I was afraid that you'd taken too strong a dose," said Angel.

He still held the vial in his hand.

"Not likely! Abbot Littlejohn told me no more than five drops."

"If you take more than the prescribed dose," said Angel, "you know what will happen."

249

"You must sleep a long time," said Rochelle. "It must be dangerous. Maybe you'd die. It's not something to mess around with."

Angel looked at her. She'd taken off her dress and her body rose up straight, flourishing and robust, but marked at all the fragile places with wrinkles and cracks of imperceptible appearance. Her breasts sagged in the white bra's flimsy tissue and sinewy bluish veins popped out of her fleshy thighs. Smiling, she lowered her head, and her eyes met those of the young man as she slipped into the sheets.

"Sit down by me," she said.

"Let's each take half the bottle..." murmured Angel.

He sat next to her and continued.

"We too should be able to escape like that."

"Escape what?" said Rochelle. "Life is good."

"You loved Anne..."

"Of course," said Rochelle. "Don't start again. Can't you see that it hurts me when you talk to me about those things?"

"I can't take any more of this desert where everyone comes to die."

She laid back on the pillow.

"Not everyone."

"Sure... Petereater, Pippo, the intern, Anne, the inspector... you and I."

"Not us," said Rochelle. "We're alive."

"To die together, side by side..." said Angel. "Like in a novel..."

"Gently intertwined," said Rochelle. "It's a pleasant image, don't you think? I've read about it."

"Just like that, one after the other," said Angel.

"That's only in novels," said Rochelle. "It doesn't exist."

"It'd be nice..." said Angel.

She crossed her arms beneath her head and was thinking.

"It'd also be like a movie," she said. "You think we could die like that?"

"Maybe not," said Angel. "Unfortunately."

250

"It'd be like a movie I saw," said Rochelle. "They died from love, lying side by side. Could you die of love for me?"

"I think that I could have," said Angel.

"You really could? That's funny..."

"I don't think we can do it with this," said Angel, uncorking the vial.

"No? We'd just sleep?"

"Probably."

"Let's try," said Rochelle. "It would be so lovely to doze off right now. I'd like to have another dream."

"There are drugs," said Angel, "that make you dream like that all the time."

"It's true," said Rochelle. "Maybe this is one?"

"Probably," said Angel.

"I want it..." said Rochelle. "I want to dream that same dream. I can't sleep all alone."

She shot him an inquisitive glance. He'd lowered his head and was looking at the vial.

"Shall we each take a little?" she said.

"We can escape that way too," repeated Angel.

"This is fun," said Rochelle, sitting down. "I really like these kinds of things. Getting a little drunk, or taking drugs and really not knowing anymore what you're doing."

"I think Littlejohn exaggerated," said Angel. "If we each take half the bottle, I'm sure we'll have some incredible dreams."

"So you'll stay with me?" said Rochelle.

"But... It's just not the proper thing..." said Angel.

She laughed.

"You're being idiotic. Who's going to come?"

"Amadis was waiting for you."

"Hey..." said Rochelle. "After the shock that I've had I'm not going to work now. Give me the vial."

"Careful," he said. "The entire thing would be dangerous."

"We're sharing!..." said Rochelle.

251

She took the vial from Angel's hand and brought it to her lips. She stopped just when she was ready to drink.

"You'll stay with me?" she said.

"Yes..." said Angel.

He was as white as chalk. Rochelle drank half the vial and handed it back to him.

"Tastes bad," she said. "Your turn..."

Angel held the vial in his hand. His eyes remained fixed on hers.

"What's with you?" she asked. "Aren't you feeling well?"

"I'm thinking of Anne..." he said.

"Oh, not again!... Just shut up, please!"

There was silence.

"Drink," she said. "And come close to me. This is nice."

"I'm going to do it," said Angel.

"Does it take a long time to fall asleep?" she asked.

"Not too long," said Angel, softly.

"Come on," said Rochelle. "Hold me."

He sat at the bedside and slipped his arm around the back of the young woman who made an effort to sit up.

"I can't move my legs anymore," she said. "But there's no pain. It's pleasant."

"Did you like Anne?" asked Angel.

"I liked him a lot. I like you a lot, too."

She moved about weakly.

"I'm heavy."

"No."

"I liked Anne... but not too much," she murmured. "I'm a fool."

"You weren't a fool," Angel murmured, as softly as she had.

"Foolish enough... Are you going to drink that soon?"

"I'm going to..."

"Hold me... " she finished with a sigh.

She let her head fall on Angel's chest. From above he saw her dark and delicate hair and her light skin between the heavy strands. He took the flask that was still in her left hand and held the chin of the young woman. He lifted her head and pulled back his hand. The head fell softly back.

He used his force to free himself and he stretched her out on the bed. Rochelle's eyes were closed.

He watched the branch of a hepatrol in front of the window, its abundant orange flowers tossing themselves about silently, casting spots upon the sunlight in the room.

Angel took the brown bottle and stood near the bed. He looked at Rochelle's body, the face ripe with horror, and he felt in his right hand the effort he had made to lift her up in her bed. The effort he had made to push Anne into the blackness.

He didn't hear Abbot Littlejohn enter, but he yielded to the pressure of the fingers on his shoulder and followed him down the hall.

X

They descended what remained of the staircase. Angel was still holding on to the brown vial and Littlejohn walked behind him, saying nothing. The odor of red flowers filled the breach between the two halves of the hotel. The last step now came to an end above the rails and one after the other they stumbled over the sharp pebbles. Angel made an effort to walk on the crossbeams, whose surface was smoother and more convenient. Then Littlejohn jumped from the track onto the sandy dunes and Angel followed him. He was now seeing with his entire head, not just his eyes, and he would soon awaken. He felt his torpor build inside him, a torpor that he would soon vanquish in one

253

fell swoop. But he still needed someone to break through, which is what Littlejohn was coming to do. He would, then, drink the little bottle.

"What were you planning on doing?" said Littlejohn.

"You're going to explain it to me..." said Angel.

"It's for you to find out," said Littlejohn. "I'd love to take a look at what it is, once you'll have found it, but you're going to have to find it alone."

"I can't find it while I'm sleeping," said Angel. "Right now, I'm sleeping. Like Rochelle."

"No one can die without you feeling the need to go on and on about it," said Littlejohn.

"When one's responsible for something, that's normal."

"You think you're responsible for something?"

"Certainly," said Angel.

"You're able to kill someone and still you can't seem to wake up..."

"But that's different. I was sleeping when I killed them."

"Of course not," said Littlejohn. "That's badly worded. They died so that you might awaken."

"I know," said Angel. "I understand. I have to drink what's remaining. But right now, I'm at peace."

Littlejohn stopped, turned around towards Angel, and looked him straight in the eyes.

"What did you say?"

"That I was going to drink the rest," said Angel. "I loved Anne and Rochelle and now they're dead."

Littlejohn looked at his right hand, tightening it up into a fist two or three times. He rolled up his sleeve and said:

"Watch out!..."

Angel saw a black mass land smack on his nose. He waivered and fell in a sitting position on the sand. His head rang out with the clear sound of a silver bell. Blood flowed from his nose.

"Damn!..." he said, like someone with a cold.

"That better?" asked Littlejohn. "May I?"

He took his rosary.

"How many stars have you seen?"

"Three hundred ten," said Angel.

"Let's make it... four."

He said the rosary four times with the virtuosity he often displayed on such occasions.

"Where's my bottle?" said Angel, brusquely.

The little brown vial had spilled onto the sand and a humid spot spread out beneath the neck. The sand around it started to turn black, and a devious little smoke rose up.

Angel held his head out over his widespread legs as dark drops of blood riddled the ground.

"Leave it be!" said Littlejohn. "Or do you want some more?"

"I don't care," said Angel. "There are other ways to die."

"Yeah," said Littlejohn. "And other ways to smash someone in the face, too. I'm warning you."

"You can't hang around forever," said Angel.

"Certainly not. That would be useless."

"Rochelle..." murmured Angel.

"Don't you look sharp," said Littlejohn. "Sighing some woman's name while blood's pissing out your nose. Rochelle's no more. Enough already. Why do you think I gave her the vial?"

"I don't know," said Angel. "So then my presence here is meaningless? Once again?"

"That bothers you, huh?"

Angel tried to think. The things in his head weren't moving all that quickly, but they were vibrating so closely together that he had a hard time distinguishing them.

"Why didn't you drink it right away?"

"I'll start over..." said Angel.

"Go ahead. Here's another."

The abbot dug into his pocket and brought out another brown vial exactly the same as the first. Angel held out his hand and took it, then he opened it and poured a few

255

drops onto the sand. It made a minuscule spot and a yellow smoke curled its way up lazily into the still air.

Angel dropped the cork and held the vial tightly in his fist. He wiped his nose with his sleeve and looked, disgusted, at the streak on his forearm. He had lost his nerve.

"Blow your nose," said Littlejohn.

"I don't have a handkerchief," said Angel.

"You are, without a doubt, correct," said Littlejohn. "You're not good for much and you see nothing."

"I see this sand," said Angel. "This railroad... this roadbed... this hotel cut in two... all this work that serves no purpose..."

"You can say that again," said Littlejohn. "That's certainly something worth saying."

"I see... I don't know. Anne and Rochelle... You're going to punch me in the nose again."

"No," said Littlejohn... "What else do you see?"

Angel's face seemed to grow brighter, little by little.

"There was the sea," he said. "When we came. The two kids on deck. The birds."

"Just this sun," said Littlejohn. "That's not enough for you?"

"It's O.K...." said Angel slowly. "There's the hermit and the negress."

"And that girl of Athanagore's..."

"Let me look," said Angel. "There are tons of things to see."

He looked at the vial.

"But Anne and Rochelle are visible as well," he murmured.

"One sees what one wants," said Littlejohn. "And seeing is just fine, but it's not enough."

"Maybe we can do things... " said Angel. "Help people..."

He snickered.

"Right away we'd be stopped," he said. "Also, we're able to kill Anne and Rochelle, you understand..."

"No doubt," said Littlejohn.

"And make railroads that serve no purpose."

"Of course," said Littlejohn.

"And so?..."

"And so is that all you see?"

Littlejohn sat on the sand next to Angel.

"Well, drink then," he said. "If you haven't got anymore imagination than that..."

The two of them remained silent. Angel's face was haggard and he continued searching.

"I don't know," he said. "I find things to see, to feel, but not yet anything to do. I can't not know that which I've already done..."

"You're a pain in the ass to the both of us," said Littlejohn. "Stop quibbling and drink."

Angel dropped the vial. Littlejohn made no attempt to retrieve it and it quickly emptied. Angel was tense and stiff, and then his muscles relaxed and he let drop his inert hands. He picked up his head and sniffled.

"I don't know..." he said. "To see, that's enough for me to begin with. We must see really far once we no longer desire anything."

"Are you sure that you're seeing?" said Littlejohn.

"I see loads of things," said Angel. "There are so many things to see."

"Once you've seen a lot," said Littlejohn, "you'll know what it is you have to do."

"You know what it is you have to do..." said Angel.

"It's simple..." said Littlejohn.

Angel said nothing. He was working on something in his head.

"Professor Petereater took off into the black zone," he said.

"Would have been the same for you, if you'd drunk," said Littlejohn. "That too, you see, is something we can do."

"But is that better?" said Angel.

"Me, I consider it a failure," said Littlejohn. "But after all, it serves as an example. We need examples of things that fail."

He took a moment to collect his thoughts.

"A little prayer?" he proposed. "I'll grab you, you grab me by the head..."

"The first one who laughs gets a fairy in his bed..."

"If you laugh, bang, bang. Amen," concluded the abbot.

"It should be Amadis singing that one," said Angel.

"My boy," said Littlejohn. "You're sarcastic and malicious."

They rose. The train, near ready, was lying on the rails in front of them and the truck drivers pounded out heavy hammer-blows upon the steel of the boiler, making the black iron resonate under the sun.

XI

But it seems strange to me that Boris, a serious young man, would have had in 1889 the bizarre idea of copying such balderdash.

Ch. Chassé, *Les sources d'Ubu Roi,*
Floury, p. 44.

Director Dudu had called together all the personnel and they were crammed onto the provisional platform hastily erected by Carlo and Marin. The train was composed of two cars. Located there were Carlo, Marin, their respective families, and that bastard Arland. The three truck drivers, one of whom was charged with tossing the coal into the boiler, were also on board as well as Amadis himself and Dupont, Athanagore's black servant (who had received a special invitation and seemed worried, for Amadis had reserved for him a special compartment where the two would find themselves alone, face to face). There was a loud blast from a whistle and everyone scrambled towards the steps.

Angel and Abbot Littlejohn watched from on top of the dune. Athanagore and his workers hadn't bothered to show up and the hermit was probably off screwing the negress.

Director Dudu appeared at the door of the reserved compartment and lowered his hand three times to signal the departure. The brakes cried out, vapors puffed, and the convoy moved ahead bit by bit with a joyful noise, hand-kerchiefs waving from the windows.

"You should be there," said Littlejohn.

"I'm no longer a part of the Company," said Angel. "That train disgusts me."

"I'm aware that it serves no purpose," said Littlejohn.

They watched the locomotive work its way between the two parts of the hotel, now in ruins. The shellac on the roofs of the cars was made shiny by the sun and the demol-ished facade was studded with red hepatrols.

"Why is it resonating like that, on the rails?" said Littlejohn. "It's almost like it's hollow."

"That's the sound it normally makes on top of the roadbed," said Angel.

The train disappeared, but they could see smoke rising in the air like balls of white cotton.

"It'll come back," explained Angel.

"I thought as much," said the abbot.

They waited in silence, on the look out for the hurried respiration of the machine which had vanished into the dis-tance. Then the noise made itself heard again.

There was a muffled rumbling at the moment when the machine, moving backwards, once again penetrated the hotel. The convoy seemed to waiver on the rails which,

259

with one fell swoop, suddenly plunged into the earth. The locomotive vanished. An immense crackle extended along the tracks, getting closer and closer, and the cars appeared to be sucked up by the sand. The ground collapsed amidst the din of grinding stone, and the track slowly sunk away like a road covered over by the tide. The sand that had accumulated on both sides subsided into oblique patches, into waves which, starting at the bottom of the incline seemed to vanquish the summit, climbing back up the slope in a single stride while the yellow grains of sand rolled down the length of the embankment.

Abbot Littlejohn, aghast with horror, had seized Angel's arm and the two men saw the sand inexorably fill the enormous rift created before their eyes. There was one last jolt at the base of the hotel and a gigantic puff of steam and smoke silently exploded while a rainfall of sand covered the building. In an instant, the smoke started to wear thin in front of the sun, and the sharp, green blades of grass bustled about gently as a current of air passed by.

"I knew it," said Angel. "I thought about it the other day... and I forgot."

"They built it right over a hole," said Littlejohn.

"Over Athanagore's excavations..." said Angel. "It was there... at two degrees from the arc of the meridian... and Rochelle is dead, too... and I forgot..."

"There's nothing we can do," said Littlejohn. "Let's hope that the archaeologist got out of there..."

"It's my fault," said Angel.

"Stop thinking that you're responsible for the whole world," said Littlejohn. "You're partially responsible for yourself and that's enough. It's their fault as well as yours. It's also Amadis' fault, and the archaeologist's. And Anne's as well. Come on. We'll go see if they're alive."

Angel followed Littlejohn. His eyes were dry. He seemed to be regaining his strength.

"Let's go," he said. "Let's see this through to the end."

XII

Angel was waiting for bus 975. He was on the ground, his back up against the post of the stop sign, and Littlejohn, seated in the same position, had his back turned to him. They spoke without looking at each other. At his side, Angel had his suitcase and a large packet of letters and reports found on Amadis Dudu's desk.

"I'm sorry that the archaeologist couldn't accompany me," said Angel.

"He had a lot of work," said Littlejohn. "His material was all messed up. He's lucky that nothing happened to him and his crew."

"I know," said Angel. "Let's just hope that the bus comes!"

"It hasn't been coming at all recently," said Littlejohn.

"It'll be back," said Angel. "Doubtless the absence coincided with the driver's annual vacation."

"It is that season..." said Littlejohn.

Angel cleared his throat. He was emotional.

"I'm never going to see you again," he said. "I wanted to thank you."

"It's nothing," said the abbot. "You'll be back."

"Might I pose a question?"

"Pose away."

"You must know what I'm going to ask. Why is it that you wear a cassock?"

The abbot laughed, gently.

"That's just what I was expecting..." he said. "I'll tell you. It's the modern method."

"What method?"

"Infiltration...it's necessary..." responded Abbot Littlejohn.

"I see..." said Angel.

They heard the motor.

"It's coming..." said Littlejohn.

He stood up. Angel did the same.

"Goodbye. I'll be seeing you."

"Goodbye!..." said Angel.

Abbot Littlejohn shook his hand and left without turning around. He leaped high so that each time he floated back down his robe looked like a bell. He was all black against the sand.

Angel moved his fingers around the collar of his yellow shirt and held up a hand. The 975 stopped right in front of him. The porter was turning his box, which let loose a pleasant music.

There was only one passenger inside and he carried a little briefcase marked A.P., Antenne Pernot; he was dressed as if he were heading to his office. He maneuvered his way down the aisle with great ease and gently jumped to the bottom of the bus. He found himself face to face with the driver. The latter had just left his seat and moved closer to see what was happening. He wore a black bandanna over the eye.

"Gee whiz!" said the driver. "One getting off and one getting on!... And what about my tires! I don't have the right to take on any extra passengers."

The man with the briefcase looked at him, disturbed, and while the driver was busy putting his eye back in place with a pipe cleaner he took advantage of the moment to hastily flee the scene.

The driver touched his forehead.

"I'm starting to get used to it," he said. "That's the second one."

He went back to his seat. The porter helped Angel aboard.

"Let's go, let's go!" he said. "And no pushing!... numbers, please!..."

Angel climbed on. He placed his suitcase on the platform.

"Bags inside!..." said the porter. "Don't hold up the

service, if you please."

He hung onto the handle which he shook several times.

"Full!..." he cried.

The motor roared and the bus departed. Angel put his suitcase under a seat and came back to the platform.

The sun was shining above the sand and the grass. Tufts of spinifex scrub marked the ground. On the horizon he could vaguely make out a black and immobile strip.

The porter approached him.

"Terminus!..." said Angel.

"Fly!..." responded the porter, raising his finger towards the sky.

PASSAGE

A short time after, there was a meeting of the administrative council. Upon the insistence of the president, Ursus de Janpolent, who gave a reading of Antenne Pernot's missive, they decided to send a team of technicians and construction workers to study the possibility of creating, in Exopotamie, a single-track railroad, whose location will differ from the first in order to avoid the unfortunate mishap which marked the end of the previous undertaking. The members who were present were extremely pleased with the amount of information gathered thanks to the effort of the much missed Amadis Dudu, from whose work Antenne Pernot greatly profited, especially insofar as he was able to make sizeable cuts in salaries. The next expedition will thus be composed of the following personnel: a secretary, two engineers, two construction workers, and three truck drivers. Because the sun in Exopotamie is possessed of certain special properties, and given the nature of the ground, there's always the risk of remarkable phenomenon. One must also take into account that there are already in Exopotamie an archaeologist and his helpers, a hermit and a negress, and Abbot Littlejohn, who has many hermits to inspect. The construction workers are leaving with their families. The overall complexity is such that anything that might happen to them is truly, in spite of the knowledge already gained, impossible to predict or for that matter imagine. It's useless to try and describe it, for one may conceive of any solution.

NOTES

p.1 The author mentioned here was a descendant of Wellington's aide-de-camp Lord Raglan (1788-1855), who lost an arm at Waterloo and died of cholera at Sebastopol during the Crimean War. A bit more of a pacifist, the Lord Raglan cited here was president of the anthropology division of the British Association for the Advancement of Sciences. *Le tabou de l'inceste (The Incest Taboo)* is subtitled "Anthropological Study" and this particular quote is taken from the chapter "The Diffusion of Culture." For more on these often farcical quotes, see *Boris Vian/Colloque de Cerisy 1*, U.G.E., 1977.

p. 2 "Bateliers de la Volga" was a popular Russian song cited in *Trouble dans les andains* (Boris Vian, *Oeuvres Complètes*. Paris: Fayard, Vol. 1, p.87).

p. 2 By saying *pineute beutteure*, Vian is imitating the manner in which a French speaker would pronounce the word "peanut butter."

p. 2 This building at number six may be a reference to the "hotel particulier," 6 rue des Moulins (1st arrondissement), cited in Alphonse Boudard's *L'age d'or des maisons closes* (Paris: A. Michel, 1998), which served as a brothel for German soldiers during the occupation.

p. 6 In the French text, the name for Dr. Deadboot is *Bottine de Mourant.* Vian is playing with the name of Dr. Soulié de Morant (1878-1955), diplomat and sinologist who spent twenty-five years in China and introduced acupuncture to France.

p. 9 In the original manuscript, the highway is referred to as "la Nationale d'Embarquement," which by antithesis brings to mind "la voie du Débarquement de 1944," namely the allied landing in Normandy in 1944.

p. 13 Nuremburg, the German city, was famous for its production of toys during the middle ages. Here, Vian is referring to the interference from English radio broadcasts during World War II. In the French text, Beebeesee is "postes de téessef," a play upon the acronym T.S.F., which refers to wireless radio.

p. 16 Laporte (1881-1971) was founder of Jeunesses Communistes (The Young Communist League) and for a time a member of the Central Committee of the French Communist Party. He was the author of various works on the Russian secret police, or *L'Okhrana.*

p. 16 The character of Claude Leon is a reference to chemical engineer and jazz drummer, Leon, or "Doddy," who worked in the same office as Vian at the Office du Papier. Vian would occasionally work on his novel in the office and Claude Leon would furnish him with quotes pulled from his rather eclectic readings. It was perhaps because of his risky participation in the communist resistance that Vian chose to have a bit of fun here and land him in prison.

p. 17 Novelist and French theatre critic Jacques-Lemarchand (1908-1974) was secretary for the Prix de la pléiade and a fervent supporter of Vian's *L'Écume des jours,* which was nominated for this prestigious literary prize in 1946.

p. 18 Augustin Cabanes was a doctor who specialized in treating hemorrhoids, but was especially well known for writing dozens of tantalizing little historical tomes on obscure topics. *The History of Flagellation in Literature* (1899) is one such example.

p. 18 A play on the name of Roux-Combaluzier, used also in *Trouble dans les andains* (see *Oeuvres Complètes*, Vol.1, p.89, note 1).

p. 18 A reference to Arne Saknussemm, the bold and fantastic voyager whose runic manuscript guides the hero of Jules Verne's *Voyage to the Center of the Earth* (see note 1, *Les Fourmis, Oeuvres Complètes*, p.279). He makes another appearance in Vian's "Opéra de chambre" entitled *Une regrettable histoire*.

p. 20 This allusion to Carthaginian origins is a rather erudite double-entendre that plays with the antiphrasis *Punica fides*. It refers to Carthaginian bad faith, or insincerity - Carthage having the reputation of not standing by its word. The phrase plays with two Latin adjectives of similar spelling: punicus (Carthaginian) and puniceus (red).

p. 20 Walther is a well known maker of German handguns whose Ppk comes in calibers of either 7.65 or 9mm.

p. 26 Martell is a famous brand of cognac.

p. 26 Littlejohn has been translated rather literally. In Vian's text he is called L'abbé Petitjean. This is a reference to the real-life writer Jean "l'abbé" Grosjean, a biblical poet and Boris Vian's rival for the prix de la Pléiade in

June of 1946. While the author makes him one of the novel's funniest, most agreeable, and most original characters, we will see later on that Vian is not always so generous towards others associated with the Pléiade jury.

Petitjean is also the name of a double author, Marie and Frédéric Petitjean de la Roserie (1875-1947;1876-1949), who together wrote under the pen-name of "Delly" and published sentimental novels (cf. *L'Arrache-cœur*, chap. XII).

p. 26 In Vian's text, this game that I have translated as "one-upmanship" is called "la pouillette" - a veritably untranslatable portmanteau that is a combination of "pouilleux" (flea-bitten), "poursuite" (pursuit), and "pirouette" (pirouette).

p. 27 Loie Fuller is a pseudonym for Marie-Louise Fuller, an American dancehall artist and forerunner of Isadora Duncan. At the end of the 19th century she became famous in Paris and later throughout Europe for her "Ballets fantastiques," in which her dances were embellished through the use of veils, flowing fabric, light, and color.

p. 28 Vian is perhaps transposing the word "communist" into "conformist." Cf. *Les Fourmis,* in *Oeuvres Complètes,* Vol. 2, p.233.

p. 29 Littlejohn is constantly playing with farcical and non-sensical little transpositions of "comptines," or French nursery rhymes. For further elaboration on the comptines, see the third volume of the Fayard edition of Vian's *Oeuvres Complètes.*

p. 30 The complete title of Rossel's book is *Memoires et correspondance de Louis Rossel,* published by his sister. Rossel (1844-1871) was a student of the École

Polytechnique and later a French military officer. Because of his participation in the Commune, he was executed by a firing squad. The quote that Vian uses is from a letter in which the protestant Rossel pleads with his parents to accept his marriage to a young catholic woman.

The Commune is historically significant insofar as it is often referred to as the first "workers state." It came into being after the Franco-Prussian War, when the French Government capitulated to the Germans. On March 18th, 1871, regular French soldiers were sent to Paris to take the city back and disarm the National Guard. Instead, the soldiers fraternized with the Guard and the Parisian citizens while the frightened government fled to Versailles. Paris essentially formed its own communal government and started electing representatives and enacting social reforms. After two months, however, the exiled Versailles government regrouped and attacked the city. Tens of thousands were slaughtered in a bloody conflict and the government's power was restored.

p. 30 I've chosen to translate this term as "Prime Minister" because during the Fourth Republic in France (1947-1959), the Prime Minister was referred to as "President du Conseil." Vian actually says "Président des Conseilleurs."

p. 38 The Maison Dupont, if it ever existed, has disappeared from this street in the fourth arrondissment of Paris.

p. 44 Historian G. Cogniot, along with Paul Langevin, founded this journal whose colleagues included many brilliant left-wing intellectuals of the time. In his work "Chroniques du Menteur" (Chronicles of a Liar), Vian associates Cogniot's keen mind with that of Molière. The

271

short story was rejected by *Les Temps Modernes* in September of 1948. See *Chroniques du Menteur*, C. Bourgois, 1972, p. 107.

p.44 Petereater is of course called "Mangemanche" in the original text. It is important to point out because he was the doctor who looked after Chloë in *L'Écume des jours*.

P. 45 Jabes was a schoolmate and friend of Vian at the École centrale and a member of the model plane club in Ville-d'Avray. For more see N. Arnaud, *Les Vies parallèles de Boris Vian*, Paris: Livres de poche, 1998, pp.59-60.

p. 47 In France, a Palme Académique is an award for excellence in education, not a real palm tree.

p. 48 Claudel (1868-1955), poet, playwright, and Christian diplomat, is one of Vian's most intimate enemies. This is almost certainly because of Claudel's religious inspiration and pompous style. Vian makes numerous farcical references to him, for example in *L'Écume des jours*, (vol.2, p. 147, *Oeuvres Complètes*) and in "Éléments d'une biographie de Boris Vian[…]" (See B. Vian, *Romans, Nouvelles, oeuvres diverses, Le Livre de poche "La Pochothèque"*, 1991, p.1309, note 17).

p. 48 *La Pensée catholique (Catholic Thought)*, or "Cahiers de synthèse doctrinale" published its first volume in 1946. *Le Pèlerin* is a more popular publication of Bayard Presse.

p. 49 Vian's play on words with the term "Heezgot" is untranslatable here. Vian makes reference to a real-life engineer, the Finnish Kylälä, whose name phonetically resembles the sound of the French phrase "qu'il a là," which means roughly "that he has there" (thus the translation into "Heezgot").

Kylälä invented an intake and exhaust system for
steam engines around 1919, and Chapelon, whose name
is also deformed in the text, was a student at the École
centrale and an engineer (as was Vian himself) who also
happened to be an inspector of railroad materials. He
published *Notes sur les échappements de locomotives*
(Dunod, 1938), in which he discusses the patents of his
predecessor as well as his own improvements. It is funny
that Vian, who adored the dieresis, forgot to use it when
he spelled the Finn's name.

p. 49 Like the Bottine de Mourant line (note 5, p. 268),
the word "Ping" is a farcical reference to the fictional
China conjured up by the title.

p. 57 In Greek mythology, Morpheus, the God of dreams,
is the son of Hypnos, the God of sleep.

p. 60 This passage contains a whimsical reference to Sir
Arthur Stanley Eddington (1882-1944), British physicist,
mathematician, and astronomer who specialized in the
evolution of stars and the theory of relativity.

p. 62 The works of the specialist René Escourrou, a doctor of science, were certainly on hand where Vian and
Leon worked at the Office du Papier. The quote is pulled
from the chapter entitled "Pâtes chimiques."

p. 62 "Sit tibi terra levis" is a rather inexact quote from
Tibullus: "May you find the earth weightless." It should
read Terra sit super ossa levis (May the earth be light on
your bones).

p. 63 γνωθι σε∝υτον is the well-known Socratic slogan,
"Know thyself." Vian was well schooled in the classics.

p. 64 Charles de Foucauld (not Foucault), a freethinking officer who later became a missionary in the Sahara (1858-1916). This is perhaps a model for Claude Leon.

p. 66 Isidore Isou is the echolalic pseudonym employed by Jean Isidore Goldstein (1925-), who immigrated from Romania to France in 1945. The Father of Lettrist poetry, his aim was a total redefinition of art in which complete interpretive liberty was key. He was a close friend of Gabriel Pomerand and a central player among the postwar Saint-Germain-des-Prés crowd. He organized demonstrations and was published by Gallimard, thanks to the support of Paulhan and Queneau. His revolutionary conception of art was furthermore a major source of inspiration for the Situationists, who helped rock Paris in May of '68. He remains to this day faithful to his revolutionary conception of art.

p. 70 Giuseppe Barrizone, called "Pippo," or "La Pipe," was the Italian gardener and factotum for the Vian family during its time of splendor. He was also a former chef and had a lovely tenor voice (cf. N. Arnaud, op. cit. pp. 47-48).

p. 70 "Facce la barba à sept houres c'to matteigno?" is an Italian translation of the phrase with which Barrizone greeted Boris's father every morning: "Zavez fait la barbe à sept heures c' matin?" (Did you trim your beard at seven this morning?). The dialect which Vian imitates is that of Nice, which differs from the standard Italian: *Fate la barba{...} questa mattina?*

p. 71 Henry was Director of Agriculture in the colonies and wrote technical manuals on cotton, rubber, etc.

p. 73 Janpolent is a phonetic reworking of Jean Paulhan

(1884-1968), the director of *Nouvelle Revue française* and the "eminence grise" of French literature for three decades. Here, Vian exacts his revenge - Paulhan voted against him while on the jury of the Prix de la pléiade (See the note on p. 269 concerning Littlejean).

p. 84 Nicolas is, of course, Colin's valet in *L'Écume des jours*. In the beginning chapter he is following one of Gouffé's recipes in order to prepare an eel dish. For more, consult the notes in *Oeuvres Complètes*, Vol. 2, p. 24 and p. 26.

Jacques Loustalot, also known as "le Major," was a very close friend of Vian's and often appeared as a character in the author's early novels. See *Trouble dans les andains* and *Vercoquin et le plancton*.

p. 84 Brachet and Dumarqué were authors of a very successful mathematics textbook, *Arithmétique et notions d'algèbre*, published in 1933 and followed by numerous reprintings.

p. 88 Arland refers to Marcel Arland, another "beau salaud" (real bastard) who also sided against Vian in the prix de la Pléiade voting. In the original text, Vian had changed the name to *Orland*, but he decided to use Arland's true name for the 1956 edition. The names Arrelent and Poland had already been used in the short story "Les bons élèves" (1946).

p. 89 The reference to the castaway is an allusion to the legendary Greek hero Philoctetes, abandoned on an island because of a disgusting wound on his foot (see the eponymous tragedy penned by Sophocles). The danger of navigating through reefs also calls to mind the passage from *The Odyssey* involving Scylla and Charybdis.

p. 98 Véron was a professor at l'École centrale and Vian could very well have been his student. In this quote, Véron is making a humoristic comparison between the dilution of gasses with air and the dilution of wine with water. Vian also refers to this work in *L'Écume des jours*, noting how Pythagorean philosophers believed fire to be composed of tetrahedrons (See *Oeuvres Complètes*, Vol. 2, p.182, note 1).

p. 103 In *L'Écume des jours*, Petereater (Mangemanche) had already demonstrated his love for jazz and was known to adapt song titles to fit the specific situation (cf. *Oeuvres Complètes*, vol. 2, pp. 112 and 115). *Show me the way to go home* is, of course, the popular American drinking song and *Taking a Chance for Love* truly is a Vernon Duke composition which was recorded by, among others, the great trumpeter and bebop innovator Dizzy Gillespie.

p. 106 Orthopompe is a completely fictional character. His name is comprised of two Greek words: "ortho," which means "right" or "straight," and "pomp," meaning of course "pomp" or "ceremony."

p. 107 With the reference to the taxi Vian definitely wants to conjure up the image of the American taxicab, whose yellow and black colors recall the image of the American taxi used on the cover of the *Série noire* books. They were essentially pulp crime novels.

p. 108 Once again, some phonetic wordplay; by typing "*Britiche Muséomme*," Vian is spelling out the way in which a francophone would pronounce the words "British Museum."

p. 113 *Le Chant de Maldoror* is the revolutionary master-work – André Breton called it the "definitive apocalypse"

– of Isidore Ducasse, better known to American readers as Lautréamont (1846-1870), whose complete body of work was published in 1938. The third *chant* (ode, hymn) deals with the idea of divine providence gone mad.

p. 114 The astrolabe, here transformed into a fictional constellation, was invented by Hipparchus in the 2nd century B.C. and was a sort of precursor to the sextant. It was also the name of the boat of famed explorer Dumont d'Urville. The Big Dipper and Orion are, of course, used for navigation at night.

p. 121 The fourth chapter of this Victor Hugo novel (*Notre-Dame-de-Paris*) is entitled "La cruche cassé" (The Broken Jug), and in it we find the poet Gringoire, who has been hauled off to *la cour des miracles* (a neighborhood in Paris reputed for its shady characters) where he is forced by the King of Thieves to marry Esmeralda. In a Bohemian ritual, she tosses a clay pot to the ground and it breaks into four pieces, determining a four-year marriage.

p. 122 Nefourpitonh is another portmanteau and pun that combines the name of 14th century B.C. Egyptian princess Nefertiti with two French terms: "fourrer son nez," which means "to pick one's nose," and "piton," which is a slang term for nose. Perhaps Vian was thinking of Pascal's famous phrase about another Egyptian queen: "Had Cleopatra's nose been shorter, the whole face of the world would have been different."

p. 122 The first line spoken by the abbot is a combination of two latin quotes; tanquam adeo calls to mind certain phrases by Cicero and Virgil, for example the Aeneid, ode III, verse 567; the rest of the line refers to the slogan of Paris, established in 1268: "Le navire flotte et ne sombre pas" (The ship floats and does not sink). The rejoinder spoken by Copper is part of the Christian liturgy, the reply to *Dominus vobiscum* (May God be with you), and translates as "And with your spirit."

p. 124 Cointreau is the famed liqueur of Anjou, created in 1849. With the French text, Vian has created a sentence, which when spoken, sounds like the title of Henry Miller's "scandalous" novel *Tropic of Cancer*. (The original French reads "Voyons si ce Cointreau pique dès qu'on sert") Miller's book was translated to French in 1945 and was, like Vian's *J'irai cracher sur vos tombes*, the object of numerous lawsuits.

p. 125 Arquebuse is a liquor named after *l'eau d'Arquebuse*, which was used as a dressing for wounds. It was created from a base of thirty-three plants macerated in alcohol and aged in oak casks.

p. 125 This church, Saint-Philippe-du-Roule, located at one of the most beautiful crossroads along the Rue du Faubourg-Saint-Honoré (8th arrondissement), was built according to the designs of J.F. Chalgrin between 1774 and 1778. It was the first of Paris's neo-antique churches and was situated in one of the most chic neighborhoods in the capital.

p. 129 Leverrier is perhaps a rather burlesque allusion to Urbain Le Verrier (1811-1877), astronomer, man of politics, and discoverer of the orbit of Neptune.

p. 129 "Comely Curtis…" is another variation (and another very liberal translation) on a French nursery rhyme, or comptine.

p. 132 The rhyme on this page starts with the words, "A little scotch, a little gin…" In the French text, Vian is cre-

ating a variation and a vaguely erotic poem: "Une poule
sur un mur/Qui picote du pain dur/Picoti, picota/Lèv'la
queue et puis s'en va."

p. 150 This little song of Pippo's recalls some of the events
of World War I. Guillermo refers to William II of
Germany (1888-1941), who abdicated in 1918 and Vitto
is a reference to Victor Emmanuel III (1869-1974), king
of Italy from 1900 to 1945. In the French text, there is
also a reference to Bernhard von Bülow (1849-1929), the
German diplomat who tried to dissuade Italy from joining
forces with the allies. Trento and Trieste are Austrian terri-
tories which Italian nationalists sought to reclaim, and
Annuzio was an Italian writer with fascist tendencies who
in 1919 siezed both Dalmatia and Fiume. Translations of
song lyrics are, in the name of lyricism, usually rather liberal, and mine is no exception. To see the original, consult
Vian's *Oeuvres Complètes*, Vol. 3, p. 165.

p. 162 George Withrow was an Oxford professor, and this
work was originally written and published in English in
1949 under the title *The Structure of the Universe: An
Introduction to Cosmology.*

p. 167 Saint Simeon was a Christian ascetic and the first
of the stylites: He spent twenty-six years of his life standing atop a column. In July of 1945, Vian made a few
notes for a project entitled "Tragédie sur Saint Siméon
Stylite."

p. 167 In the manuscript and first version of the novel
Vian used the word "Yanks" (Amerlauds) instead of
"backward fools" (arriérés). He often ridiculed the rather
cultish fervor expressed by the Americans for the father of
psychoanalysis.

p. 181 Vian is reworking a surreal little children's song called *Une souris verte (A Green Mouse)*. Lazare Carnot (1753-1823), general and founder of the Armies of the Republic, was a politically astute and learned man who dedicated the later years of his life to science. He was one of the founders of modern geometry.

p. 182 Two Latin quotes in the epic tradition once again underscore Vian's knowledge of the classics. The first, "Magni nominis umbra," is from the *Pharsalia* of Lucan (39-65), book I, line 135, and reads, "the shadow of a mighty name." The passage describes Pompey's waning efforts in his fight with Caesar. The second, "Jam proximus ardet Ucalegon," comes from Virgil (70-19 B.C.E.), lines 311-312 of the *Aeneid*, and reads, "Ucalegon burns next." It reminds us of Aeneas, and his flight from Troy as the Greeks enter the city.

p. 183 Vian, though quite the pacifist, did in fact possess a handgun of this caliber (7.65 mm) which was manufactured by Herstal.

p. 187 The Valley of the Kings is a famous archaeological site in Egypt, the burial grounds of the pharaoh.

p. 187 The Eudists were an order instituted by Saint Jean Eudes (1601-1680) to administer the "Bon Pasteur" seminaries and institutes, which handled the rehabilitation of prostitutes.

p. 192 Vian owned a copy of this handbook, *Précis de Prestidigitation*, written by the "master magician" Bruce Elliot. The 1952 edition, translated into French by Pierre Delanoë, has a preface by Orson Welles.

p. 193 "Black, Brown, and Beige" is the famous forty-five

minute suite by Duke Ellington, which recounts the history of African-Americans in the United States.

p. 195 The term "bayou wax" is an allusion to Louisiana and another in a series of references to jazz which underlines once again Petereater's love of the music.

p. 197 Karpathian cyanide has two possible references. The first is to Dracula, which Vian transposed as "Drencula" in an unfinished erotic story (See *Oeuvres Complètes*, V.5, p.493). The second possible reference is to Jules Verne's *Château des Carpathes*.

p. 200 François de Curel was a famous French playwright. *Le Repas du Lion* (The Lion's meal), his third play, focuses on the social conflicts which arise between workers and their superiors. In Vian's story "Le figurant," Claude Leon, whom we already know as the source of this novel's epigraphs, also shows himself to be concerned with these types of social issues.

p. 216 Boris Vian explored the theme of female homosexuality in his novel *Elles se rendent pas compte* (1950).

p. 221 See the note from page 276 concerning the yellow and black taxi. In the original manuscript, the taxi was a Peugeot, a product of the Montbéliard factory and itself a condemned vehicle because of its numerous technical problems.

p. 223 Another sarcastic reference to Marcel Arland (See the note on p. 275).

p. 232 Nine years later, in 1955, Vian would be in charge of creating a catalog of the jazz recordings of the Philips company (For more, consult Noël Arnaud's *Les vies paral-*

lèles de Boris Vian, op. cit., p.447).

p. 244 An approximate quote from Baudelaire's personal notes written between 1855 and 1862. It is essentially an aphorism that Vian jotted down in his diary on January 3, 1947: "Nous aimons les femmes à proportion qu'elles nous sont plus étrangères. Aimer les femmes intelligentes est un plaisir de pédéraste. Ainsi la bestialité exclut la pédérastie." Translation: *We love women insofar as they are foreign to us. The love of an intelligent woman is the fancy of a homosexual. Thus this is precisely why bestiality and homosexuality are mutually exclusive.* (Baudelaire, *Oeuvres Complètes,* Gallimard, Editions de la Pléiade, 1975, p. 653).

p. 250 For some, this romantic notion of dying side by side may conjure up Cocteau's *L'Éternel Retour* (1943), based on the legend of Tristan and Isolde.

p. 258 This nonsensical little exchange between Angel and Littlejohn is based on a popular little French tune, "La Barbichette." It may also serve as another commentary on Amadis Dudu's lifestyle. For more, see the Fayard edition of Vian's *Oeuvres Complètes,* Vol. 3, p. 267.

p. 258 Chassé (1883-1965) was a writer and columnist interested in art and literature from the turn of the century. Vian offered a critique of this particular work, under the pen name of Hugo Hachebuisson, in the publication *Les amis des arts,* no.4, March 12, 1945 (cf. *La Belle Époque,* Le Livre du poche, 1998, pp. 87-88).

p. 263 Because of Vian's fondness for Latin, I have decided to translate "terminus" rather literally. In French, the phrase is usually followed by the porter saying, "Last stop!" or "Everyone off!"

The novel comes to a close with a final bit of wordplay that brings to mind the game of chance called *Pigeon, vole!* (Pigeon, fly!). The game consists of spitting out a series of nouns in rapid succession, and when a flying object is named it is followed by the rejoinder "vole!" p. 264 In the original manuscript and first typed draft, Vian adds to this list of future personnel, "a foreman, a doctor, and his assistant," which underscores even more strongly the idea of an identical new beginning.

BOOKS

TamTam Book Series:

I Spit on Your Graves
  - Boris Vian

Evguénie Sokolov
  - Serge Gainsbourg

Considerations on the Assassination of Gérard Lebovici
  -Guy Debord

Foam of the Daze (L'Écume des jours)
  - Boris Vian

Autumn in Peking
  - Boris Vian

Forthcoming:

The Lyrics of Serge Gainsbourg
  -Serge Gainsbourg

For further information about these titles and authors:

www.tamtambooks.com